Misunderstood

HEALING JASON SUTTER

Misunderstood

⚡ HEALING JASON SUTTER ⚡

JAY SHERFEY

iUniverse LLC

Bloomington

Misunderstood: Healing Jason Sutter

iUniverse books may be ordered through booksellers or by contacting:

iUniverse
1663 Liberty Drive
Bloomington, IN 47403
www.iuniverse.com
1-800-Authors (1-800-288-4677)

ISBN: 978-1-4620-5962-1 (sc)
ISBN: 978-1-4620-5964-5 (hc)
ISBN: 978-1-4620-5963-8 (e)

Printed in the United States of America

iUniverse rev. date: 07/24/2013

With heartfelt gratitude, I want to thank,

- My wife, Claudia, my daughter, Kirstin, and my son, John for the alone-time I needed to finish this work.

- My sister, Sara, who offered valuable feedback.

- My coworkers who graciously volunteered to read an early draft and offer guidance.

- My friends at restaurants where most of the writing was done who read and offered advice.

- The good people at iUniverse who pleasantly drove me to make the final revisions. Their insistance made the book better.

- My writing mentor, Fran Bellerive, who has been nudging, cajoling, guiding and editing this story from the beginning. I could not have made it without her.

Prologue

/

November, 1960

Hang-dog tired, Jason Sutter fell into the rickety chair next to his mother and rested his head on her shoulder. He didn't think he could get up again. His legs felt sore and stiff. This was the fourth house in the last two days.

Jason had been a good soldier. His father, Robert, had told him to buck up, not complain, and do anything he was asked. It had been hard for the eleven-year-old not to whine about being hungry and tired, but he managed. *It would have helped*, he thought, *if they told me what was going on*. He figured they were on the run, but from whom or what he had no idea.

His mother reached over and caressed his cheek. He loved the feel of her soft hand on his face. His eyes scanned the room. This place was as dirty and old as the last. The faded wallpaper hung down in places. The only furniture was the scarred table and the beat-up, old chairs on which they sat. The place smelled funny too, like when something in the refrigerator goes bad.

Jason worried about his father. He stood by the door with his eyes closed. But his head moved swiftly like a deer whose ears chase the elusive sound of danger. In the last week, Jason had watched as the dark circles and deep lines grew around his father's eyes and over his cheeks. He no longer walked upright but staggered forward like he suffered under a heavy load.

1

He looked sick. But his mother had not changed. Jason thought that his father had given up part of himself to keep her strong.

In a corner stood two people Jason knew well, Sarah Stiles and her son, Seth. He could not remember a time when they were not around. Sarah was the picture of a Midwestern, no-nonsense grandmother, with her gray hair pulled back into a tight bun. She was steady and reliable in any task. Seth stood strong too, a barrel with arms and legs and a sharp intellect. Jason grinned as he remembered Seth as someone who could make him laugh. The Stileses waited grimly, watching Jason's father.

His mother dropped her hand from his cheek, but Jason caught it in his. He sat up, held her hand in his lap, and looked up into her sad eyes. "Mom?" He placed the question gently in her mind.

She did not answer but turned away.

"This place is no longer safe." Jason barely recognized his father's weary voice. "We do not have much time."

Jason leaned forward to see his father limp to the table. The set of his jaw, the certainty in his eyes, told Jason that something bad was about to happen. He looked from one parent to the other for comfort.

"It's the only way," Robert Sutter stuttered. He did not look at his son but turned to Sarah Stiles. Jason felt his despair.

"Are you ready to do what must be done?"

"Yes," Sarah said. She and Seth nodded. "We know what to do."

Jason watched his father caress his mom's shoulder. He leaned down to whisper gently in her ear. "Now, Beth." He stumbled back a few steps.

Jason looked at his mom questioningly when she pulled her hand from his grasp. She turned to him and coaxed him to face her so that their knees touched. Her soft, warm hands caressed his cheeks.

Jason watched a single tear escape the corner of his mother's eye. "Mom?" he whispered. When his mother's caress became a hard clamp on his head, he knew something was wrong.

Chapter 1

⚡

December 1962

A car rolled down the tree-lined street in Franklin Chase, a bedroom community south of Philadelphia. Street lights glowed in the early evening hours beneath a winter-darkened sky. Wreaths hung on front doors. Strings of multicolored lights outlined homes. Occasional plastic Santas, sleighs, and reindeer dashed across front lawns. A Ford Fairlane pulled up to the curb of a large Victorian house shrouded in darkness. Its rumbling engine stopped. Silence took back the neighborhood.

Will Grossman shivered in his old car. He doubted he would get his few dollars back for food and gas. The evening grew darker, colder. The car's windows fogged as winter crept in through cracked weather-stripping. Frustrated, he pounded the steering wheel. "And on the Friday before Christmas, for Christ's sake!" The steering wheel took another blow.

Will was not a giving man. He thought, *Tonight's overtime at the Department of Social Services had better pay off with an IOU or two at the office.* After a deep breath, he calmed. He reached up, turned the rearview mirror, and examined his teeth. He removed a black leather glove and ran a forefinger over his incisors. *A winning smile never hurt,* he thought. Affable and pleasant looking with a loud laugh, Will lurched through life glad-handing all the right people. To get ahead, he'd grinned ear to ear through whatever abuse.

Satisfied, he pushed the mirror back. The police cruiser's headlights

3

lit the fogged rear windshield. "Let's get this over with," Will said as he pulled up his coat collar and put on his glove. He grabbed his notebook and an overstuffed grocery bag, and got out to greet the officers. One sat behind the wheel. The other, out of the car on the sidewalk, restrained a boy struggling to break free.

"Thanks for bringing him over," Will said to the policeman. "I appreciate it." The officer nodded as the child thrashed against the policeman's hold.

Will watched the boy with a modicum of sympathy. His deliveries, as he saw them, included troubled kids, mentally ill adults, drunks, and drug addicts in withdrawal. To Will, their pitiful souls were not worth much. Before him on the sidewalk squirmed another one. Without further delay, he turned and headed toward the house.

After taking the steps two at a time, Will rapped the tarnished brass knocker twice. The officer dragged the boy onto the porch. A weak light spilled out as the door opened.

"Well, Lydia, here he is." Will stepped out of the dark, cold evening with a holiday smile. He handed Lydia Dubois a paper bag with the boy's clothes and medicine. Lydia frowned.

"He got his last dose about an hour ago," Will said. "I expect he will be asleep in a bit." He removed his gloves and unbuttoned his wool overcoat. The boy fought the officer's grasp as they stood inside the door.

"What's he taking, Will?" Lydia rummaged through the bag, looking for the pill bottles. Her mousy brown hair tied back in a long ponytail highlighted the harsh angles of her face. When she managed a smile, it looked painful.

"Chlor something or other. Check the label. It's something new. They told me he's on a pretty high dose."

The boy had given up the struggle; he slumped against the officer. The medication had worked its magic.

"My, my," Lydia said, struck by the quick change. "If you would lay him down on the sofa right over there, Officer, I would be grateful." The policeman gently cradled the boy and set him on the cushions. He then excused himself, saying something about other duties, and closed the door as he went.

"Okay, Will, how bad?" Lydia eyed him suspiciously, wary of being used with no potential gain. Lydia, her husband, Frank, and Will worked as a team to do what appeared to be the right thing. In reality they skimmed money from the state allowances intended for their foster children's necessities. When the kids needed less medication, they worked every angle to keep the prescriptions at high levels so they could sell the excess.

"You know, Frank, and I can handle only so much." Eleven foster children lived in the huge, rundown Victorian house.

"I won't lie to you," Will said as he stared across the room at the unconscious child. "He's a bad case." He paused and scratched his chin. "If there'd been any beds in the state ward, I would've taken him there. There'll be no backin' off on meds for a long time."

"So we're the Social Service's saviors, their only hope and last resort?" Lydia grinned. Will nodded and gave a thumbs-up. "Well then, will the Department pony up more money to help out?" Lydia's mouth twitched.

"I knew you'd ask." Will smiled. "Started the paperwork before we picked up the boy. Give it a few weeks, and I'll know what can be done. My bosses, thanks to me, are well aware of the difficult situation. They owe you for this one. In the meantime, don't hesitate to use the emergency room or the cops if you need them. Be sure to document everything. His name's Jason Sutter. He's thirteen years old. We have no records of any family. Looks like no one will be asking about him."

"Gotcha."

Frank and Lydia Dubois were well matched. Both had graduated from the foster care system they now gamed. They took care of themselves first. Yet no child in their care suffered injuries or abuse; bad things happening cut into their cash flow.

Lydia went over to the couch and looked down on the boy. She could not tell whether he had black or brown hair; it was cut too close to the scalp. With his clothes being several sizes too big, he struck her as small for his age, but angelic, asleep in her living room.

"It may take some time, but this little angel will pay off, I'm sure."

☆   ☆   ☆

After a month, Frank Dubois had had enough. He glared at Lydia. They stood at either side of Jason's closed bedroom door like police ready to rush a criminal hideout.

"Have you been holding back on the pills again?" Frank asked Lydia. They heard Jason stomping around in the room, screaming.

Lydia said, furiously, "I did what we always do with the kids' pills." She fixed her green eyes on Frank and smiled. He shivered at the pure malignancy of her expression. A hard slam against the door startled Frank.

"Will warned us about backing off too soon." Frank mumbled as he withered under Lydia's grotesque grin.

"Yeah, well, Will's not around to consult." Lydia produced the key and prepared to go in. "So just shut up about the meds and get your butt in gear."

She paused. Maybe she *had* pushed the experiment too far. "Okay. From now on, I'll give 'im his full dose." She could not afford to alienate Frank.

He nodded.

Lydia unlocked the door. Frank went first. Jason was standing on his bed, pounding the wall with his fists. Frank pulled the boy's legs out from under him, and he collapsed on the bed. Frank fell across his chest. Lydia dove on his legs.

"Give me his pills," hissed Frank through gritted teeth. Controlling the boy took all his effort. One of Jason's arms lay trapped beneath Frank's body. The other Frank held firmly in one hand. Lydia reached into her dress pocket and slapped the pills into the palm of Frank's free hand.

"Hey, kid!" yelled Frank. He smacked Jason's cheek several times, harder each time, to get his attention. Jason's eyes focused; his mouth opened to speak. Frank quickly forced the pills into his mouth, pushed his chin up, and clamped the boy's mouth shut. The child's eyes stared frantic; he arched his back. Finally he swallowed and lay still.

"Thought he was about to choke for a minute there." Frank relaxed, and in that instant an arm pulled free and a clenched fist punched Frank in the face. "Damn it!" He grabbed the arm and doubled his effort to restrain the boy. Blood dripped from his nose onto his shirt.

"I want this psycho the hell out of here!" screamed Frank. "I'm gonna lose my job if I have to keep running home like this!" His manager at the car parts warehouse had started to notice his long lunches and sudden absences. Sweat rolled off Frank's forehead into his large, owl-like eyes. It stung, making him angrier. He moved his gangly body for better leverage and held Jason's arms tighter.

"Don't be hasty," said Lydia. "Give it more time. I see a gold mine here." A leg almost escaped from beneath her. She threw her weight forward, regaining control. "We have to manage!"

"No more experiments!" Frank came across as comical to Lydia. With blood flowing from his nose over his lips, it bubbled when he yelled.

"Oh, all right." She chuckled. "No more experiments." Frank stared, shocked that Lydia found the situation humorous.

"Get this kid out of the house now!" he yelled.

Banished to the large toolshed in the backyard with an old, worn comforter and cot, plus a rusty bucket for urine, Jason, fully drugged, didn't even feel the cold.

Life in the Dubois house followed a combination of strategic planning and reaction to unexpected events. Lydia's experiments with medication often led to the unexpected. With Jason out of the way in the shed, Lydia felt confident that their money machine was back on track. She stood at the kitchen sink and prepared the cups for Jason's evening pills. The scream from upstairs demanded her immediate attention. She set the cups on the windowsill.

After jogging up the stairs, Lydia found two girls fighting furiously. The smaller of the two had the larger girl by a ponytail. She snapped back her head and made a supreme effort to whirl her around the room. The bigger child had her hands on her hair, desperate to ease the pain and free herself. She didn't have the leverage and screamed. Lydia entered the melee and broke the ironlike grip of the younger girl. They separated.

"You little freak!" screamed the bigger girl. Tears flowed.

The smaller girl smiled, saying nothing. Lydia's mouth twitched. She respected the girl's callousness in victory.

"You," she said with a nod to the older girl, "to the kitchen. You," she said as she pointed to the smaller, "stay exactly where you are. Nobody eats until you both calm down." Lydia could not remember their names. She needed Frank, still at work, who had a knack for dealing with children. Lydia followed the girl to the kitchen and began to prepare dinner. The pills on the windowsill were forgotten.

Chapter 2

Bored and frustrated faces pressed against the windows in the school cafeteria. A hard rain lashed the playground in that afternoon. The wind-whipped droplets looked like snakes slithering back and forth across the blacktop. The storm had delayed the buses.

Jason pulled back from the window. He looked around. *No better time than now,* he thought. Arthur Dresden sat with his gang, but something struck Jason as different. The usual anger and threatening looks were missing. Russ, his best friend, had said complaints from Dresden's usual targets had stopped. He didn't know what to make of it.

✣　　✣　　✣

Jason remembered the first time he confronted Dresden. It was the day he took tests to see if he could manage a regular classroom. Due to his psychotic diagnosis, Jason had missed two years of school. No records of his past life existed. After several hours of testing, he sought sanctuary on a bench near the swings. In the quiet of the empty playground, Jason wondered what would become of him; the testing, in his opinion, had not gone well.

The lunch bell rang, and children flooded the playground. Groups formed quickly according to age. The boys formed teams for basketball or kickball; the girls gathered around the tables to talk. A few stood; some sat alone and watched. Others buried their heads in books. One group of boys did not participate in the sports. Instead they stalked the area for targets. Their leader, Dresden, was an older boy with short, black hair who wore denim jeans and a jacket with the collar pulled up. He sauntered around the playground with his gang in his wake, like he owned the place.

Jason sat alone, not paying much attention. With his telepathy barely controlled, the many new voices screeched in his head. The pain was tolerable; if he remained focused, the volume dropped. If left alone, he would be fine.

"Who're you?" The yell came from behind. Jason jumped up and spun around. It was Dresden.

"Jason. I'm new here." He felt threatened. His head ached. "Who're you?"

Dresden smiled malevolently and said, "I'm the boss around here." The playground quieted; the other kids watched. "You got a quarter?"

"No, I don't have any money." Jason lost control of the voices; they flashed into his awareness. He ignored invaders and focused on this new problem.

"Then I'll just make sure you remember it tomorrow." Dresden pulled back his arm, his fist clenched. It shot forward but didn't land. Dresden lay on the ground, his arms crossed over his face. Jason stood ready to fight, not realizing, he had already won.

A flash of lightning and pounding thunder brought Jason back to the cafeteria. He had to know what really happened at the first meeting with Dresden. He gathered his determination and approached the bully and his gang. He waited to be recognized. With hands in his pockets, he looked at them; they crowded around their leader. A sudden increase in the pounding of the rain against the windows drew his attention.

"I was wondering when you'd come back," Dresden said. Jason's focus snapped back. "Okay, guys, get lost. Sutter and me got stuff to settle." Six boys evacuated the area. Jason, nervous, sat across from the larger boy, recalled Russ's advice: "He'll want to get back on top. So you can expect to get ambushed or somethin'. The best thing to do, and believe me I know what I'm talkin' about, is take the hit, dive, and don't get up. Dresden gets what he wants, and everyone knows you're playin' along. Ya know?" Jason hoped it wouldn't come to punches.

Jason looked Dresden in the eye and said, "I need to talk about what happened that first day in the playground." He sat on his hands. His left leg twitched. "I know it wasn't anything I did. I mean, I'm no match for you." Afraid, he dropped his eyes. They locked onto a crack of the dark-stained, picnic-like table; it ran the length of the tabletop.

"Look, Sutter, get to the point." Dresden pulled a large set of keys from the pocket of his denim jacket. With the fingers of one hand he flipped through the lot one by one.

"What happened?" asked Jason. He looked up. "What did you see that made you step back?"

"I should just pound you into the dirt." Dresden half laughed. Each key turned over the ring and fell against the next with a distinctive, metallic clink. "But I won't." He shook the keys after the last one fell and began flipping through them again. He thought for a moment. "I saw my dad comin' at me drunk, dangerous. Course, it wasn't him. How could it be?" He paused. The keys came over the top of the ring faster; they clinked louder. "I don't argue when I see 'im like that. I get the hell out of the way. So I got out of the way and tripped."

He slapped the keys down on the table. Jason jumped at the sound but kept eye contact. Dresden continued. "I have a question for *you*. How'd you do it? An' even worse, how come I care 'bout things I didn't before. I could just take whatever I wanted from these sheep. All of sudden I feel bad about it. What the rat's ass did you do to me?"

"So far as I know, I didn't do anything." Jason brought his hands up, his palms facing out. He shook his head to stress his ignorance. "I'm sorry about the way your dad is. It's not right."

"You did somethin', Sutter." He started with the keys again.

Jason remained silent. He knew he was guilty as charged. Instead of receiving thoughts, he had planted one. He had created an image so real Dresden ran from it. How? Both of his legs started to dance under the table. White knuckled, his hands grasped the table's edge. This constant ignorance made him wish he didn't have the mental abilities he'd discovered over the last few months.

The key flipping stopped. Dresden glared into Jason's face. "You say a word of this to anyone and I'll bury you. Got me?"

"Yeah." Jason nodded. "Got you." He released the table, stood, and turned to go.

"One more thing." Jason froze. "Tell the Russell runt that he's got guts. I respect that."

"I'll tell 'im." As Jason headed back to Russ and Suzy, he felt Dresden's eyes, following him.

☆　　☆　　☆

"What is it with adults?" Jason said as he sat down with his friends. The storm continued to rage. Suzy was the first kid he'd met living in the Dubois house after he'd gotten out from under the fog caused by his medication. Those he'd met before Suzy existed in a drugged haze. Everything was a blur until his mind cleared.

"Did he really say he thought I had guts?" Russ smiled ear to ear.

"Yes, Russ, but you're missing my point." Jason watched Russ try to get serious by losing his smile. He failed. It popped right back. Jason shook his head, annoyed.

"What do you mean, Jason?" Suzy asked. She pulled her shoulder-length brown hair back behind her ear.

"Dresden's got one parent who beats him up. Rachel has one who scares her to death." Rachel, like Suzy, was a Dubois foster child. "Lydia and Frank are scary. I mean, the kids in our house are there because of screwed-up adults. Believe me, I know. I've seen them." Jason's fisted hands lightly pounded the table. "Even you, Suzy, must have had some trouble." Suzy looked down and said nothing. "And Mr. Downing, the teacher who sat with me during the tests, had learning beaten into him. Aren't there any good parents out there?"

"Well, yeah," Russ said, still smiling. "My parents are okay. You wouldn't want them hangin' 'round too much, but they're not scary. Funny scary, maybe." Russ glanced down at his hands and chuckled. "My dad trying to be hip when my oldest sister's friends come over is pretty weird." A laugh escaped his control. Suzy giggled, watching Russ.

Jason counted Russ as the person he could trust the most. Their first meeting, however, had not been auspicious.

If the sixth-grade class had a president, Russell Wyatt would be it. He stood up to Arthur Dresden a number of times and wound up bloodied on the ground. Every kid in the class respected his fearlessness, and most liked him. He was the all-American, likable kid with freckles, reddish-brown hair, an energetic, loud mouth, and enough smarts to impress the teachers. When Jason stepped off the bus for his first day of class, Russell had followed him.

"Hey, new kid!" Russ yelled. Jason's playground battle with Dresden had been the day before.

Jason turned, not knowing what to expect. He hoped Rachel would give him some tips, since they were in the same class. She didn't say two words to him on the bus, even when he tried to be nice.

"Yeah?" Jason turned and watched Russ approach. With all the other kids so close, he did not dare expend any more energy reading this person. He'd learned only a few weeks earlier that he could read minds. When the urge to use the bathroom had awakened him and the door was unlocked early on a Saturday morning, Jason had crossed the backyard from the shed to the house, only to collapse in the grass with a blast of damaged kids' thoughts and dreams overwhelming his ability to move. Jason had discovered then that every errant thought within a given distance flashed in his consciousness. It took considerable focus to allow only one mind into his thoughts.

"The name's Russell Wyatt. You can call me Russ." He looked Jason up and down and wondered how this skinny kid had overpowered Dresden. "You're a hero. You're our hero after what you did yesterday."

"I don't want to be a hero. I just want to be normal." Jason rubbed his forehead; his head throbbed.

"Too late. You will likely find yourself surrounded by kids wanting to be safe. I can help with that if you want." Russ cocked an eyebrow.

Jason almost smiled. "Oh? You have a plan?"

"You stick with me, and you won't be crowded. All we have to do is get the word around that you expect something in return for guarding us from the bully. A fee to—"

"Forget it. I don't want to be like Dresden." Jason stepped back, turned from Russ, and headed to an empty corner of the playground.

Russ cut off his escape with a few quick steps. "You're right. You're right. Stupid idea." Russ thought for a second. He massaged his chin with his right hand. Suddenly he held up his hands and pointed his index fingers at Jason. "Hey, what about this? We get Dresden to be your bodyguard and …" Jason stopped listening, desperate for quiet. He pushed by Russell to get away.

"Hey, I was only tryin' to help!" Russ watched him go, and then he saw Rachel nearby. "Rachel, what's his problem?"

"He's a real nutcase. Had to be put in a straitjacket a couple of times. Somehow he managed to get into school to ruin it for the rest of us." She set off to join a group of girls who waited for her.

"Very interesting." Russell moved among his friends and let the new kid be by himself. He would make a connection as an act of self-preservation.

✳ ✳ ✳

As they waited for the storm to subside, Russ and Suzy stared at Jason, not understanding his frustration with adults.

Jason frowned at his friend; he was serious. "I have got to meet your parents, Russ. I need to know there are some good ones out there."

"Speak of the devil," said Russ, as he caught sight of a sky-blue Pontiac Le Mans pulling up to the playground gate. "Here's your chance. That's my mom. C'mon."

"Wait, wait! What about Suzy?" Jason asked.

"Sure, sure, c'mon." Russ gathered up his stuff and headed to the door.

"Can I go find Rachel?" asked Suzy. "She'll want a lift too."

"Yeah, but hurry," Russ said. Suzy ran off to find her friend.

Rachel did not like Jason, because his crazy wall pounding—his violence—upset her very much. Driven to try to understand why he was not liked, one night Jason entered her sleeping mind. Afterward he still did not get why she remained angry at him. But Rachel had others—her family—as the target of her rage.

Minutes later, Russ rushed out of the door into the storm with Suzy, Rachel, and Jason hot on his heels. He dove into the front seat while the others piled into the back—all soaked to the skin.

"The more the merrier," said the sweetest voice Jason had ever heard. His heart melted as he looked into smiling green eyes. Russell's mother turned out to be as opposite to Lydia Dubois as dark is to light. Her dark auburn hair hung straight down, wet from the rain. "So I finally get to meet the infamous Jason Sutter. I'm Peg Wyatt." She held out her hand over the back of the front seat. Jason shook it. The floral smell in the car was intoxicating. He inhaled, held his breath, and let it go slowly.

"What is that smell," he whispered.

"Perfume," Suzy said in Jason's ear. "I don't know which one. Something with roses maybe." Jason didn't care. He could not get enough of it and continued to breathe it in.

"Now, you are?" asked Mrs. Wyatt energetically to the other two occupants in the rear seat. Suzy and Rachel introduced themselves and thanked her for the lift. Finished with the introductions, she turned around, started the engine, and headed to the Dubois house.

"What?" Mrs. Wyatt asked. She looked down between her and Russ. "Ha! Everyone, this little bundle of joy whom I overlooked is my youngest, Patti." A small hand shot up over the middle of the front seat.

Jason did a double take as the small, outstretched hand disappeared from view. He leaned forward, sensing something. With his head over the back of the front seat, he looked down into bright, blue eyes and a cheery smile. Like her mother's, the four-year-old's wet hair hung down dripping.

"So, Jason, did Russ mention he's got his first game of the season coming up this weekend?" Mrs. Wyatt concentrated again on her driving, leaning forward. The lashing rain turned the windshield opaque. The wipers barely kept up.

"No, he never mentioned it." Jason fell back into his seat and glanced at his friend.

"I just forgot." Russ shrugged. "Ya know? There's a lot goin' on these days."

"What do you play?" Rachel asked.

"Baseball. I'm the catcher."

Rachel nodded, making it clear she understood what Russ was talking about.

"You keep up with baseball?" Russ asked her, surprised.

"Had to in my family. My dad was a nut about ..." Rachel spoke the last words in a whisper and then looked down. She swiped away imagined crumbs on her plaid skirt.

"Oh!" Suzy said excitedly, filling the uncomfortable silence. "Can we go watch you play?"

"It will be up to Mrs. Dubois," Mrs. Wyatt said before Russ could answer. "I will talk to her and see. Would you want to come too, Rachel? I know Jason wants to."

"You bet," Jason said. He wondered what had caused Rachel to become silent and if she was still mad at him.

"Yes, Mrs. Wyatt. I would love to go," Rachel said. Any reason to get away from the house was a good thing. She turned to Suzy and smiled. But as she looked at Jason, her smile fell. Jason mouthed the words "I'm sorry." She thought for a moment and then nodded and accepted his apology.

"There you go," Mrs. Wyatt said. She reached over and patted Russ's knee. "A cheering section just for you, other than Dad and me." She laughed, and everyone laughed with her. The mood in the car was light and full of cheer.

The lightness faded when they reached the Dubois house. The kids dashed from the backseat into the house. On the porch, Jason turned and waved good-bye. He was happy that Russ had such a wonderful mother and family. He could only watch but not have what he wanted so much. No one noticed the single tear as it escaped down his cheek.

✶   ✶   ✶

In an office over a drugstore on Main Street, Robert Sylvester—Sly Dog to his business associates—was talking on the phone. He ran his fingers through his blond-brown hair and pulled it back off his aviator glasses. His index finger scratched the beginnings of a moustache that never grew fuller.

"Yeah, yeah, I've heard all this before." Sly shook his head. He stood and gazed down on the street below his office and watched the rain come down. His string-bean physique made him look weak, especially in his signature outfit: tight blue jeans with a white business shirt and a bright-red tie. He used this misdirection to his advantage. Though Sly was thirty-eight years old, he was all muscle, so he looked much younger. On more than one occasion, a competitor wound up bleeding and unconscious in an alley because he thought Sly was an easy target.

"We need to meet. My client is disappointed. Ya know what I mean?" Sly turned back to the desk and leaned over to pick up a pencil. He tapped it on the desk's edge.

"What can I do?" whined Frank.

Sly did not like Frank Dubois, but he appreciated Lydia. A smile crossed his face as he remembered the first time she approached him. After an acquittal on drug charges because the cops got sloppy with the evidence, Sly stumbled into this frightening woman on the courthouse steps. She was dressed in business attire, like one of his meaner grammar school teachers; she wore a dark-blue dress and her hair was pulled back hard. He had to admit this woman knew her stuff. She quoted Sly's record as well as where he lived and worked. There was something about her that drew him and repelled him at the same time.

"Look, fool," she said, looking evil, "I've got prescription drugs to unload, and you got access to the market."

"Why should I talk to you?" He started to walk away. Sly got the feeling that this hellion was wired, that she worked for the cops.

"Don't be stupid." She glared at him. She read the situation clearly. "You aren't worth the trouble to trap. Walk with me down to the corner." She nodded in the direction she meant and spoke in a pleasant tone. "I've got a deal for you."

Sly followed her. He figured there might be something in it for him.

The deal they cut that day lasted five years. There had been ups and downs in the flow of drugs, but things worked out for Lydia in Sly's world. No one got rich, but the income was steady, and it all remained under the radar so the police never became an issue. Lydia was lucky.

"The kids are better," Frank said. His whine brought Sly back from his reverie. "The damn doctors won't write the prescriptions the way we want."

Frank stood in his living room and tried to explain why the pill count came in shy of expectations.

"Well then, Franky, we have a problem," Sly said as he twirled a pencil through his fingers. In the last few months he'd dealt more with Frank; he had a bad feeling about this guy. "Got a repulsive streak of Boy Scout in him," he had complained to Lydia years earlier.

"Don't worry about him," she'd said. "Worry about me. He does what he's told."

Sly followed her lead. He hoped Lydia's luck would hold up. But the numbers—the pill counts—did not lie.

Sly leaned against the edge of the desk and said to Frank, "Ya don't want a visit from those guys in Philly." He had built a small but successful illegal prescription drug exchange with heavy-hitter drug lords in Philadelphia. The big boys did not pay much attention to the smalltime hoods if they delivered in cash or contraband to their schedule. A delivery was due, and Dubois was short on the contraband.

"Okay." Frank thought fast, rubbing the back of his neck. "We've done a kickback before to ease the situation. Will that do?"

"Might. Don't know." Sly sat in his chair and then tossed the pencil onto the desk. "At the next exchange, I'll give you their direction. Where and when?"

When Frank hung up, the meeting arrangements were set. He felt sick. His and Lydia's goldmine had begun to look more like an empty pit with dangers lurking in the shadows. He wanted out. Lydia would not hear of it. He feared that the whole situation could get very ugly.

Chapter 3

J ason sat in Dr. Lipton's waiting room beside Frank. He fretted about making a good show to keep the medications coming. Frank flipped magazine pages and worried about getting to work late. Both walked softly when it came to Lydia. She was dangerous and destructive. When it became obvious that Jason didn't need his mind-numbing drugs, Lydia set him straight.

It was the morning Jason first met Suzy. He was sitting with Suzy on the steps of the back porch, talking about his learning to read. When Suzy left the porch to get ready for school, Lydia slid through the open screen door, careful not to spill the steaming coffee from the mug she carried. She stood over him, staring down at the back of his head.

"Feeling well enough for school, are you?" Lydia spoke the words as though it was a great inconvenience. She had overheard the children's conversation and was acting to take advantage of it.

"Yeah." Jason had hoped she would go away if he ignored her. It didn't work; Lydia wanted something.

"We need to make a deal." Lydia set her cup of coffee on the wooden railing. "Frank and I will make sure you get what you want—if you do what we ask."

"What do you want me to do?" He turned and looked up at her. His first impulse was to run and hide. But he remained still; his expression remained calm.

"Your meds are almost gone. Seems like you don't need them anymore.

How that's come about, I guess, will remain a mystery. The shrink doctor wants to see you before he renews the prescription. You want school. We want the meds." She folded her arms and waited.

"If I refuse, 'cause like you say, I don't need 'em anymore?" Jason stood to face her.

"Let's put it this way: make it hard for us,"—she nodded at the shed—"and we can put the lock back on the shed door. We'll just ask the shrink to make a house call … which he won't. He'll just give us what we want anyway." She smiled. "Remember, everyone believes you are out of your mind and that we are your one best hope of comin' around."

"Fine," Jason said. He could not tolerate imprisonment in the shed any more. "I'll fake it."

"Good. We have an understanding." She picked up her coffee cup and finished it. "You're a smart kid when you're not rattling the walls screaming." She started to turn away, but turned back. "By the way, watch your back with that Suzy. She damned near ripped a girl's hair out and left her bleeding in a couple of places." Lydia shook her head, chuckled, and then left.

☆　☆　☆

A week later Jason went for tests to find out what he could do.

Called into the office, he sat before Dr. Lipton. It was time to make good on the deal.

"Do you think about your parents?" Dr. Lipton sounded very friendly. With glasses low on his nose, he looked at Jason over the tops. His hair was white, short, and thinning in front. He wore a dark-blue suit with a red-striped tie. Jason felt comfortable with what he sensed of the doctor's thoughts and regretted that he had to trick him.

But the doctor's question had caught him off guard. Jason stopped twitching; he thought it made him look crazier. Which would help the deal with Lydia: saying he thought about his parents every day or lying?

He decided to lie. "No, I don't."

"Do you remember what they look like?" The doctor scribbled on his pad. "Do you have any pictures?" He glanced up.

"No. I … I can't remember them at all." This time he didn't have to lie. Jason knew he had parents like everyone else. Why couldn't he remember their faces?

"Let's try a different direction, shall we?" Lipton placed his pad and pen on his desk. He picked up his pipe. Tapping down the tobacco, he took out a lighter and lit it. "What have you determined about you?" He drew the flame into the bowl. Fragrant smoke filled the room.

"I know my name, if that's what you mean." Jason grasped the edge of his seat on either side. He lifted himself slightly, uncomfortable.

"No, no." The doctor laughed. "I hope you know your own name. I mean things like, when is your birthday? Have you attended any other schools before? Do you like to read or play a sport? That kind of thing."

Jason felt suddenly very sad and stared at the floor. Controlling the telepathic gate that allowed the screams and cries from others to explode on his consciousness exhausted him. The items the doctor listed had never entered his thoughts.

"I … I don't know any of those things. I just wanted the voices to go away. I can't remember a time when I could care about anything else."

"Well." Dr. Lipton pointed at him with his pipe. "You seem stable right now. We will have to work on this together. You can't go through life not knowing these simple things. For now, we will keep your medication at the current level to help with the symptoms and allow us to open your memory. I will try to track down some information on you and your family. We will meet next week and for the next number of weeks. What do you think?"

"That would be great," he said. He knew Frank and Lydia would be happy with no change to the meds, and he would have someone with a calm mind to talk to. Also, the possibility of finding his family excited him. Maybe he had found the right person in the right place to open doors.

✳   ✳   ✳

On Friday before Russ's game, Frank dropped Jason at Russ's house for dinner. Lydia insisted he go and attend the game with Suzy and Rachel the next day. Jason couldn't figure her angle, but he didn't argue.

On the threshold of Russ's house, Jason found it impossible to waste any time thinking about his foster mother. Seeing Peg Wyatt again was his priority. He stood at the opened door, stunned by the glorious chaos in the Wyatt house. An ordinary wall of sound struck him: loud voices, laughter, and music. This was very different from the museum quiet punctuated by occasional screams at the Dubois house.

Russ pulled him into the house. "C'mon into the kitchen and say hello to my mom. Then I'll show you my room, and we can kill some time before dinner."

Jason followed Russ to the back of the house. They passed the living room on the right and the stairway upstairs on the left. Mrs. Wyatt bounced around her kitchen like a ball in a pinball machine; she sought key ingredients over the oven, looked through pots and pans in the island drawers across from the sink, and checked the state of the meat roasting in the oven. Patti played on the floor near the island, dressing her dolls in different hats and dresses.

"I hope you like roast beef?" Mrs. Wyatt asked when she looked up and found Russ and Jason watching her.

"I love it." Jason was not quite sure he had ever had roast beef, but it smelled wonderful. Lydia and Frank did not serve anything like it. Jason suddenly turned his head and looked down on Russ's sister, sitting on the floor. "Sorry, what'd you say?"

Patti looked up at her mother.

"I think Patti wants to ask a question," Jason said as he looked at Mrs. Wyatt.

It suddenly became very quiet. Mrs. Wyatt stopped what she was doing. Her expression saddened. Jason looked to Russ and back to his mother.

"I'm sorry, Jason," said Mrs. Wyatt. "Patti does not … can't talk. You caught me off guard."

Jason sensed that she believed it was her fault. "I'm sorry. I just saw her looking up at you. I thought she was about to say something." Jason glanced at Russ for help to fix this.

"It's okay, Jason. You didn't know." Mrs. Wyatt wiped her hands on a red-and-white checked kitchen towel, went over to Patti, and smiled down at her. "Now, my little munchkin, I bet you wanted to know about the mashed potatoes." The awkward moment passed in an instant. She looked up over her shoulder and said to Jason, "She loves her mashed potatoes and gravy." She cradled her daughter's cheek in her hand, stood up, and got back to work.

"Mom, Jason and me are going upstairs." Russ tugged Jason's shirt.

"Okay. Dinner will be ready in about thirty minutes." She pulled a ricer down from the top shelf over the oven and checked the huge pot of potatoes boiling on the stove.

The boys retraced their steps to the stairway and reached Russ's room at the top of the stairs. As he opened the door, Russ said, "I got lucky. With all sisters, I get a room to myself." Jason was amazed. The walls and the blanket on his bed were an ocean blue. Dark-blue curtains hung from rods over the windows. Model airplanes twisted slowly on their wires from the ceiling. One partially completed model lay on the desk, which sat before one of the two windows in the room.

"Did you do those?" Jason pointed up at the World War II bomber models.

"Nah, those have been hanging there since I was five. My dad did those. He actually flew a B-25 and later a B-17 in the war." Russ looked at the planes, proud of his dad.

"War?" Jason knew nothing of the war.

"Man! I keep forgetting you're from another planet." Russ shook his head. "World War II? Adolf Hitler? The atom bomb? Pearl Harbor?" Jason shook his head. "Let's just forget it. But if my dad starts talking about the war act like you know, okay?"

"Yeah." Jason walked around the room. He examined and touched everything. On the desk was the unfinished model of a P-51 Mustang fighter plane, according to the box lid. He stopped. "Russ, I have to tell you something." He ran his finger over the plastic wing of the plane.

"What? I shoulda warned you about Patti?" Russ sounded defensive.

"No, I just wanted you to know that your mother is … well … kinda like me." Jason turned and looked at his friend. Russ just stared back at him.

"You have got to be kidding."

"Nope." Jason turned to face his friend. "She is not as ... loud or powerful, I guess, as I am, but it's there." He grinned, amused by Russ's reaction. "How often does she do things for you without asking and get them right. And does she know when you're telling a lie?"

"Damn, she always knows. I can't get away with anything." Russ sat on his bed, shocked and dismayed.

"Your sister is better at it." Jason watched Russ's reaction and would have laughed if the issue were not so serious. "Downstairs in the kitchen, Patti clearly asked about the mashed potatoes, but not with words. I heard here clearly, and your mother picked up on it. Patti knows she is different, but your mom doesn't know that she has this ability too."

"You're telling me that my sister and my mother can read minds? More to the point, my mind?" Russ put his head in his hands, thoroughly amazed and distressed by the possibilities.

"Yes, but like I said, your mother is not that strong and doesn't know she can do it. Patti knows." Jason walked over and sat on the bed with his friend.

"Why don't you bring Patti up here?" Jason said. "She would love to play with her big brother. Believe me, I know." Jason nudged Russ to get him moving to the kitchen. In short order, the three kids were on the floor, quietly playing with Chutes and Ladders.

Mrs. Wyatt put the finishing touches on her dinner. She gathered the last of the pots and pans, and placed them in the sink full of soapy water. As she dried her hands and started to put the platter on the dining room table, she heard a child's laughter. The platter dropped the last inch with a thud, and juices splashed the table cloth. She had never heard it but knew that laugh instinctively. She ignored the food and slowly started upstairs to her son's room. Outside the door on the landing, she stopped and listened. She heard it again, unmistakable.

"I climb the ladder," said Patti, as if she had always spoken.

"Oh, hi, Mom," Russ said.

Mrs. Wyatt stood on the threshold and put her hand to her mouth, trying to choke back tears. They came regardless, as she rushed into the room and picked up her daughter and held her.

"No cry, Mommy," Patti said. She put her tiny hands on her mother's cheeks.

"How … how did this happen?" Mrs. Wyatt looked down at the two boys, stunned by her reaction.

"Not hear me, Mommy," said the little girl into her mother's ear. "So Jas'n said to blow my things. So I blow 'em and ev'r'body hear 'em."

Dinner turned into an odd combination of tears and laughter, uncomfortable but not in a bad way. Harry Wyatt climbed up from his basement sanctuary where broken things returned fixed. He gently caressed his wife's hand, and she talked quietly with their miraculous daughter.

"First," said Mr. Wyatt, standing at the head of the table, "let me express my gratitude and our indebtedness to you, Jason. What appeared to be such a small thing to you, none of the best doctors could do. So—"

"Okay, Dad," said Angie, Russ's eldest sister. "Like, I'm really happy that Patti has found her voice and everything, but what about our bet?"

Angie was taller than Russ with long, auburn hair like her mother. She also had her mother's green eyes and high cheekbones. Jason could not tell who was the prettier, her or her mother. Even the second sister, Jeena, would turn heads. Jeena sat quietly. She looked up often and smiled, as her mother engaged Patti in conversation.

"Well, Angelina, I don't think this is the time." Mr. Wyatt was annoyed by his eldest daughter.

"No, Harry," said Mrs. Wyatt. "Patti and I are just fine. Go ahead and pay attention to the girls. I need you to stand in for me for a while." They shared a smile. He nodded and sat.

"Okay, who's hungry?" The platters waltzed around the table, and everyone took their fill. Patti got a mountain of mashed potatoes with gravy pouring over the top like lava from a volcano. Talk sprouted up randomly about anything and everything. They knew, however, not to disturb the quiet talk at the end of the table.

"So was Kennedy the right choice?" asked Mr. Wyatt, as the food platters made the rounds.

"He looks good, but I bet Nixon would've been better." Russ loaded his plate, turned to Jason, and winked.

"What?!" Angie almost tossed a spoonful of green beans at her brother. "You little … What do you know?" Angie put on a hang-dog face and said, "'My wife wears a good wool Republican coat.' Give me a break!"

"Better the crook ya know, sis," Russ said. He pointed his potato-laden fork her way.

Jason sat and ate; the free-for-all left him dumbstruck. His eyes followed the discussion back and forth like a spectator at a tennis tournament. They had … something. None of the kids at the Dubois house shared it. He took each bite slowly and thought about it. The roast beef, however, distracted him. It felt miraculous on his tongue. The mashed potatoes were an adventure to his palate. This new world of flavors devoured his attention.

"The Beatles will be bigger than Elvis," Angie said over everyone else. Jason froze with the last piece of meat dangling on his fork halfway to his mouth. Before another energetic give-and-take could start, he gobbled it.

"Bigger than Elvis, fine," said Mr. Wyatt. He wiped his mouth with his napkin and then slapped it down next to his plate. "Bigger than Sinatra? I don't think so." Jason wondered who these people might be.

"Dad, you are so out of touch," Angie said. She rolled her eyes.

"What do you think, Jason?" Mr. Wyatt asked. "And here's the bet." Jason nodded with the forkful of mashed potatoes in his mouth. "Angie is a deal maker. When she heard Russ had a new friend coming over, she had two questions: One, 'Is he cute?'"

"Dad!" A bright pink blossomed on Angie's cheeks

He continued, enjoying his daughter's embarrassment. "Then she asked, 'Do you wanna bet he picks my music over yours?'" He turned to his daughter and grinned. "Well, is he?"

"Cuter than the others." She held her father's eye defiantly and then looked Jason over unabashedly. Jason felt like he stood naked before a crowd. "Which do you like best?" she finally asked.

"I … uh." He gulped a mouthful of corn. "I don't really know who they are." The table exploded. Russ shook his head and laughed. For the rest of the evening, Jason was chained to the record player in the living room, where he listened to current, popular music, and tunes from the forties and fifties.

Patti sat with her mother and occasionally looked over at Jason, communicating her thoughts. Jason responded in kind, intent on "Love Me Do." He had learned two things. First, he liked Sinatra best. When he said so, Mr. Wyatt did a kind of funny dance to celebrate his win over his daughter. He rocked at the waist, side to side, while he turned slowly in a circle.

Russ chuckled at his dad and said to Jason, "See what I mean. This is so embarrassing."

Angie took losing the bet better when Jason said he thought the Beatles would be more popular than Elvis Presley. She stuck out her tongue at her father, who laughed and gave her a big hug. Angie couldn't stay mad at him very long; she smiled when he danced with her to one of Sinatra's slow ballads.

All through the evening, Jason's mind raced. *There were others like me! How long until they find me or I stumble onto more of them?* He held this thought and watched Mr. Wyatt and his daughter dance slowly in their living room. Before too long, Jeena cut in. Angie graciously shared their father's attention.

It suddenly occurred to Jason that these people cared about each other. That was the something that he and the other inmates at the Dubois house missed.

I care about you, Jason, whispered in his mind. He smiled and looked back over his shoulder into the dining room.

Thanks, Patti. I care about you too. Jason responded.

Patti waved at Jason, as she and her mother sat cheek to cheek. He waved and then prayed he would have a chance to share that kind of moment with his mom.

☆   ☆   ☆

At the Dubois house, while Jason sorted out the music debate at Russ's house, Frank and Lydia stood at the kitchen sink. They looked out of the window at the empty toolshed. Frank drank coffee in his T-shirt and navy-blue work pants. Lydia, in her usual yellow dress, arms crossed, stared at the shed door, impatient that the boy was not in it, secured.

"We got lucky, ya know?" Frank turned from the window and sat down at the kitchen table.

"Meaning?" Lydia hated when Frank thought luck had anything to do with living. Her left foot tapped. Lydia heartily believed in making and taking advantage of opportunities. Luck was for the lazy.

"I called the drugstore after I put the kids' lunch bags together yesterday morning." Frank said as he stared into his cup and swirled his coffee. "The pharmacist said sudden withdrawal from the stuff the kid was taking could be life threatening. At the least, a patient would shake involuntarily for days, accompanied by bouts of vomiting and diarrhea. Worst case,"—Frank looked up—"he stops breathing and goes into cardiac arrest. Like I said, we got lucky we didn't find him dead."

"So he shoulda been sicker for longer. That what you're saying?" Lydia turned to Frank.

"Yeah, I guess … when ya think about it." The words came out slowly. He had lost his train of thought, stunned by her lack of concern. "I should still be cleaning up a mess." *Or burying a body.* Frank sipped his coffee.

"So we have a little mystery." Lydia returned her attention to the shed. "He's suddenly a fairly normal kid after months of insanity and then doesn't die when we stop the meds all at once." She shook her head slowly. "Let's keep a close eye on the boy. Maybe he might get sick again. We don't want any undue attention brought our way."

"His unused pills ready to go with the others?" Frank stood up. He needed a good book and the isolation of his reading nook in the basement.

"All in the bag." Lydia shrugged her left shoulder to indicate the cabinet to the left of the sink. "We might make better money this time."

Frank nodded then headed downstairs. He left his cup on the table and left Lydia to her strategic thinking. He shook his head, unable to get rid of the image of the hollow eyes that had stared back at him from the shed door weeks before. The boy had been seriously sick.

☆ ☆ ☆

Frank remembered the dead grass being wet and slippery as the March weather began to give way to the onset of spring. They crossed the backyard to the shed. Lydia released the lock. The door swung open.

"Whoa," Frank said, standing at the door with Lydia. He wrinkled his nose at the smell of vomit. "Somebody was sick last night."

"Take care of it," Lydia ordered. Frank handed her the usual two cups of medication, stepped into the shed, passed Jason, and grabbed the bucket. He held it at arm's length as he crossed the yard. When he returned, Lydia and Jason had not moved; they stared at each other without speaking.

Lydia broke the silence and eye contact first. "You sick?"

"Yeah. Tough night." Jason leaned against the door frame.

Frank saw the exhaustion in the dark circles under the boy's eyes. *He must have been retching most of the night,* he thought. Jason watched Lydia and the key to the lock on the toolshed door she held in her right hand.

"Here." Lydia held out the usual cups.

"No!" Jason backed away a step. "That's what made me sick."

"Hmm." The corners of Lydia's mouth twitched ever so slightly. "Well, the shed's still standing. That counts for somethin'." Frank walked up to Jason and handed him the cleaned bucket.

"Thanks," said Jason.

"Go use the bathroom," Lydia said. The pills slid into her pocket.

Frank felt sorry for the kid, but he knew that asking Lydia why she did anything might cause an uproar. He noted that Jason's hair had grown a few inches, dark brown and wavy. He was a good-looking kid.

"No pills?" Frank humbly addressed Lydia. "Worth a try, I guess." She waved him off and watched the boy carefully.

Frank witnessed Jason set the bucket by the door and start across the slippery, snow-covered yard unassisted. Jason stumbled on the porch steps and held his head as though a sudden intense headache stopped him. He steadied himself by grabbing the step railing. With great effort, Jason took the last two steps as one and entered the kitchen. Frank thought that the kid handled himself pretty well getting to and from the bathroom without a breakdown. Back in the shed, the lock clicked. Frank and Lydia walked away.

Maybe, thought Frank, *he isn't a psycho after all*. Frank had misgivings about keeping him locked up all day.

"You don't have to feed me or lock me in," Jason said the next day when Frank brought him lunch while Lydia looked on. The boy looked from one adult to the other. "I'm okay. I won't cause any more trouble. I can take care of myself." This sudden clarity and reasonable request shocked both.

"I don't know," Frank said. He glanced Lydia's way. She looked the boy up and down and considered the risk. An opportunity for extra money rang the cash register in her head. Frank knew the crooked smile playing on her lips.

"Fine. We'll give this little miracle a trial run starting …" Her foot tapped the ground. "Wednesday. As long as we have no trouble between now and then, the lock comes off." She turned abruptly and walked back to the house. Frank pushed the door shut, slammed the metal latch into place, and closed the lock. He turned toward the house.

"Wait," Jason called through the door. "What day is it today?"

Frank stopped and glanced back at the shed. "It's Monday," he yelled. Then he scooted across the yard to catch up with Lydia.

Two days of the regular routine dragged as Frank hung around at meal time. He made sure the boy could feed and control himself. At noontime Wednesday, true to her word, Lydia removed the lock. Silent, she tossed him a brown bag lunch, looked him in the eye, nodded, and left.

Frank watched from the porch as Jason walked out of his prison and around the yard. Taking a deep breath of the frosty air, he settled on the ground and leaned back against the big oak tree next to the shed. The boy smiled and opened the bag. Peanut butter again, always peanut butter, but Frank saw the big bite and Jason's closed-eyed satisfaction.

Frank turned away and went back into the house, wondering what Jason Sutter would do with his unfettered freedom.

✧   ✧   ✧

The crack of the bat echoed around the field the day after Jason's dinner with Russ's family. The ball sailed over the left-field fence, and the Shiller's Saloon Bulldogs took a two-run lead over the Jackson Used Cars Rockets. Russ, wearing the white with red striping of the Rockets, threw his catcher's glove down in disgust. A cloud of dust erupted around home plate.

"Explain what just happened," Suzy said. She, Jason, and Rachel sat in the bleachers along the third base line.

"That kid," Rachel said as she pointed at the boy who rounded third base, "just hit a homerun, a homer." The boy in the gray with green stripes of the Bulldogs made a cross-eyed face at the third baseman as he passed.

Frank Dubois sat quietly two rows up. He looked around, searching for a face the crowd. Harry and Peg Wyatt sat with him. They had tried to start a conversation with Frank, but his one-word answers told them he would rather be left alone. So they focused on the game.

Jason only half listened to Rachel's explanation; he breathed deep the fresh air and enjoyed the day's warmth. The sun stood high in a cloudless sky. The mild, late-April weather got people out of their houses to do yard work, enjoy a picnic, or go to a baseball game. Jason was able to control the mental chatter, even though he sat surrounded by raucous fans. The exercises Russ and Suzy had forced on him helped.

Chapter 4

E arlier, near the end of March, as the winter cold loosened its grip, Suzy had sought out Jason in the playground. It was his first full day of school.

"So how did it go?" she asked. She came up short when the flame-haired boy stepped from behind him. "Who's this?"

"A new friend," said Jason. "Suzy, this is Russ." He placed his hand on Russ's shoulder. "Russ, Suzy."

"Hi," said Russ. "That pink blouse looks kinda nice on you." He winked at Jason then broadcasted his winning smile at Suzy.

Happy with the unexpected compliment, she mumbled, "Thanks."

Both turned their attention to Jason.

"Well?" asked Suzy.

"Okay," he said. "I need to tell my only two friends in the world some stuff about me. We only have about ten minutes before the buses load up. Listen carefully. You have got to promise never to tell anyone else, ever. If you do, well, our friendship is over. You understand, right?" He looked at both with a stern expression to make his point.

They nodded. Jason launched into a detailed description of all he could remember of his psychic abilities and how he had stumbled into them. His arms and hands punctuated his words as he laid out his painful rise from the ashes of a drugged existence to his current state of self-awareness.

"I knew it!" screamed Suzy, grinning ear to ear. "I knew there was something. I knew it."

"Calm down, Suzy," Jason said. He looked around to see if anyone had noticed her outburst.

"So you're saying you have powers like Sue Storm of the Fantastic Four?" Russ asked.

"Fantastic Four? What's that?" asked Jason.

"Oh man, how can you not know the Fantastic Four? How about Spiderman or the X-Men?" Jason shook his head. Russ stared in disbelief. "You've been living under a rock."

"Okay. Okay." Jason brought his hand to his forehead. Weariness had begun its slow assault. He needed to sleep. "Let's not make too big a thing out of this. Tell me what they are."

"Here, I'll show you." Russ reached into his book bag and pulled out a comic book. He handed Jason the latest Fantastic Four edition. On the cover, a woman in a blue costume with the number four emblazoned on her chest was using her mind to throw a force field around another blue-costumed character, protecting him from a blast of light energy. Russ looked over his shoulder and then asked, "Can you do that?"

"I have no idea." Jason studied the picture and wondered.

"What can you do?"

"It's like I told you, not much. It's hard just to get the noise level down. You have no idea how much you are hitting me with right now." He pointed to Russ. "It's hard work to stop it."

"What do you get from me, Jason?" Suzy asked.

"Well, that's the strange part." He turned to face her. "I don't get anything. Maybe that's why it's easy to be near you."

Suzy beamed. She threw her arms around him, pinning his arms to his sides.

"Suzy?" Jason said through clenched teeth, "I can't breathe." She let him go and stood back. He rubbed his arms and stared at her. "You're strong for your size."

"Hey, where does that leave me?" demanded Russ, who stood there with his hands apart, his palms facing up. "I'm not gonna hug ya."

"We're friends, and we have to help each other," Jason said. "I'll help you with your problems. You help me with all the things I don't know but should if I had been in school. How's that?"

"Pretty slim to my way of thinking," Russ said. "What you need is a manager." He stepped forward and put his arm around Jason's shoulders and waved his other, palm out, to invite Jason and Suzy to share his vision. "Someone to run interference for you. A good talker. An idea man."

"What now, idea man?" Jason asked with a laugh.

"Don't know yet, but I'll work something out."

"Okay. You're the manager, and Suzy helps me learn more about what I do." He threw one arm around Russ's shoulders and the other arm around Suzy's. From now on they would be a team.

Russ stepped away, bursting with energy. "Wait, wait! I got an idea." He faced them. "How about you practice what you already can do. Ya know, so you can do it better." He smiled and raised his eyebrows.

"That's how I got this far," Jason said. It felt good to be around Suzy and Russ. He wasn't so alone anymore.

"You need to do push-ups and sit-ups," Russ said. When Jason began to object, Russ waved his arm to dismiss it. "Like my old man always says, 'You wanna get stronger, you hav'ta work at it.'"

"Oh, I think I get it," Suzy said as she nodded at Russ.

"Like you just said," Russ replied. "You're working hard now to keep the noise from my brilliant thoughts getting too loud in your head."

"Yeah," Suzy said, and continued his line of thought. "Let in all the thoughts. Let the noise get loud, then shut it off the best you can, as fast as you can."

"Do that, my man, ten times, rest. Then do it again." Russ grinned and pointed at Jason. "You'll work up a good sweat. That's what I'm getting at. Work up a good sweat."

For weeks Jason did exactly that to near collapse. Suzy and Russ drilled him ruthlessly.

Chapter 5

Jason sat in the bleachers and watched the game while the random thoughts of hundreds of people barely registered. He could be a regular guy and enjoy a game.

Baseball amazed Jason. Everything was a new experience. When he entered the stadium, the intense green of the grass surprised him. His gaze gravitated to the perfect field as he moved with the crowd into the stands. The wind brushed the field with its soft, warm breath. It felt good to be in this place of such ordered greenness. He just wanted to lie back in the new grass and feel it against his bare skin.

The townspeople called the field Amber Stadium, but it was more a ball field with walls along the outfield perimeter and bleachers along the base lines to accommodate a few hundred people. No changing rooms or showers—the kids came in their uniforms or suited up in the parking lot. One section of the lot catered to the food vendors who hawked hot dogs, beer, popcorn, and more.

"The board says two outs," Jason said to Rachel. He nodded toward the scoreboard over the center-field fence. He thought for a moment and scratched his head. "So that was the first two guys who batted. One got tagged at the first base and the other missed the ball too many times. Right?"

Rachel looked shocked that a boy could know so little about baseball. "Jason, under what—?"

"I know. I know. Rock." He shook his head. "I get a lot of that. But when did I get a chance to learn? Ya know?" He glared at her.

"Yeah, you're right." She paused and looked out over the field. "Sorry." She turned back and said, "When you swing and miss the ball three times, it's called a strikeout."

All focus returned to the field and the next batter.

"Hey," said Frank, who stood in the aisle next to Jason. "I'm goin' to the concessions. Stay out of trouble. I'll be right back." They nodded, stunned for a second. They had forgotten he was there.

Another crack of the bat, and everyone's attention sailed with the ball. The outfielder backpedaled and snatched the ball and then banged into the fence. The green, wooden wall bowed with the contact. The fielder held up his glove to show the caught ball. The crowd applauded; it ended the fourth inning.

"Okay," Rachel said, turning to her two students, "any more questions?" Jason and Suzy had many. Patiently she answered them.

Before the game started, at two o'clock that Saturday afternoon, Russ, his parents, Frank, Suzy, Rachel, and Jason ate hot dogs and drank sodas in the parking lot. The carnival atmosphere infected everyone. Even Frank, a constant worrier, enjoyed himself. He even pulled out his wallet and offered to contribute to the costs.

"No, no. My treat." Mr. Wyatt waved him off. Frank nodded his thanks.

"Look," said Russ, who helped Jason doctor his hot dog. "It's like this. Do you like mustard, ketchup, relish? What?"

"Uh …" Jason said, shrugging. He looked at the dog in the bun and then at his friend. "What's the yellow stuff most have on theirs?"

"That's mustard." Russ grabbed a yellow squeeze bottle, turned it over, and spread a line on Jason's. "You eat it like this." He took a large bite from one end.

Jason followed his example. "That's good" came out as "Thass gud." Mustard coated his upper lip.

Russ laughed. "You got a load of yellow on your mouth." Then he wiped his hand across his mouth, pantomiming what Jason should do.

"Thanks." Jason wiped his mouth and smiled. Russ shook his head and chuckled at Jason's mustard covered teeth.

☆   ☆   ☆

The fifth inning of the game started with the Rockets at bat. Russ led the batting order.

"No hitter! No hitter!" yelled the catcher, squatting behind home.

"No hitter, my butt," Russ said calmly. He took a few practice swings and then smacked the first pitch into short centerfield for a base hit. A wall of noise erupted. The Rockets were thought to be outmatched by the Bulldogs. But the underdogs could count on support from the crowd. The first-base coach whispered in Russ's ear as he tossed his batting helmet to the side and put on his red cap. Russ nodded and then took a lead off the first-base bag.

Jason leaned over Suzy to ask Rachel a question: "What was that discussion all about?"

"He probably told Russ to wait on the long ball and then tag up." She leaned toward Jason but never took her eyes off the field. "If the ball is hit on the ground, he should make it hard for the other team to make a double play."

"How does he do that?" Jason watched the next batter, a big kid, as he stepped to the plate.

"He runs to second and gets in the way of the second baseman's line of sight to the first baseman, if he can," Rachel said in a loud voice.

The batter swung at the first pitch. It thwacked into the catcher's glove for a strike. He connected with the ball on the next pitch. The ground ball streaked up the middle of the infield across the second-base bag into the outfield for a stand-up single. The centerfielder rushed the ball. Russ ignored the third-base coach who signaled him to stop at second base. Russ charged and rounded second base for third. The centerfielder picked up the ball and threw it to the shortstop, who hesitated. He fired the ball to the third baseman. Russ slid into third base, stirring up a cloud of dust. The ball came in high.

"Safe!" called the umpire.

Russ jumped up and knocked the dirt and dust off his uniform. Everyone jumped to their feet and clapped. Shrill whistles echoed across the stadium. Russ took off his hat and held it high to thank the fans for their support. He put it back on and focused.

"You're next!" Russ screamed at the opposing catcher. "Comin' right at ya!" The loudest applauds and screams came from Jason and Russ's parents.

"Hey! Lansing!" Russ called to the Bulldog's pitcher. "You still wearin' your sister's pretty pink underwear for luck?" Laughter erupted in the stands. The pitcher ignored him; the next batter came up. Russ continued to razz the pitcher and the other players to throw off their game.

Jason, distracted, stopped laughing. At the end of the bleachers on the other side of the field, Frank and a tall, thin man in a dark jacket were talking. Jason watched the two interact several hundred feet away. The man gestured wildly with his hands. Frank held his hand to his head. It looked like he was receiving some very bad news. Trouble for Frank meant problems for the whole Dubois house. This meeting could not be good.

Jason focused on the man in the jacket. He tried to read his body language. There was no way he could get into someone's mind so far away. Jason blocked out the game and the cheering crowd, and focused on the drama across the field. He put his hand behind his ear as though he might hear something. Suddenly, like shooting through a tunnel at high speed, Jason flew into Frank's mind. He looked at the slim guy through Frank's eyes.

"… agreed to it, but the Philly bosses are not happy, Franky. Not happy at all," Sly said. "Up to now this venture has been low volume but high profits with little or no costs. The profitability isn't there now."

Jason wondered what "not happy" meant. Who was not happy?

"I know," Frank said, "but what could we do? Next month doesn't look much better." Frank started to pace.

"If I was you, I would leave for a while." Sly opened the bag Frank had handed to him and counted the cash and small bags of prescription pills. "I'll try and put in a good word after all these years of good business but … it may not go too far. Deal's a deal."

"Thanks. Anything you can do, since there's no leavin' for us." Frank turned and headed back to the main entrance. Sly walked to the parking lot.

Suzy tugged on Jason's arm. With a great whoosh, like a vacuum, he was sucked back into his seat next to her. "Where were you?" she asked, annoyed. "Russ's team just took the lead. You missed it."

"Frank's in some sort of trouble." Jason rubbed his eyes. He found it hard to focus. "Lydia too, probably, which means we all are." His sudden departure down the tunnel with an equally unexpected return had left Jason queasy. It took several minutes for the effects to go away.

"C'mon, get up," Suzy insisted. "You can tell me later."

A jubilant Russ and the big kid jumped up and down. His third teammate crossed the plate. They gave him a big hug. Jason clapped and cheered along with everyone else.

✶   ✶   ✶

Later that night, Jason lay awake on his cot in the toolshed. The whole gang except Frank, who had stolen away to the house, celebrated the Rocket win at the local diner after the game. Russ's father agreed to get Jason, Suzy, and Rachel home when Frank begged off.

Jason smiled as he remembered the laughter and the food. He had eaten too much and felt like a two-pound sausage in a one-pound casing. His notebook lay open across his chest. The list of things that he knew little about grew ever longer.

I can reach much further now. I have no idea how I do it. Maybe total concentration?

Peg and Patti, Russ's mother and younger sister. I'm not the only one.

Thoughts and pictures swirled in his mind as he drifted off. He worried about coming trouble. Suzy never got the chance to talk with him about Frank. Tired, he closed his notebook and placed it on the floor beneath the cot. He decided to stop fretting about what was outside of his control. His brain calmed further, like tiny ripples in a pool. Little by little, he became unaware and slept.

☆   ☆   ☆

The word on the street among the drug dealers spread like wildfire. Dubois had failed again to come up with the drugs or enough cash. Sly took the call at his desk late Tuesday night.

"Don't say a word."

Sly knew better than to argue. The man on the other end of the phone meant business.

"It will happen soon. Maybe no one gets hurt … bad, but maybe bad things happen to people who don't deliver. It's not the money. It's the principle."

"Okay." Sly shook his head. He hoped none of the kids got in the way.

"You warn these sorry-ass people and you will be on the list as well." The man hung up.

Sly laid the receiver down. There was nothing he could do or would do. He had warned Lydia and Frank that things looked shaky. The lack of promised profitability was an issue for the mob. Frank took this warning seriously. Sly had frowned on Frank's noble nature but now saw him as a reasonable guy. Frank wanted to bail, as Sly advised.

Sly sat forward at his desk and started to tap a pencil on the blotter. He stared at the phone. *Should I?*

"Just pay off these guys," Frank had said the previous December. Lydia had glared at him, her foot tapping. She claimed she had a new kid on the line. He would bring in a new type of drug worth loads. She wanted the deal, and she damn near took off Frank's head in front of Sly when he disagreed. It was clear who ruled in that house.

"You wanted it," Sly whispered. "You got it." He dropped the pencil and turned off the light on his desk. "To hell with you."

Chapter 6

A n older, distinguished-looking man with thinning, gray-streaked, brown hair relaxed on a wooden, deck chair. He lounged, eyes closed, legs crossed, and enjoyed the early spring weather, as if he were vacationing on an ocean going liner. His hat, a fedora, which he usually wore at a rakish angle, rested on his knee. An expensive gray overcoat draped over his shoulders. The three-piece suit beneath confirmed his wealth, as did the gold watch chain that linked the pockets of his vest.

The man's attire was not an oddity given his location. He took his leisure beside the concrete steps of the Morgan Guaranty Trust offices in New York City where Broad Street and Wall Street met. He faced the New York Stock Exchange, and over his right shoulder, across Wall Street, the bronze statue of the first US president looked out on the ever-changing city.

Near noontime, the heavy traffic, both on foot (brokers off to power lunches) and automotive (trucks and vans making deliveries further uptown and down), passed the gentleman without noticing him. The grandfathers of some of the scurrying men might recall an odd, old man comfortably decked out near the exchange in the 1920s. Rodney Davenport grinned at the thought. His smile faded, and he concentrated.

"C'mon, norman," he whispered. "C'mon. Give me something." A powerful telepath, Rodney weaved in and out of the minds of the Wall Street movers and shakers. Everyone without psychic ability was norman.

Timing was everything. The scheming, the trickery, had to be at the front of the brain to be useful. He found it. His minions, who waited on the trading floor, received his orders and sprang into action. They bought. They sold. A mountain of money would be made that day.

With his goal achieved, Rodney relaxed until a shadow fell on him. He ignored it. A norman had become aware of him while his focus was elsewhere.

"Rod, we need to talk," said the young woman. Rodney opened one eye and glared at this annoyance. She wore jeans and a brown bomber jacket. Her shoulder-length chestnut hair was caught up in a white, knit beret. "We have a situation and it looks—"

Rodney raised his hand, stopping her from uttering another word. He opened both eyes and stood, then pushed his arms into his overcoat and reached down to collect the deck chair. It folded conveniently into his grasp. A black limousine appeared at the curb next to them. The driver dashed around the front, took the chair from Rodney, and stowed it in the trunk. He then held the door open as Rodney and his companion got in. In seconds he was behind the wheel, and the limo joined the northbound traffic. They were heading for Rodney's office in the Empire State Building.

"Never," said Rodney through gritted teeth. He stared out of his window at the passing scene. "Never give norman an opportunity to overhear our business." He was furious at such a stupid lack of security.

"I know that, but …" she sat forward and glared at the financial leader of all the US Communities.

Rodney felt her pull in his mind, her determination to make her point, and he allowed it. He turned to face her.

She blurted out, "A search-and-destroy action may be necessary."

"I see." He did not believe it. "Are you sure, Samantha?" It had been more than a decade since the last kill mission. Mistakes had been made in the past. It caused senseless mayhem.

"Activity has been detected." Samantha Black sat back but maintained her psychic exertions to get her point across. She relaxed a bit when she sensed she had his undivided attention. "At first the energy detected was small but constant. It reached a higher level over the last week, and remained constant. We have to act."

"Have to?" Irritated, Rodney slammed Samantha with a thought. *To whom did she think she was talking?* She collapsed against the limo seat. All of her strength drained away. "Where?"

"Somewhere," she choked out, unable to move, "south of Philadelphia."

"Strength level?"

"Five at the least." Samantha gasped for air. "I … I apologize. This seemed important."

"It is." Rodney let his anger subside. He examined her, considering her worth to his organization. Samantha was gifted. Within her limited range, enemies had no chance of survival. She never gave or asked for quarter. *A tool worth keeping,* he finally decided. Her impudence would go unpunished but not forgotten. He released her.

"I want Constance and Riley," Rodney said, turning away from her. "We need to plan. Philadelphia is a long reach."

"I'm on it," Samantha said as she pushed herself up slowly. She hurt all over.

"We will meet at the Tarrytown house when ready." The limo pulled to the curb at Twenty-Third Street and Broadway next to the Flatiron Building.

"Consider it done." She grasped the door handle and then stopped. "I almost forgot." She pulled a folded piece of paper from her back pocket. She held it out, her hand shaking. "From Community Central."

He glanced at the sheet and then up at Samantha. A laugh almost escaped his lips. He admired how she played politics. In time she would probably replace him. But he might have to kill her first.

"She wants what?" The message on the paper, he knew, was no secret.

Samantha unfolded the note and read, "To the Northeast Community Leader from Community Central, blah, blah, blah." She took a breath. "All power greater than level four is to be destroyed with prejudice. No exceptions. Yours truly …" She knew better than to speak the name.

"Stupid woman," Rodney whispered. "States the obvious," he said louder. "Make the appropriate response."

Samantha nodded and stepped out of the limo. Rodney watched her walk away until she disappeared among the trees of Madison Square Park. As the limo pulled away from the curb, his fist pounded the seat. He needed to release his fury at the woman who had ruled the Communities with an iron fist since the end of their war. He would not have been so upset if it had been his own iron fist. Toward that end he worked diligently. It was only a matter of time. He calmed when he remembered that part of the mountain of money made that day would go to his efforts to unseat the current regime.

"It belongs in New York anyway." He settled back into the black leather, thankful for norman's conniving ways. Their greed opened doors for his kind's financing. Funny, he thought, how the norman world war overlapped their revolution. The psychic battles had expended a great amount of blood and destruction on American soil. He dismissed the thought and moved on. The wheels in his head spun; he worked out the logistics for that day's money and the upcoming assassination.

Chapter 7

"Found some," called Suzy on her hands and knees. The early morning sun poured through a break in the thick clouds and reflected off a brass casing. The glint had caught her eye. She stood and brushed the dirt off the knees of her blue jeans and then held up the shiny, round piece of metal.

"Great!" Jason came over and looked at the five casings. Suzy handed them over. He looked at the oak tree next to the toolshed, where he had discovered the bullet hole at daybreak. Suzy had joined him in the search for the second hole and happened on the casings.

The Philly boys, whom Sly had warned Frank about at the game a week before, had visited the house during the night. Nothing had prepared them for a confrontation with a gifted psychic who operated on instinct, unable to control himself. Jason remembered little of the night's happenings. He thought shots had been fired, but he could not be sure until the evidence rested in his hand.

As the morning warmed, Jason dumped his blanket in the toolshed. He dressed in an old, plaid shirt and jeans to continue the search. He found an extra pair of clean socks in the folded pile of clothes on the benchtop. The old ones were stiff and uncomfortable. He stepped out of the shed and looked up. Clouds gathered in the sky, and Jason hoped the rain would hold off until they finished the investigation.

"So," said Suzy, scouring the ground for more clues, "how did you know those guys were here?"

"Don't know." Jason stood next to her and stared off into the distance. He tried to remember but shook his head. "I was asleep on the cot one minute. The next I'm standing by the old oak, staring at an empty yard. Then you came out of the kitchen wondering, what I was doing?"

Suzy looked up at him from her search of the ground. "Yeah, sometimes I get up in the night to get a drink or something to eat." She returned her attention to the ground. "I never heard any shots. I just saw you standing by the tree."

"Yeah." Jason shook his head. "I don't know anything about that. Maybe I did it. I just don't know."

She asked, as her hand parted the weeds, "How did you know what to do?"

"I have no idea." Jason, frustrated, kicked a small stone that sailed into the wooden fence. "But ... it seems I'm not supposed to know how things work yet." He took a deep breath and let it out slowly; then he bent over to study the ground for more clues. He moved away from Suzy. "Wish I knew though, 'cause it worked real well. I'm still alive."

After twenty minutes, Jason abandoned the ground investigation and started to look over the shed for holes that should not be there. *When will I get total control?* he wondered. A forlorn sigh escaped. He ran his hands over the rough surface of the shed wall, found nothing, and stood to consider what to do next. Suzy came over and sat on the shed threshold.

She looked up. "What's that on your neck?" Suzy noticed what looked like a scar.

"What?" Jason brought his hand up and felt around under his chin.

"There's a swirl or something there." Suzy came close and touched the spot. "It might be fading."

"Let's find those bullets and worry about this later." Jason went over the same area around the oak tree where he found the first bullet hole. Suzy rose and looked everywhere else. Jason stomped across the yard to the porch without finding anything new. He sat on the steps and thought. He scanned the whole backyard.

Suzy suddenly bent down and pick something up near the shed. "Hey, Jason. Your shed is falling to pieces." She brought him a six-inch-long wood chip with one straight edge and the other torn up. A small, round indentation could be seen along the ragged edge.

"Suzy, you're brilliant!" he cried. "This is it." He dashed to the shed and examined the corners where the walls came together. Suzy watched. The second bullet hole was then easy to find. Jason fit the piece Suzy handed him into a damaged corner closest to the oak tree about four feet from the ground. Jason jumped and held his fists high in victory. Suzy laughed.

Jason dashed into the toolshed and sat on the door stoop, his notebook and pencil in hand. Suzy took a seat, cross-legged, on the ground in front of him. As his hands shook with excitement, he drew a simple picture of the tree, himself, and where he thought the assailants might have been.

"Look." He drew two lines from stick figures armed with guns through a figure to the tree. He was the figure. He showed the drawing to Suzy.

"You should be dead?" She looked puzzled, concerned.

"I should be. But I think I know what happened. Look at the back of my neck. Do you see another swirl?" Jason bent over and turned his head to let Suzy examine him. She stood up and peered over his bowed head. "Lift up my hair in the back. It might be hidden."

"Part of it is." Suzy pushed the hair up from his hairline and found a match to the swirl in the front. It was faint and hard to see. "It's definitely fading, Jason."

"Oh … my … God! This is great!" Jason set aside his notebook and jumped up. As he paced, he built a picture in his imagination of what had happened.

"What? What?" Suzy's eyes followed him around the yard.

"These guys didn't expect to find anyone in the yard. They saw me and drew their pistols. I was distracted." Jason looked at her. "Some defense control kicked in. I don't know how, but one bullet passed through me without doing any damage and lodged in the tree. The second was deflected by some action and hit the shed directly to my right. I must have done it."

"So you're like a superhero or something?" she asked, excited. She mimicked Russ's reaction.

"Don't know for sure." He stopped moving. "It does mean I have some more stuff to add to my list of what I can do but don't know how." Jason returned to the stoop and his notebook, turned to the page with the list, and scribbled.

"Hey, what's that?" asked Suzy. She walked to the gate and reached down between the garbage cans. She strained to heft a rusted can with both hands. It had a domed lid that screwed on. Jason went over and supported the underside with one hand. With the other he grabbed the handle and took it from her. Suzy did not argue. It was heavy.

"Gas," she said. The smell of fuel inundated the immediate area. "Frank keeps his gas for the lawn mower in the garage on the other side of the house. This isn't his." She spoke with certainty. Jason nodded.

"Let's put it behind the shed for now." Jason went to the back of the shed where he hid it. He didn't want a lot of hysterics. It was important that this episode remain secret.

"So," Suzy said, "those guys were going to start a fire and burn down the house or maybe just the toolshed."

"Let's not think on it." Jason took her hand and pulled her to the front of the shed. "It doesn't matter right now anyway. It's over."

Suzy shuffled her feet and wondered if this was the right time to ask. She gathered her resolve. "Jason, can we talk?"

Jason was scribbling in his notebook. The sun shone brightly below the edge of dark clouds. "I thought we were," he said, not looking up. He took a deep breath and focused on the page.

"I mean about how angry I got over what you did to Rachel."

Jason froze and glanced up at Suzy. "What about it?" He felt bad about what had happened.

☆   ☆   ☆

On the Sunday night after he started school, while everyone in the house slept, Jason, unable to understand Rachel's hostility, sat on the rug outside her bedroom. He felt stronger after several days of practices with Suzy and Russ, who had proved to be strict taskmasters. Russ's ideas worked.

Frustrated with Rachel's treatment on his first day back to school,

Jason decided to invade her sleeping mind and find out why she hated him. The trick would be how to do it.

Closing his eyes, he dropped his defenses. Images surged at him, as always. Like wind-whipped waves, the horrors crashed against him. He allowed them to come, no longer frightened. After a time, he shifted and sorted through the voices and pictures until he heard Rachel's name. She dreamt:

She stood at a second-story bedroom window, looking out. She turned when she heard the clicking. She saw the gap between the inner and outer walls of the house around the window.

"Rachel," said a voice, cajoling, soothing. She ignored it.

Large ant-like bugs crawled between the walls, causing the clicking. She watched them move around and over each other and was disgusted by their presence. She turned around, and on the other side of her unmade bed a woman stood. She wore a white nightgown. Her brown hair flowed over her shoulders. She looked sad.

"I can't help you with them." The woman shook her head. "It is all too much."

"Rachel," the calm voice called again. Rachel, more curious than frightened, moved away from the window, where she could see the bugs in the wall.

"Go away," she yelled to the voice. "Just go away." The tapping grew louder. Bugs came out and covered the walls inside her room. She began to fear what was happening.

"You know I won't," insisted the voice.

Rachel froze where she was; the bugs skittered about the room. The woman disappeared. Something else entered the room, something she feared.

"Help me, Rachel. Only you can help me." The voice was sad, disappointed. It whispered from behind.

"I don't want to help you." Rachel spun around and cried, afraid to move. The bugs were everywhere, crawling out of the walls. Like disembodied hands, they scrambled. They tapped along every surface. She cringed. The spider-hands brushed her bare legs repeatedly. Then they began to gather at her feet, as if waiting for a signal.

"Rachel! Defend yourself!" Jason called out, forgetting his primary mission. He had to do something to help.

"How?" she cried. "He's too strong, too big."

"With this." In the middle of the room appeared a golden sword. It hung in midair. "Take it! Defend yourself!"

Rachel stared at it.

"Take the sword."

Jason unsheathed the weapon and placed it in her hand. Rachel, unaware of Jason watching her dream unfold, saw only the sword come to her on its own. "Defend yourself!" he said again.

Rachel grasped the hilt. The spider-hands made their move. They dropped from the ceiling and landed on her. Others crawled up her legs.

"Get off!" Her voice was weak. She swung the sword halfheartedly at one of the spider-hands and knocked it away. It fell on its back, flipped over, and came back. "No!" Rachel called louder, feeling stronger. She swung hard and knocked another across the room. She grasped the sword in both hands and began to hack at the hands. She drove them off her body.

"No you don't. You won't hurt me again …"

Rachel awoke. She sat up startled and breathless. Jason shot across the rug backward and slammed his head against the opposite wall. He brought his hand up and rubbed the back of his skull, shocked by the force that had thrown him out of Rachel's dream. He sensed her waking thoughts through his headache. Her nightmare faded. She collapsed on her pillow.

"Oh, somebody," she sobbed, forlorn. "Somebody help me." Jason felt her desperate call but remained frozen in fear. If only he knew how to make her feel better or to help her go back to sleep. Instead he quietly stole away.

What had he done? How had he gotten thrown across the floor?

✫   ✫   ✫

At the toolshed with Suzy, Jason shook off his guilt feelings associated with Rachel. He set aside his notebook, curious about what Suzy wanted. He waited.

"Looks like Rachel got over being mad … but I wanted to know, to ask …" She turned to the shed wall and, nervous, kicked a sideboard.

Jason felt defensive, so he said, "Rachel never knew I was in her head. She got mad for no reason 'cause I asked her about her parents at lunch, if you will recall."

"But!" Suzy yelled annoyed. Jason had missed her point. "I need to ask you something."

"Ask me what?" Jason felt a sudden gust of wind blow through the backyard. The first drops of the promised storm tapped on the ground.

"Why you never tried to, ya know, read me?" Her eyes met his.

"I never needed to, Suzy." Jason sat up straighter and pulled up his knees. "You never caused me any problems. In fact, you have been my one true friend in this house. Yeah, you worked me to death with the exercises, but I trust you." He smiled. She did not return it.

"Will you try now?" she asked. "I think it's important."

Jason stood up and considered her. After a moment, he waved her into the shed. "I'm not sure this is such a good idea." Jason shook his head worried. "But go ahead and lie down on the cot." He pointed to his bed, with the comforter balled up at the foot. "Close your eyes. You won't go to sleep." Suzy did as instructed.

Jason sat on the floor next to her cross-legged. He concentrated and met a strong block to his entry. Suzy's mind, unlike Rachel's, which tossed him out after an easy entry, would not let him in.

"I want you to picture something," he said. "It can be anything. Just get a good, solid view of it in your mind." His own face came to him in a flash. Eating spaghetti on the back porch streamed by. It occurred to him to ride their good times together. He sensed that he had made it past the barrier. As her memories of him faded, like a curtain sweeping closed, total darkness enveloped her mind.

Jason waited. A path presented itself. He would not force anything as he had with Rachel. A spotlight on a round, four-legged, wooden table appeared. The sound of cards shuffling echoed about the space.

"You don't belong here," said a woman who sat at the table. She studied the rows of cards laid out before her. She wore a white summer dress.

"I was invited." Jason walked over to the table. She moved a queen of hearts to the king of hearts.

"Well, this is as far as you go." She looked up. Jason thought she was attractive, even without makeup. She resembled Suzy, especially around the eyes.

"You're her mother?" He pulled out a chair and sat directly across from her. She smiled but did not answer. "What game are you playing?"

"A version of solitaire." She placed her hands on the table on either side of the cards and scanned the columns. She shook her head. "No winner here." She looked up and winked. Gathering the cards, she shuffled and asked, "How do you stand it?" She put the deck in front of her with her palms down on either side.

"What do you mean?" Jason looked her in the eye. "Oh," he suddenly understood, "you mean the voices and stuff."

"I never could." Sadness came to her eyes. "Never found a way."

"I worked a long time to get it quiet in here." Jason tapped his forefinger against his temple. A kitchen in hues of gray started to appear. Transparent at first, it became more opaque.

The woman picked up the cards and smiled slyly. "Do you feel lucky?" She shuffled. Her hands changed. She now had bright-red nail polish that matched her lipstick. Her dress morphed into a fancy, black, sleeveless gown.

"I am not sure what you mean?" Jason smiled at her. His fingers drummed the table.

"Are you willing to bet something of value to win something of greater value? Do you feel lucky?" Her eyes flashed her challenge.

He ignored her question. "Why are you here?" He placed both hands flat on the table.

"Is that what you want?" She raised an eyebrow.

"To bet?" Jason was not sure what he was doing. Nervous, his fingers drummed louder. "Yes."

"Fine. If I lose, you find out why I am here. If I win," she said and blew him a kiss, "I get to be with you and learn how you did it." The cards shuffled with a sudden intensity. "Is it a bet?"

"Okay." Jason knew Suzy watched from somewhere, and he believed his friend would not hurt him. The white metal kitchen cabinets, the counters, and appliances solidified around them.

"One card down." She dealt. "Four cards up." Jason showed three kings and the two of diamonds. Her cards showed three aces and a jack of hearts. Smiling, she looked at him, confident in her hole card.

"What wins?" Jason asked.

She picked up her hole card and then flipped it onto her face-up cards. The jack of spades slid into place with the other jack. "Full boat."

Without hesitation, Jason turned over his facedown card. He did not look at it. His eyes never left hers.

"We have a winner!" she yelled. She stood up and walked to a door that had not been there before. As she passed the counter, she picked up something from behind the blender and left the room. The door slammed behind her. Jason looked down and saw the fourth king.

The gunshot startled him. He sat paralyzed, as he had with Rachel, not knowing what to do. He sensed the launch out of her mind coming.

For Pete's sake, not again.

✫   ✫   ✫

The morning storm gave way to a sunny afternoon. Jason sat at the kitchen table with his head resting on his folded arms. A blinding headache paralyzed him. It was noon, only a few hours since Jason and Suzy had found the bullet holes and casings. Jason's hand flat on the table gently hid the chipped piece of wood from the shed. He ignored Lydia when she entered the kitchen. He wondered what had happened to Suzy.

"You slept in, huh?" Lydia stood over Jason. "That's from your shrink." She slid an opened envelope across the table. "I kept the original, but you can have the copy. When you leave us, you can have the original back." Lydia left the kitchen without another word.

Jason kept his eyes closed and sat up. He willed the pain to go away. It did not, but he squinted anyway to locate the envelope and pulled out the sheet of shiny paper. The official-looking, black-and-white document stated that it was the birth certificate of Jason Anthony Sutter born October 12, 1949, to Robert Joshua and Elizabeth Claudia Sutter. He stared at it a long time. He whispered their names, but their faces never came. Because of his work with his psychiatrist, Dr. Lipton, this was not a shock. But his sudden despair and tears surprised him.

Jason caressed the bullet-chipped sliver blasted from the toolshed. He clung to the copy of his birth certificate, intent on saving it in his notebook. As an afterthought, he turned over the envelope. It was addressed to him at 49 Hickory Lane, Franklin Chase, Pennsylvania. In all the time he lived in the house, it had never occurred to him to question where in the world he might be.

"Good morning, Jason," Frank said with a grin. He held a broom with a blue handle and a copper-colored dustpan. "You were up and about last night." This was not a guess but a statement of fact.

"What makes you think that?" Jason felt nauseated. He folded the papers and put them back in the envelope. He prayed Frank would be quick. His head hurt worse, and he was desperate to get back to his cot to wait out the pain.

Frank held in a laugh. "Well, the dirty footprints running across the kitchen floor right up to Suzy's room and ending by her bed might be considered a dead giveaway." He leaned the broom against the table and stuck the hollow handle of the dustpan on the end. Frank pulled out a chair and sat. "You wanna tell me exactly what you were doing parading around the house last night?"

"She couldn't sleep and woke me up to talk for a while." Jason put his head back on his arms. It did not hurt as much. "I got her back to bed." He turned his head and looked at Frank. "Sorry about tracking in dirt."

"Hmm." Frank interlaced his fingers as if in prayer and leaned forward on the table. "That jives with what Suzy said. So I guess you are off the hook … except to clean up the mess." Frank stood. "Okay?"

"Yeah, I'll get right to it." Jason waited for a response, but none came. When he looked for Frank, he saw a hand with two white pills in the palm.

"Here, these will help with the headache." Frank gazed down on him.

"These are aspirin." Jason reached over and popped them in his mouth. Frank had a glass of water ready. Jason sipped it.

"Thanks," he said. Frank nodded.

"Don't forget to clean up those prints." Frank turned and left the kitchen.

Jason waited for the aspirin to have an effect before he tried to stand and do any cleaning. It took about thirty minutes. The pain relinquished its hold slowly. As he rose to his feet, he felt a little better and grabbed the broom. He pulled the dustpan off the top and shoved the handle into his back pocket. When he looked at the floor, he saw the unmistakable signs of his passage. The linoleum was easy to sweep, but clearing his tracks from the rug in the hall and up the steps brought on a sweat. The harder he swept, the faster his headache faded. He ended his efforts at Suzy's door, which was open. His tracks in her room had been cleaned up.

"Where is everybody?" he whispered. He had encountered none of the residents as he cleaned his way through the house. Even Frank and Lydia had magically disappeared.

Done with his chore and his headache significantly diminished, Jason went to the front room, where Frank stored books by the hundreds. The stacks lined the walls and covered much of a large, mahogany desk at the center of the room. Jason had discovered this room when he first scouted the house in the early hours after he possessed the mental strength to suppress the dreams and thoughts of the sleeping inmates.

He leaned the broom with the pan stuck on the handle against the wall. He found a large text with maps of the States. There was just enough room on the desk to open the book. He searched for Pennsylvania and discovered it was a large state with thousands of towns and cities. He pulled up a chair, determined to find Franklin Chase. Jason started with towns around Philadelphia and got lucky. He located the town fifteen miles to the southwest.

"Hey, Jason," said Rachel happily. She was headed to the kitchen, carrying a large box. He looked up. Suzy came down behind her with her own full box. At the bottom steps, she stopped.

"Hi, Jason," she said, animated. She took a deep breath and hoisted her box higher and followed Rachel into the kitchen. Jason replaced the book of maps and snuck after them. He peered around the corner. They sat at the table and drank glasses of cherry Kool-Aid from a pitcher taken from the fridge. They talked avidly about their plans for the day. A column of boxes stacked by the back door waited for their attention.

"Um, excuse me, but … Where is everybody?" Jason asked as he walked into the room.

"Some went to climb on the rocks in the park," Rachel said. She sipped from her glass and then added, "Some went with Frank to the carwash."

Jason took a chair opposite her. "If you don't mind, Rachel, I need to talk to Suzy for a minute." He sensed a strong camaraderie between these two, like the feelings he experienced among Russ's sisters.

"Sure, Jason." Rachel shrugged. "Just don't take too long." She gulped the last of her drink, put the glass in the sink, and headed back upstairs.

Suzy lit up when Jason turned his attention to her. "We got the okay from Lydia to share a room," she said. "So we're working on setting it up today. Getting rid of old junk. Isn't that great, Jason?"

"Suzy, that's amazing. I'm really, really glad." He put his hands on the table palms down, fingers spread. This new relationship between Suzy and Rachel added to the growing list of unexpected outcomes when he squatted in someone's mind. "What happened this morning in the shed?"

Suzy downed her Kool-Aid and then held her empty glass with both hands. She stared for a moment at the blood-red dregs at the bottom.

"I … I hurt you, I think," Suzy said, embarrassed. She took a deep breath. "Do you remember anything?"

"I remember a woman. Was she your mother?" Jason leaned forward and brought his hands together, fingers interlaced.

"Yes." She hung her head, afraid of where this might go. "It's the way I remember her."

"She killed herself?" asked Jason. He closed his eyes and tried to remember all that had happened.

"What?" Suzy looked up, shocked.

"In the room next to the kitchen," Jason whispered the last few words, suddenly uncomfortable. He opened his eyes but could not look at her. It felt like betrayal. Something you know someone is not ready to hear. *Stop now!* He couldn't.

"Your mom picked up a gun on the counter, then walked into the next room. I heard a shot. At least I think it was."

"She went to the garage," Suzy said in a shaky voice. "My mom heard voices all the time. She—"

"Couldn't take it anymore." Jason finished her thought. Suzy nodded.

"And this has been your secret?"

She nodded again. They sat quietly for a time.

"I'm sorry." Jason unclasped his hands, leaned across the table, and caressed one of Suzy's.

She pulled back and looked away. "We get used to it," she said, very serious. "Don't we?" She looked at Jason.

"Yeah, I guess we do." Jason raised his eyebrows, surprised. These things aged a girl or a boy too fast. He took a deep breath and then blew it out. He glanced at the table and then at Suzy. "She said some stuff."

"About me?" She turned back to him and leaned forward.

"Not exactly." His fingers tapped a nervous cadence. Suzy sat back. "She said she could jump into my mind. She would have to be like me to do that. Do you think she was?"

"I don't know," she whispered, her eyes sad.

"Okay." Jason pushed back his seat and grasped the table's edge. He had decided to change the subject. "Do you remember your father at all?"

She smiled and then frowned. "Why?"

"Well, he never came up. I was wondering." Jason struck a Dr. Lipton pose, relaxed back in the chair, and crossed his legs.

"Yes and no." Suzy stood. "It isn't very clear." She picked up her glass, stood, and placed it in the sink. "He just suddenly wasn't there."

Jason stood too, wondering why his father left no trail in his thoughts. Suzy and he had some not-so-good things in common.

"It's just so weird," he said, thinking of Suzy, "how you aren't cramming thoughts down my throat like everyone else. Ya know?"

Suzy smiled. "It's a good thing, right?"

"A very good thing." Jason grinned.

"I should get back to Rachel." Suzy returned to the table, picked up the pitcher, and returned it to the refrigerator.

When she got to the archway to the hall, Jason called to her. "It wasn't your fault, ya know. What happened to your mom, I mean." He had no idea why this needed to be said. It was obvious. Suzy turned back to him for a moment and then ran to him. She gave him a hug and kissed his cheek.

"Thanks," she whispered and dashed back upstairs to work with Rachel on their new room. The first salvo of laughter broke the silent gloom on the second floor of the Dubois house.

"Not so obvious, I guess," Jason said to himself.

Chapter 8

Weeks earlier, Jason sat in Dr. Lipton's waiting room for his regular appointment. Russ's Fantastic Four comic book lay open in his lap on top of his notebook. The week before had gone well. He had impressed his teacher with a bit of writing. Jason kept the paper with "Outstanding" written across the top.

☆   ☆   ☆

It had happened so quickly on his first day in Mrs. Needham's classroom before Russ or Suzy knew of his telepathic abilities.

"Class, I want three paragraphs on what you hope to do over the summer. Be descriptive. I want details. You have twenty minutes. A few of you will read your papers in front of the class." The perfect school marm—granny glasses low on her nose and gray hair pulled back in a bun—Mrs. Needham listed what she wanted on the blackboard.

"The Needle is famous for this sort of thing," Russ whispered to Jason.

"Who's the smartest kid in class?" Jason asked in a panic.

"Easy. The girl two rows over sitting in the front." Russ pulled several sheets of paper and a pen out of his desk.

"Too far away. Someone closer," Jason demanded.

"Rodney," said Russ slowly, wondering if Rachel was right. This Jason kid might be nuts. "Three rows to the right. That guy." Russ pointed.

Jason arranged paper and pen on his desk then closed his eyes, searching for the right boy's mind. After a few moments, the name appeared printed across the top of a page in his mind's eye. He had no idea what to do next. His hands barely formed the letters on the page as Rodney sped far ahead of his ability to keep up. Jason, eyes closed, concentrated as hard as possible on what he wanted to do. His right hand twitched repeatedly, making scribbles on the page. Suddenly his hand moved to the beginning of a line like a typewriter carriage, and words flowed out in a clear, neat handwriting. Jason opened his eyes and was delighted then concerned. He no longer controlled his hand. The words were Rodney's and the penmanship, Jason bet, would look exactly like his also.

It took five minutes of significant effort to disconnect from the boy. Sweat poured down Jason's forehead. He wondered if this mind stuff would ever get easier. With half of the time left and a silent prayer that he had picked up some writing ability, Jason started his own few paragraphs.

☆   ☆   ☆

Jason recalled he had written quickly after he stole the ability to put words on paper from the boy a few rows over. For a scary few minutes, the other student had controlled his hand, and Jason could not get it back. He had finally regained control and scribbled the first thing that came to mind. He finished as papers were collected. Mrs. Needham's positive reaction to his honest expectations for the summer surprised him. *Maybe honesty works best,* he thought. He wondered if it would have worked with Rachel Sunday night.

"Let's see," said Dr. Lipton. He brought Jason from the waiting room and had him sit down. "You've had a week or so at school that you seemed to have survived fairly well. You have impressed your teacher. Mrs. Needham, is it?" He pulled his pipe from the jar on his desk and started to fill it. "So tell me what you think about your time in the classroom."

"I had to read something I wrote in front of the class." Jason sat on his hands. He always felt nervous with Dr. Lipton.

"This, I believe?" He handed Jason a piece of paper.

He took it in his right hand and scanned the page. "Yes," Jason said, "this is it. How did you get it?" Jason wasn't sure he liked the intrusion.

"When you have a patient on significant medications, it is important to keep up with his day-to-day activities. I made a few phone calls. Mrs. Needham mailed me this copy. I must admit, aside from being a very honest statement, it is unusual for someone with your diagnosis. The drug you take would make this very difficult. You are a mystery, Mr. Sutter." He reached over and took back the paper. He sat back and crossed his legs.

"I just wrote what was in my head. It wasn't any big deal," Jason said, shrugging his shoulders. He worried about where Dr. Lipton headed.

"'I do not hope for much this summer. If I make a few friends …' This is very good, Jason." Lipton looked up at him. "It shows an awareness and recognition of what we all need. Nothing grandiose. Nothing paranoid. Do you know what I mean by paranoid?" He uncrossed his legs and sat forward, studying his patient.

"Frank, my foster father, used that word once when talking to me." Jason stared blankly. He remembered his first venture outside the house to the grocery store. "No, I didn't know what he meant."

"You don't write about people coming after you or trying to get you." The doctor tapped the paper with the mouthpiece of his pipe.

"Well, I did have a problem with the school's bully." Jason shifted in his seat.

"Does the bully have a name?" Lipton looked at him with one eyebrow raised.

"Arthur Dresden." Jason tapped the floor with his feet.

"Can he be seen by other people? Does he bully other children?"

"Yes." Jason worried about messing up the deal with Frank and Lydia and folded his arms across his chest. These questions better not cause Dr. Lipton to question the need for the medication.

"That is not paranoia. That, my boy, is reality. I have been told you handled the situation to your advantage, but no one can tell me exactly how. Can you help me?" The doctor sat back in his chair, placed Jason's writing on his desk, and picked up his lighter.

"I stood up to him," said Jason. He gave a brief description of what happened but left out most of what Dresden had told him on that stormy day in the school lunchroom. He ended with, "Dresden slipped trying to punch me and fell over backward."

"That's all?" Lipton stopped in midlight, the lighter turned to the side, the flame pointing skyward.

"That's it." Jason smiled unconvincingly.

"I have dealt with bullies a few times." The doctor finished lighting his tobacco. He took the pipe out of his mouth and leaned forward in his chair. "I have never known one to slip and not come back up angrier and more violent to save face. I have seen them knocked down whereupon they get up and run away. You didn't knock him down?" The look on his face told Jason that the doctor had trouble believing his story.

"No." Jason stared at him.

"Well, I now have another mystery to solve." Lipton's eyes smiled like he knew something that amused him. Mysteries about a patient's behavior, however, bothered him. He sensed he would get no further and let the subject drop.

Jason kept quiet. The silence stretched. Lipton finally put the pipe between his lips and sat back.

"Made any new friends?" Jason told the doctor about Suzy and Russ. "Good. Good." He paused and set the pipe in its stand at the corner of his desk. "Is that a subject notebook from school, or your journal?" Lipton pointed at the notebook in Jason's lap.

"I write about private stuff." Jason clutched it tightly.

"Can I have a look at it?" Lipton asked calmly. Jason froze. He couldn't let him see it. The doctor read the fear and said, "Maybe when you trust me better."

"Okay," Jason said, relieved. "I'll do that."

"Now, I need your help." He gathered his notes and scanned the pages. "Your teacher reports that you are doing very well. No outbursts. No loss of control. No falling asleep during class. No dull affect. But Frank and Lydia have left messages for me saying that you have improved only marginally. Why are you having a problem at home?"

Jason replied, "It's not really home, is it?" Thinking quickly, he added,

"They both have a way of getting me all angry and stuff. I don't remember much about those times."

"I see. Well, maybe in time we can help you remember." Dr. Lipton turned back to his desk and reached for a different file. "I have some news for you." He rifled through the stack of papers and found the one he wanted. "I have a line on one of your parents—your mother, to be specific. She has been treated in a mental institution in upstate New York."

Stunned, Jason did not know what to say. "Where exactly?" he blurted out.

"Elizabeth Sutter is in …" Dr. Lipton sat back and searched the paper. "A state institution in or near Poughkeepsie, New York. Must be Hudson River State." He leaned forward and handed over the paper. Jason looked over the page and discovered his mother's name. When Lipton observed Jason's eyes water, he nodded. He made a note concerning this normal behavior in his notepad. Jason quickly wiped his eyes and smiled; he handed back the page.

Dr. Lipton said, "I will keep looking into your family situation—try to get some records, if possible. I have a few friends up that way. You try to remember better what happens in your foster home, and I'll keep digging. That sound like something you can do?"

Jason nodded. "It's … it's a deal," he choked out with a smile.

"Now," Dr. Lipton continued, "what can you tell me about the other children in the house and how you relate to them?"

Jason talked about the laundry and the problems with the kids, but always in the back of his mind he heard the doctor's voice: "I also have a line on one of your parents." His mother lived.

☆   ☆   ☆

The end of school came the following Tuesday, which was much too quick for Jason.

"Settle down now. Settle down." The school's principal, Mr. Harris, addressed the school assembly before the summer vacation started. Hundreds of bored students, row after row across the high-gloss wooden floor, endured in the metal folding chairs. Partially obscured behind the podium, Mr. Harris stood center stage, with the retractable basketball backboard directly over his head. He looked oddly out of place in his starched, white shirt and bright-red bow tie.

"This is the last assembly before summer vacation and ..." He waited for the applause, the catcalls, and the whistling to stop. "We have a few announcements." He flipped a few pages and began, "There are awards that need to be presented. I am very proud—"

"Oh man," Russ whispered Jason, "you look awful. What happened?" The dark circles under Jason's eyes had caught his attention.

"Another headache." Jason groaned from the incessant ache. "I've been trying for days. It hurts, and I can't move even the smallest thing, not a twig, a leaf, a scrap of paper."

"Maybe you can't—or you can't yet. Know what I mean?" Russ scanned the immediate rows, always on the lookout for something interesting. A hum from the hundreds of whispered exchanges filled the gym. Only the teachers paid attention to Mr. Harris.

"Maybe." Jason sighed. Quiet for a moment, he looked up at the stage. Then he said, "Oh yeah, I didn't tell you about our visitors, did I?" He quietly brought Russ up to speed on what he thought had happened over the past weekend. He left out the part about Suzy's mother.

"Lemme see." Russ looked under Jason's chin to see the swirling pattern. "It's gone, but you think the bullet went right through without touching?"

"Yep."

"Wow, man, you need your own comic book. This is getting too good." Russ could hardly keep still in his chair. Mr. Harris droned on. "And the other bullet you knocked away from you?"

"Apparently." Jason reached into his pocket and pulled out the wood chip. He held it up so Russ could see the half-moon indentation from the bullet.

"Oh momma!" Several shushes filled the air. Quietly he said, "Like ... this is evidence." Russ just stared, amazed.

"Yeah, but it doesn't help," Jason whispered. He put the piece away.

"We're having lunch once the assembly is over." Russ looked at his shoes, lost in thought for a moment. "Let's see what Suzy has to say." Jason never got the chance to respond.

"… and the final award for perfect attendance goes to Russell Wyatt. Where are you, Russ? Come on up here." Mr. Harris and the teachers started clapping energetically with only a smattering of applause coming from the students.

"This is so embarrassing. Remind me to be sick at least once next year. It saves on nerd attacks." Russ got up and, from his seat far back in the auditorium, walked up to the stage. He waved and laughed, ignoring the sniggering.

"Lastly," said Mr. Harris as Russ paraded back to his seat, holding his award envelope high, "due to a large number of new first-graders coming in September, it has been decided that the sixth grade will move to Jackson Middle School. Your parents have been notified."

"Hey," Russ said back in his seat, "doesn't that mean Suzy will be in the same school with us?"

"Yep." Jason smiled. This was a welcomed surprise.

Russ opened his envelope and whistled. "A five-buck gift certificate to Hagarty's Drug Store. I'm rich. Finally, something useful!"

☆   ☆   ☆

Jason shot off the school bus and down the side of the house through the gate in the chain-link fence. He pushed open the shed door and tossed his books on the work table. He turned and froze. Lydia sat on his cot; she turned a page of his notebook. He had been in a hurry to catch the bus that morning and had forgotten to hide it.

"So there is more to you, as I suspected," she said quietly. Jason choked. He could think of nothing to say. Scared and frantic, he sought a solution. The noise in his head started to build. "I think we need to rethink how best to use your talents." She looked up from the notebook with an evil smile.

A new rush of fear and revulsion flooded Jason. *This is wrong. This cannot happen. How can I stop it?* All this and more passed through his conscious mind. A hiss like a radio between stations blasted in his head; a dull ache became acute. He closed his eyes to the pain and staggered against the bench. When he opened them, the notebook lay where he had left it, but Lydia had disappeared. The pain in Jason's head did likewise. The noise levels dropped to tolerable levels and then wasted away to nothing.

"Oh no!" he said. "What did I do now?" He heard the back door slam and peered out of the open shed door. Frank walked across the yard with a can of something in his hand. He entered the shed.

"Jason, you may want to leave for a while." Frank started to shake the can.

"Why?" Jason spoke quietly, not understanding what might be about to happen.

"Lydia wants me to get rid of the spiders. She's got issues with spiders." Frank chuckled at Lydia's arachnid discomfort.

"If you don't mind, I prefer you didn't. I won't be able to be in here for a long time, and I don't really mind them." Jason stood by the cot, picked up his notebook, and stacked it among his other books.

"Well, you'll have to do your own housekeeping, if you know what I mean?" Frank took a look around. "Not that there is much to do out here."

"Yeah, I'll take care of it." Jason dropped his books back on the cot and turned to Frank. "Did Lydia want anything else done?" He studied him. Had Lydia discussed the notebook with Frank?

"Nope." He said matter-of-factly and left.

Jason followed a few moments later and looked for Lydia in the kitchen. He had to know what she planned to do. She stood at the sink, gazing out of the window. She took no notice of Jason as he stood inside the kitchen by the back door.

"Lydia?" Jason called. She turned slowly.

"Jason," she said with a grin. Her face struck Jason as wrong: a pleasant smile and no anger flashing in her eyes. "I was just watching you cross the yard." She spoke very deliberately. "I was wondering why I had come to the kitchen. It had something to do with you, but it has flown out of my mind. Can you remind me?"

"The spiders, maybe?"

"There was something else … but …" She turned back to the window. After a few minutes with no further response from Lydia, Jason left the kitchen and went to the shed. Her memory of their confrontation in the shed had evaporated. How? Jason let the thought hang while he considered the shed layout in search of a better place to hide his notebook. He did not want to carry it with him all the time. Where the tabletop touched the supporting legs, there was a half-inch gap stretching from one leg to the other. The notebook fit snugly in the gap and was hidden by the tabletop. The only way to find it was to crouch low and look up under the table.

Jason pulled the notebook from its new hiding place and opened it on the workbench. His fifth entry read, "Somehow I have erased Lydia's memory of the notebook and its contents." He placed his pencil beside the page, folded his arms, and rested his head on the workbench.

When will this get easier?

Chapter 9

"So how have you been?" Dr. Lipton fussed with his notebook, flipping pages. He was looking for something. Since their last meeting, he had moved his desk away from the window to the opposite wall. His bookshelves, which had stood together last week, now graced either side of his desk. He looked oddly uncomfortable, searching the desk for missing items.

"I've been okay." Jason spoke cautiously. He was uneasy, as was Dr. Lipton, with the new office configuration. At least he sat in his usual chair. With both of his hands, he brushed back hair from his eyes. "Thanks for the letter."

"Oh, good. You received it." Finding his last entry, Dr. Lipton crossed his legs and entered a new line. The pencil broke. "Another few pieces of the puzzle put in place, eh?" He went through three drawers before he found a new no. 2 in the fourth. "How have you been getting on with your foster parents?"

"Doctor? You've moved things around." Jason sat on his hands and pushed up.

"Ah, you noticed." He smiled like a child caught in the act.

"It's hard not to, ya know?" Jason scanned the office.

"Well, I find it very important to upset the status quo in small ways. It changes the way I think about things." He set his notebook aside on the desk. "I was getting too comfortable with the old layout. It is a good idea to mix things up."

Jason looked at the shelves of books. "I never noticed your collection of books. Am I in there somewhere?" He leaned forward to read some of the titles.

"Excellent question." Dr. Lipton swung around to his desk and picked up his pipe. "They represent my apprenticeship." He glanced at them, following Jason's gaze. "They hold the data that applied years ago. We hope and pray it still applies, but … I have discovered it is largely outdated." He turned back to Jason. "No, you are definitely not in those texts." He picked up a small metallic object and spun through the spiral of tools, finding the one to tap down the tobacco in his pipe. "Now, back to my original question: How are you and your foster parent's getting along?"

"Better in some ways. I can't complain." Jason thought it strange that he should mention them so early in their session.

"Good." Lipton patted his jacket pockets before he found and pulled out his lighter. "Several weeks ago I informed your foster father that maybe you no longer needed such strong medication. He did not take it very well at the time, but he has acquiesced recently. What do you think?" He flicked the lighter.

"I don't think I need it so much." Jason wanted to add that he hadn't taken it in months, since the lock came off the shed door. The sweet tobacco aroma filled the room. Jason inhaled deeply; the smell of burning pipe tobacco comforted him.

"Would you say you are symptom-free?" The doctor cocked an eyebrow and waited.

"Yeah. I haven't crashed any walls or doors in a long time."

"No voices? You have been sleeping normally?" Lipton pulled on his pipe and held it. He released the bluish smoke slowly.

"No voices or anything like that." *No uncontrolled voices,* he thought. "And I've been sleeping okay." He glanced around the office again, looking for more changes.

"Good." Dr. Lipton stared at the coals in the pipe bowl. "I think, Mr. Sutter, considering where we started and given these rather extraordinary outcomes, I no longer see the need for you and I to meet."

Jason choked. He was going to be abandoned by one of the few safe adults in his life.

"You are obviously," continued Dr. Lipton, "out of trouble. How and why has eluded me." He tapped down the tobacco. "I am tempted to try to keep you as a patient to try to unravel this mystery, but the State of Pennsylvania does not want to pay for my time."

"Why not?" Jason's heart pounded in his chest. "You have helped me a lot." He felt his world break into pieces. No safe place existed. The good doctor was a constant when other adults failed. "I … I … Please, don't do this!"

"Hmmm." Dr. Lipton fired up the lighter again, inhaled, and pulled the flame into the bowl. "Professionally, you are a miracle defying long-held dogma." He waved his hand toward the shelves of books. "You are a poster boy to our misunderstanding of psychosis. Personally I find myself caring about what happens to you." He uncrossed his legs and leaned forward in his chair. "I like you. And … there is something about you that I am missing. Maybe if I knew what that was, I could help you even more." He put the pipe back in his mouth and sat back to wait for a response.

"I …" Jason wanted to tell him everything, to keep him in his life. If appointments stopped, he'd feel lost—completely on his own. "There's this … thing." He stopped, certain that nothing should be said about his abilities. He changed direction. "I don't have many friends, and I counted on you as one of them. Not seeing you anymore really stinks."

"Well, we agree on that point. Here." Dr. Lipton smiled and gave him a card. "If you want to talk to me or need something, call the number on the card. I do not want to lose contact."

"Thanks," Jason said, his eyes watering. He stared at the card. His thumbs rubbed the card, feeling the reality of it in his hand. He stuffed it in his pocket. This would go directly into his notebook for safekeeping. It may become a life preserver to be used in case of emergency.

Dr. Lipton continued. "I intend to keep searching for information on your parents. I will keep you informed on my progress." Jason nodded.

They did not speak for a while. Finally the doctor said, "Did I ever tell you about my crazy nephew?"

Jason looked up.

"Well, you must understand this was before we understood that hyperactivity was not crazy. We, like others, took self-control as a sign of sanity much too far. But Timothy cured me. It was 1955 as I recall ..."

Jason barely paid attention, crushed by the weight on his heart. His mother, his father, and now Dr. Lipton had abandoned him. It wasn't fair. If he could change places with Russ and give up his telepathic abilities, he would do it in a second.

✵   ✵   ✵

On the drive back to the house, Frank sensed that Jason was upset. The phone rang as they entered the house. Frank picked up the receiver. He watched Jason trudge down the hall to the kitchen.

"Hello," Frank said, worried about the boy. He heard the screen door slam. Jason headed to the shed.

"Franky, Franky, what am I going to do with you?" Sly sat at his desk with his feet on the top, opened drawer. "The guys up Philly-way are done with you. They figure you're a lyin' bastard, not worth a bullet."

"Lying? What are you talking about?" All concerns about Jason vanished. Frank sat at the desk in the front room, upright and scared. Sweat darkened the back of his white shirt.

"I'm not stupid, Franky." Sly considered his fingernails; he needed to improve his grooming. "You had firepower backing you up. Surprised the Philly boys and me."

"What? Firepower?" asked Frank, confused.

"Okay, Franky. You want to keep it secret. I can play that game. It's your funeral." Sly leaned forward and picked up a toothpick. He worked his teeth.

"Sly, what is going on?" Frank felt like he was in a car sliding uncontrolled on a patch of ice. Nothing could be done to avoid a wreck.

"They want nothing more to do with you or me," Sly said. "We both got screwed."

"What does that mean?" Frank began to hope that the whole drug business might be over.

"All the drug deals are at an end. Our relationship will also disappear. Just as well, don't you think?" Sly sat up and started to flip through envelopes on his desk. His lips held the toothpick at the side of his mouth.

"You mean we are out of this business?" Frank smiled, and relief flooded his body.

"Out, free and clear, except …" Sly sat still to deliver this last message.

"Except what?" Frank was frantic, taken aback.

"Except that, and this is them talkin', Franky—" Sly paused. "They said that revenge is a dish best served cold."

"Damn." Relief evaporated. Frank held his head in his free hand. The other was white knuckled around the receiver.

"Can't say when anything might happen, but you were never any big deal with them."

"So if we're no big deal, they'll just forget about us, right?" Frank closed his eyes and prayed for Sly to throw him a life preserver.

"Well, they got bigger fish to fry, if ya know what I mean." Sly pulled the toothpick from his teeth and tossed it into the green waste can next to his desk. "So … it could be that you're one fly they won't bother swatting." Sly yawned.

Frank did not feel comforted. "Okay, Sly. I appreciate the call."

"We've done some pretty good business over the years, Franky. It was the least I could do."

"You gonna land on your feet?" Frank knew he would feel worse if Lydia's and his actions got someone else hurt, even Sly.

"Me?" Sly pulled the receiver from his ear and stared at it. He did not know what to do with anyone caring about what happened to him. He smiled and put the phone back to his ear. "Always." After an uncomfortable pause he said, "Gotta go, Franky."

"Yeah, thanks." Frank hung up, sat back in his chair, and worried about what might happen. He took a deep breath and blew it out, trying to calm himself. The guys from Philly had come and gone.

He stood up and decided to walk the yard. There would be signs of a visit. Since no one was hurt and no damage done, Frank expected to find nothing. He crossed the front yard slowly. He covered the ground, the house, and the garage. The front was clear. At either side of the house, he found nothing unusual.

In the back, all looked normal except that the grass and weeds grew high around the shed. He cursed. "How many times do I have to cut this damned stuff?" It would be harder to discover any clues with all that grass. He decided that Jason could get the lawnmower and clean up his own space from then on.

"Holy jeez!" Frank came up short. He had found the gas can behind the shed. He ran his fingers through his hair, trying to remember why he would do something so stupid. The shed could go up in a flash. He caught a whiff of gasoline, grabbed the red can, and immediately took it to the garage to be stored safely. The metal cabinet, however, had its own red can. Frank put the extra can in the corner and stepped outside.

Frightened, he put two and two together. "They were gonna burn down the shed." Frank left the second gas can in the garage and ran to the backyard to perform a detailed search. His search among the weeds gave up no new information.

Frank entered the kitchen from the back porch. At the sink he rolled up his shirt sleeves and splashed water in his face. He felt sick. He grabbed a dish towel and dried himself. From the cabinet, he grabbed a glass, filled it from the faucet, and drank. His hands shook. For the first time in years, he wished he had something stronger.

"So what's the deal with Sly?" Lydia asked when she walked into the kitchen. Frank turned, startled. He put the empty glass on the counter and wiped the beads of perspiration from his forehead with the towel.

"We are out of the business." He watched her as the news moved over her face. First her jaw clinched; then she frowned; and finally a vein popped up on her right temple. Frank looked on, amazed at how her reactions never changed.

"Get that lowlife on the phone now!" she yelled. Her fisted hands clung tight against her sides.

"The mob paid us a visit." Frank spoke calmly. "They didn't do anything. At least not yet, but they were here."

Lydia stopped in mid-rant. "You're sure?" Frank nodded. "Why didn't they do something?" she asked.

"Maybe just checking the landscape. They left a full can of gas behind." Frank tilted his head toward the backyard.

"Where?" Lydia moved next to him and stared out the window.

"Behind the shed." Frank tossed the damp towel onto the counter. "Looks like they intended to scare us. Burn down the shed, maybe."

"Yeah, but they didn't." Lydia's anger eased. "The kid was in the shed when they were here. He must know something. Maybe ..." She tapped her clenched fist on the counter.

Frank turned to her. "The kid's out back. I'll ask him."

The gears in Lydia's head turned. She stared at the shed.

"What?" Frank asked.

"That kid ... something ... but I can't remember." Lydia stepped away from the counter. She paced around the kitchen and then stopped and turned abruptly. "Something is goin' on. I don't know what, but something."

"Well, we'll have a lot more time to find out." Frank rolled down his sleeves and buttoned the cuffs. "School's over. We never did get Will to set him up with any overnight camp like the other kids. So he's ours for four weeks."

"Yeah, but I'm not happy about the drugs. It went right to our bank account, to my safety net." Lydia looked pained.

"Well, your safety net might have gotten someone killed." Frank said the words hesitantly. "Maybe me. Is it really worth it?"

"Yes!" She turned and left the room before Frank could say another word.

✲   ✲   ✲

School was over. At the breakfast table the next day, the kids at the Dubois house laughed, joked with each other, and talked about plans for things to do at camp.

"I'll meet you out back in a minute," Suzy said on her way to her room. She leaned over to speak softly into Jason's ear. Jason was eating his morning cereal, so he turned around with the spoon in his mouth and gave her a thumbs-up. He gulped the last few mouthfuls, got up, and grabbed a bunch of books he had stowed under his chair. After dumping the dishes in the sink, he headed to his detached bedroom. Halfway there, he noted the red lawnmower by the shed and the gas can beside it.

At the shed door, he tossed some books onto the tool bench and was about to turn away when someone called to him from inside the shed.

"Jason," called Frank, "come on in and sit for minute. I need to talk to you."

Jason entered. Frank sat on his cot with his hands clasped in front of him. His elbows rested on his knees. He looked troubled.

"What's up, Frank?" Jason pushed himself up to sit on the tool bench beside his book bag and gazed down at his foster father. "You taking a day off or somethin'?"

Frank ignored Jason's question. "First, Will Grossman usually works out deals with local summer camps to take our kids for a month." Frank paused. His eyes moved left then right. His interlaced fingers curled and uncurled. "Will messed up and forgot to put your name in the mix. You won't be going. You'll be staying with Lydia and me."

"Oh," said Jason. "Well, that's okay by me." He truly thought this could be a good thing.

"We're going to move you back into the house too," Frank added. "You aren't tearing things up anymore, so you should be back inside."

"Okay. Which room?" Jason pushed up with his hands, rocked forward, and slid off the bench.

"The one you started in. It has the cracked walls." Frank's foot suddenly shot out and stomped down on the floor. Jason jumped back, startled.

"Sorry," Frank said. "Just a spider." Jason nodded. More of them had appeared with the warmer weather.

"Anything else?" Jason moved to the end of the tool bench and started to unload his book bag. He blocked all of Frank's buzzing thoughts. His control had improved after the months of practice keeping the active minds at school out of his thoughts. Lately the importance of being a regular kid had taken on a higher priority.

"Yeah." Then Frank pointed at Jason. "I want you to keep the backyard in better shape. You do the lawn mowing back here." He pushed off the cot, stood, and exited the shed. But he stopped at the mower. "This is not the only gas can." He looked at Jason. "The second one came from where?" He crossed his arms over his chest.

"I found it by the garbage cans and thought it was yours." Jason started with the truth. "I put it behind the shed for safekeeping until I could let you know." That one was a lie.

Frank accepted the explanation and nodded. "You have no idea how the second can wound up by the ... garbage cans?"

"Nope."

Jason now understood. Frank feared the men who had invaded the backyard the other night and the men who sent them. What could he say? *Don't worry, Frank. I scared them off with my superpowers.*

"Sorry, Frank, I really have no idea." Jason joined him outside the shed. "How do you work this thing, anyway?"

Jason watched carefully with his hands in his pockets as Frank checked the gas level in the reservoir, set the ignition, and gave the cord a few strong pulls. It started rumbling in idle. After Frank killed the engine, Jason repeated the process. Then Frank left him to finish the job.

Jason mowed the backyard, wondering the whole time where his actions over the last few weeks might lead.

Chapter 10

Jason tromped around in the undergrowth in the park, as the kids in the Dubois house knew it. The undeveloped tract of land was the James Lewis Bird Sanctuary, a mile from the house. During the first three weeks of summer, Jason, Rachel, and Suzy clapped, whistled, and laughed, cheering Russ at his games. When there were no more games, Suzy, Russ, and Jason worked together in the toolshed. It became their clubhouse after Lydia and Frank moved Jason to his original second-floor bedroom.

Three weeks of effort to help Jason move objects with his thoughts failed. His head hurt, and the failure made him short-tempered. With Russ and all of the Dubois foster kids off to overnight camp, he was on his own for four weeks. He discovered the sanctuary on his first day alone when he explored the neighborhood.

Among the trees, the early morning air smelled fresh and clean. The sun poured through the cathedral branches interlaced high above. A choir of bird calls echoed. Jason felt peaceful. *Alone, sometimes, is a good thing,* he thought. He sat on a stone outcrop and soaked in the serenity.

☆   ☆   ☆

Jason recalled that Suzy had said, "Nice room," on the day he moved from the shed. "Why did they allow you into the house?" The room was small, but it had a window. She had jumped on the bed and laughed. Then she jumped off and went through the built-in drawers below. She opened every drawer in the small desk beneath the window. Jason paused, ignored her, and ran his fingers over the lightning-bolt plaster cracks. His history of insanity was etched in those walls.

"Not sure." He unpacked the box full of books taken from the shed and his clothes. He took special care of his notebook. A new hiding place was essential. "I overheard the guy from social services who brought me here say something about an inspection requested by my shrink. There may be some trouble with the doctor over the pills and things Lydia and Frank want so much."

Suzy stood by the bed and said, "The inspectors wouldn't like it if they found you living in a toolshed." She fell back and bounced a few times. "At least now you have a real bed. Very comfortable."

"If you haven't worn out the springs." Jason chuckled. He caught a momentary look of concern on her face. "Somethin' on your mind?"

"Well, I ... kinda told one of the younger boys who's having some trouble to come see you." Suzy smiled sheepishly. "You have a way of helping even if you don't know how it works. Everyone you've touched is better—except Lydia, of course."

"Well, Lydia's a special case." Jason pulled the drawers out of the desk and looked up under the openings. "I don't mind you telling people I might be able to help. Just let me know you're gonna do it." Not finding what he'd hoped for, he pulled one of the bed drawers out. "When's this guy gonna show up?"

"Soon, I think." As Suzy stood to go, a boy appeared at the open door. "Jason, this is Stephen. See ya later." She gave him a reassuring nod, slipped by him, and skipped down the hall.

Stephen looked twitchy, like a mouse looking out for a cat. His problem, like all the others', related to terrible adults. At twelve years old, he still wet the bed at night. Sick of the teasing from his roommates and fearful of the Frank's threats about sleeping in the backyard to save on laundry, he had sought help from Rachel and Suzy. Stephen heard them at night in their room below his. They sounded ... happy.

"Okay," Jason said. Like the other boys in the house, Stephen wore worn jeans and a T-shirt. "Lie down here. I need something from the shed. I'll be right back."

Jason never returned to his room. He nudged the boy on his bed into a deep sleep while he sat on the back-porch steps. Stephen acted as the guide as Jason entered his mind, providing his own solution. This strategy had worked well with Suzy and Rachel. The only new tack was the Etch-A-Sketch. A long row of the thin, red boxes with silver screens and white knobs appeared side by side on a control panel. They stretched forever like a mirror reflected in a mirror. Jason picked up three or four, turned them upside down, and shook. Stephen's recent memory of Jason disappeared. He awoke confused and left Jason's room, wondering why he was there. Suzy would report if the intervention helped.

Jason slid off the rock to the dirt path below. Exploring the woods felt good. It cleared his head and helped his headaches. The pain came more often lately. A thicker wall of trees beckoned. He stepped off the path, pushed through underbrush, and disappeared into a forest of evergreens.

Fighting through a thick hedgerow, he discovered an overgrown rock garden. The hedgerow encircled the remnants of the garden, whose main feature was a small fountain where water had cascaded down smooth rocks to a pool, long dried up. Overgrown with weeds and small trees trying to take root, the beauty of the place lay hidden. *A little effort,* he thought, *could bring it back.*

Jason forced his way through the dark-green wall on the other side of the rock garden. He froze. He had stumbled on a man who sat cross-legged beneath a huge oak tree; his eyes were closed. Startled, Jason made no sound. The man, only twenty feet away, did not react to his presence. In defense mode, Jason's mind reached out to touch the stranger's thoughts and grabbed whatever lay at the front of the stranger's mind. The man's history spilled into Jason's mind.

Chiang Chin, a thirty-four-year-old agriculture professor, lived and taught at the University of Taiwan. A survivor, he started life in a small village along the Yellow River in China, Zhengzhou. The Japanese war machine destroyed his village. The civil war in which he fought for Chiang Kai-Shek against Mao Tse Tung destroyed his soul. With Mao victorious, Chin and tens of thousands like him retreated across the Formosa Strait to Taiwan.

With no one to fight, Chin sought mindless work in the fields outside Taipei as a common laborer. Nightmares of corpses piled in the main square with their severed heads stacked against a wall plagued him. He became very depressed, and suicide seemed a viable solution.

It was a village elder who pointed the way to hope and forgiveness. Buddhist discipline, honest talk, and a desire to do good finally salvaged Chin. It was 1949, and he was twenty-one years old. In 1962 he entered the United States on a professor exchange program with the University of Pennsylvania.

Mildly shocked when he discovered he was not alone, Chin waited for his new companion to finish his meditations. Jason opened his eyes minutes later.

"Tell me, you have a name?" Chin rose and slipped on his sandals. Tall and thin with short, black hair, he moved with a fluidity that comes from strength and confidence. He wore a sleeveless, black sweatshirt and baggy, black pants. His arms looked muscled from long days in the field.

"Jason, sir." Jason felt stronger, refreshed. He uncrossed his legs and stood. Chin stood a head taller.

"My name, Jason, is Chiang Chin. Call me Chiang. How long have you been meditating?"

"You mean doing what we have been doing here?" Jason stared at his feet, moving a small pebble around. He felt guilty about entering Chiang's mind uninvited.

"Yes."

"Today is the first time." He looked up.

"Ah." Chin gathered his things and packed them away in a black duffel bag.

"It's amazingly calm in my head when I do this," Jason said. Hoping he had done nothing wrong, he added, "I apologize if I disturbed you, sir." He almost blurted out that he had unintentionally taken the art of meditation from his mind.

"Disturb me? No, my young friend, you did not disturb me." Chiang scanned the surrounding area. "I am here every day at this time. If you wish to join me again please do … but only if you call me Chiang."

"Yes sir. I mean, Chiang, I would like that." Relieved, Jason smiled and nodded.

Chiang nodded too. "Tomorrow then?" He threw the bulky, black bag over his shoulder.

"Yes," Jason said. He turned to follow his track back the way he had come.

Chiang watched him walk away. *Strange child*, he thought, *but very special*. Only this spot in the park had a lush, deep summer, green with late-summer flowers in full bloom. A month's growth had exploded where an hour earlier no flowering plants perfumed the air.

A few days later, Lydia confronted Frank as he sat at the kitchen table, reading the newspaper. "What is going on around here?" Arms crossed, foot tapping, her anger built as Frank slowly lowered the paper. "It feels different. Don't you get that something strange is going on?"

"The kids strike me as happier and are helping each other out. This is a new, unexpected twist. That what you mean?"

Frank felt better too but couldn't quite understand why. The house was bereft of children except for Jason. Frank recalled that they had been surprisingly cooperative and helpful with one another as they prepared to leave for camp. This was a good thing. He would not, however, contradict Lydia, who obviously did not see the benefits.

"Yeah, that's very strange. Why now?" She shook her head and sat down at the table. "Another thing bothers me. Why haven't the drug goons come back?"

"Well, maybe we aren't worth the effort." Frank closed and folded the paper. The phone conversation with Sly was fresh in his mind.

"Maybe they don't see the profit in coming after us, since we're such small potatoes."

"Those guys are never satisfied, and they get even. Why haven't we heard anything more, if the arrangement was such a bust? No, there's something goin' on." She rose from the table and looked out the window over the sink. "It has something to do with that kid."

Lydia saw Jason sitting with his back against the toolshed wall and his legs crossed. He looked asleep. She knew better.

"What? The toolshed kid?" Frank got up and joined her at the window. "What could he have done? He's only a kid—and pretty screwed up at that."

"Not screwed up enough for the shrink to keep the pills comin'." Lydia eyed Jason just sitting there. She hated him. He had something she did not understand. "Got that damned doctor to call an inspection on us. On us!"

Frank remained silent. He expected that sooner or later there would be an inspection without Will running interference. He didn't think the doctor had anything to do with it.

"I don't know," Lydia continued. "How come he's a mess in December and suddenly pretty normal a few months later?" Lydia paused. "It doesn't make any sense. Come with me. Time for a room check." Lydia left the kitchen. Frank followed.

When she reached Jason's room, she turned and said, "Let's tear this place apart."

"Looking for what?" Frank felt uneasy.

"I don't know. Something ..." Lydia grabbed either side of her head as if concentrating on something. "Arrgh. I can't remember. Look for anything like a notebook or journal."

It took them fifteen minutes to ransack Jason's room. They found nothing.

Frank surveyed the mess, scratching the back of his head. "Do we leave it like this?"

"No, let's put it back," Lydia commanded. They left no evidence that they had invaded his space.

"This thing he's been doing," Lydia said, "this just sitting like he's asleep is new."

"Yeah, I noticed." Frank stuffed the last of the socks and underwear back in the drawer under the bed. "I remember saying to myself right about the time he started this stuff, 'Kids are happier.' Course, that's okay by me. The less running around I have to do to keep up with their fighting and nutsy stuff, the better."

"The less money in our pockets. Have you forgotten?" Lydia folded her arms, challenging him to argue.

"Yeah, you're right. But I fig'red maybe we got off easy with the goons." He stood up. "Let's not look a gift horse in the mouth." Lydia's foot tapped. "Let it go, Lydia. It coulda been a whole lot worse."

"Worse? Worse … yes." She turned to Frank and then started pacing around the room. "That's it!" She stopped and snapped her fingers. "I hav'ta call Will at social services. We can turn this getting-better angle into money." She pointed at Frank to drive home her point. "We catch the worst cases and get more money to cover the poor sick children no one else wants. The kids will get better. No one will know for a time. We pocket the extra cash until the damned doctor's report on their improved conditions." She strode into the hallway.

"We have only so much room, Lydia." Frank followed her. He saw the signs of obsession. He knew no arguments could change her course.

"We ship out the new kids as their doctors become aware that they are better." She spun around to face Frank. "You get it?"

"Wait a minute." Frank frowned. His hands beat the air in time with his words for emphasis as he said, "Ship them where?"

"Let Will work that out." She turned away, not caring that Frank did not buy into this plan. "The boy needs to be kept close. He is the key. I know it. Give him chores. It will be easier to keep track of 'im."

Frank just stared after her as she rushed downstairs. The whole idea struck him as nuts. He worried that Lydia might be losing her mind.

"Okay." He called after her. "We try it for a while. But if I wind up like I did with the boy before he got better, we drop the whole thing. We're doing fine. Let's not get too greedy."

"No such thing, Frank, as too greedy," she yelled. "Let's get Will on the horn."

As Lydia dialed, the meditation in the backyard ended. Jason regained self-awareness. If he were asked about where his thoughts took him, he could not have answered. One second with controlled breathing, he calmed, and his heart slowed. The next second he left to who knew where until something kicked him back to himself. The only thing certain was that Jason felt invigorated, alive, and ready to meet whatever challenges came his way.

Jason pulled his notebook out from under him, opened it, and made some notes. He finished scribbling, rose, and returned his journal to its hiding place in the toolshed. The shed was the best place. The spiders, he noticed, were busy as ever in the ceiling corners. "Hey, guys, how're you doing?" He didn't receive or seek an answer, of course. It did his heart good to see something working should.

When he entered the kitchen, Lydia was waiting for him. "With so many of the kids at camp and such, we need you to run errands." She handed him a slip of paper. "Here's the grocery list." She walked over to the door leading down to the basement and opened it. An old fold-up cart hung from two hooks on the backside of the door. She took it down and handed it to Jason. "You know where the A&P market is, right?" He nodded. "Good, here's twenty bucks, which is plenty. See you bring back the change."

Chapter 11

"You are nothing and everything. Seek nothing first. Everything will follow." Chiang began the sessions the same way each day. After two weeks of meditating with his new, young companion, he decided it was time to discuss a few things.

"You have special talents, Jason." Chiang remained in his meditation pose, legs crossed, back straight. Concern wrinkled the older man's forehead. "Yet you have not spoken of these things."

Jason stared at him. Caught in the rays of clear, bright, morning sunlight, he felt like he stood in a spotlight. There was no place to hide.

"You are unaware, which I think is not possible or you are afraid to reveal yourself or you are playing a joke of some sort at my expense."

"I ..." Jason slowly climbed to his feet and brushed the dirt and leaves off his sweatpants. Dry mouthed and fearful, Jason realized either direction—running away or talking—might bring pain and potential danger. "It's too scary to talk about this stuff," he said, clenching his fists. "I don't really know you. Things have been ... happening. I can't deal with them all. If I talk to you, it's another thing to worry about." Jason turned to leave, his heart heavy. "I ... I hope you kinda understand."

"Wait, my young friend."

Jason hesitated. He turned his ear to listen; he did not want to see the judgment in Chiang's face.

"I believe," Chiang said, "it is time we took a meal together. Will you join me for lunch? I find it easier to talk over good food." He got to his feet and gathered his things, ignoring his pupil.

Jason swung around and eyed his meditation partner. His sense of Chiang was clear; he had been in the man's head, if only for a second. The reticence he felt with Dr. Lipton was not there. This would be the first adult he might trust with his secret or the start of a huge mistake. He decided to go, since he was hungry. He would clear his memory if necessary.

"I'll join you."

"Excellent." Chiang smiled and bowed slightly and then gestured toward the path with his upturned hand. Jason led the way. Once outside of the bird sanctuary, Chiang took the lead.

A half mile away near the local Penn State campus, Chiang knocked and entered a small white cottage; ivy grew up the wall around the windows. Jason followed. Something wonderful simmered in the kitchen. It filled the house with a seductive aroma. It lured him like sirens tempting unwary sailors. His stomach grumbled. A small, old Chinese woman stepped into the hallway directly in front of them. She wiped her hands on a dish towel.

"Mrs. Lim, may I introduce Jason, my new associate," said Chiang. He dropped his bag to the floor beneath the coat rack by the front door.

She looked the boy over and then smiled. "You are welcome, young man. Come in, come in. I have just finished preparing lunch." Before Jason could say a word, she put her arm around his shoulder and guided him to a chair at the kitchen table.

"I ... I am honored." He did not know why he spoke those words. It struck him as the right thing. Mrs. Lim stared at him, delightfully shocked to hear such unexpected courtesy from an American. She nodded her approval at Chiang.

"Mrs. Lim has been a great help to those of us who visit your country. She's mastered your culture and acts as a bridge between the old and new worlds." Chiang took a seat next to Jason. "She also makes the best dim sum on this side of the planet."

An hour later, Jason and Chiang sipped jasmine tea over their empty plates, not able to eat another bite.

"You like dim sum?" Chiang placed his cup on the table and folded his hands before him.

"It's amazing. I've never had anything like it." Jason sat back thoroughly sated.

"Mrs. Lim will be pleased to see the honor you have given her efforts." Chiang paused a moment not sure how he wanted to proceed. He did not want to scare Jason off. "Mrs. Lim is my landlady. I rent a room here."

Jason nodded. He considered eating one more dumpling.

"I teach horticulture at the university campus nearby. Do you know what that is?"

Jason shook his head.

"Plants, Jason. The how, when, where, and why of successful growth. I specialize in the growing of hardier species of plants used for food in my country."

"Oh." Jason thought this job sounded important, though exactly what Chiang did remained a mystery. He eyed the dumpling but decided against it. He would need to loosen his belt to get out of his chair.

"I want to show you something. Come into the backyard." Chiang rose, held open the back door, and waited for Jason to step onto the porch. Slowly the boy pulled himself up. He walked under Chiang's arm and then looked out over a field of incredible color.

The backyard spanned the width of the house and stretched fifty feet to a wood fence that bordered a dirt road. A path of white stones divided the yard evenly, with a garden on either side. A bench sat amid a circle of the same stones at the midpoint of the garden. The air blossomed with the sweet smell of hyacinth, orange blossom, and lilacs. The flowers in full bloom painted the yard in a spectrum of purple, white, yellow, orange, and some colors Jason had never encountered. He stood amazed. The buzzing, he realized, came from outside of his head. The bees, little black dots, hovered over and among the flowers.

Chiang laid his hand on Jason's shoulder and then stepped down to the path and waited for him to follow. He walked ahead down the center path to a spot near the fence and squatted, examining some plants. Jason was mesmerized. He felt and heard the stones crunch beneath his feet; he watched as pollen gathers moved from blossom to blossom or a butterfly crossed his line of sight. He came up to and stood behind Chiang, who crouched and gently caressed a white petal with an orange tongue along its center.

"These flowers," he said, "grow only in the soil in my country, Taiwan." He stood and walked among the two-foot stems. "They will not grow elsewhere. But here they are."

Jason stared, dumbfounded.

Chiang continued. "I planted the seeds in small paper bags of soil from Mrs. Lim's backyard and brought them with me to our meditation sessions. They grew. The ones I did not bring are there." He pointed to a row of three small, opened, brown bags propped up against the fence; nothing grew over their tops. Chiang continued his examination of the stem and leaves. "These shouldn't have been able to grow."

"So you think I did this?" Jason, stunned, had found his voice. His heart skipped a beat; his breathing was labored.

"I am a scientist, Jason." Chiang turned his head and looked at him. "I study the data provided and make conclusions based on that data. Without you, there is no growth. With you, there is growth. Somehow you have changed these plants into something new that can survive here. You changed their genes." Chiang stood, walked back up the path, and took a seat on the bench.

Minutes passed before Jason could calm his panic and trudge up the white path, kicking stones to the side. He sat and studied his sneakers. Afraid to say anything, he glanced at Chiang and then turned away. Chiang's reassuring smile did not help. Jason had to make a snap decision.

"I can do things." His wall of insecurity and fear cracked. More words leaked out. "I can do things with my thoughts. I don't know much about how. I just do things."

Before he realized it, Jason's whole story had poured out in Mrs. Lim's garden. The words gushed like the sea through a failed seawall. He gave up his fear and prayed for acceptance from just one person.

Jason meticulously ticked off the items listed in his notebook, holding up a finger for each of his demonstrated talents. Eventually the flood of words ended. It was out. Relief and fear of judgment flooded his mind until he looked up into Chiang's face.

Chiang patted his shoulder, and tears suddenly burst from the boy. *Finally*, he thought, *someone*. His arms flew around Chiang; he sobbed uncontrollably.

Shocked at first, Chiang relaxed and held his friend in silent acceptance.

☆   ☆   ☆

As the summer days passed, Frank and Lydia kept Jason busy running errands, cleaning the house, and doing yard work. It was a twenty-minute walk to the grocery store, and Jason made the trek every few days. This particular job he enjoyed.

"Well, I have found our whistler."

The next few notes of the Beach Boys' "409" faded from Jason's pursed lips as he glanced up. A pretty woman in sunglasses grinned at him. The two large cans of spaghetti sauce he held in either hand dropped into the grocery cart.

"Oh, Miss Thompson," he said. Jason stood up straight and then pulled his cart to one side, which allowed her to pass. "Yeah, it's a song I heard coming from a car in the parking lot." He returned her smile.

Miss Thompson and Mr. Downing had monitored his first tests to place him in the right class. No records existed for Jason, so the testing would allow the school to place him in the classroom where he would succeed. After his first official day in school, Miss Thompson had presented three small gifts to him to commemorate the milestone. As he climbed onto the bus, she had handed him a notebook and pencils, and she offered her smile. It was so unexpected, such a pleasant surprise, Jason could hardly speak his thanks. She became his angel.

"Doing the shopping, I see." She took a step back and pulled her cart around the corner to join Jason in the pasta and sauce aisle. Dressed for summer, Miss Thompson wore sky-blue shorts with a matching top. A large, pink purse sat in the child seat in her cart. She reached for her sunglasses and set them back on her curly, brown hair like a tiara. Jason noticed that her hair was shorter.

"Your hair looks good. I mean … you got it cut." He fumbled, embarrassed. "It looks good."

"Why, thank you, sir." She gave his shoulder a squeeze. "Most boys your age wouldn't have noticed." Removing the sunglasses, she pushed back her hair with her fingers as she held the glasses in her hand. "How is your summer shaping up?"

"Not as bad as I thought it would." Jason tucked in his yellow T-shirt and ran his fingers through his hair. It suddenly became important to look more presentable. "With doing chores and helping out with other things around the house, time is going pretty fast. It's better to be busy." A week had passed since he divulged everything to Chiang.

"Well, good." She looked at him and absentmindedly began to chew on one stem of the sunglasses. "I never did get to test you further. Did I?" Jason did not respond. "You will undoubtedly get tested in middle school. Are you keeping up with your reading?"

"Some. But I am writing more." It felt strange to talk to a teacher in the middle of the A&P. Suddenly an idea popped into his head. "Miss Thompson, I need to learn a few things about the world war and genes. Who could help me out with those?"

"Don't tell me you've never been to the library?" She frowned as she watched him slowly shake his head.

"What is it?" Jason cringed and waited for her shock at his not knowing another simple thing.

"It's a gold mine, Jason, a gold mine," she said with no hint of judgment. "It would probably be best if I took you over there. I've got tons of free time right now." She rummaged around in her purse and pulled out a small book. "Let's see. How about some day next week at noon? Wednesday, perhaps? I'll pick you up at your house. Yes?"

"It should be okay."

"Good. It's a date. Now, to finish my chores for the day." She grabbed the cart handle and spun, disappearing around the end of the aisle. Jason stared after her. Things were getting better.

✶   ✶   ✶

The following morning, finished with their meditation, Chiang and Jason sat beneath the oak tree.

"I have considered what you told me very carefully," Chiang said. "We must move slowly and see where your abilities might go." He considered Jason and then added, "Will you allow me to guide you for a while?"

"Yes." *For once, the load is not all on me.*

"Given all that we have covered over the last few days, I have a few suppositions based on the data you have provided. First, you cannot use some of your abilities with your conscious mind. This is likely a built-in, fail-safe mechanism. For example, when you run in your dreams, do you find yourself on the floor with a bloody nose having dashed into a wall?"

Jason shook his head.

"No, of course not. This is probably for your own protection. You must mature—that is to say, grow into your capabilities much like a child who gains fine motor control of his hands as he grows older. How long this will take is anyone's guess."

"And my headaches?" asked Jason.

"There are two possibilities where one or both may apply. It could be that the maturing process is in full swing. The headaches are a result. That is the best case." Chiang paused for a second. "But I am concerned, Jason. You need to know that another possibility is that another like you is trying to attack or break into your mind."

Jason uncrossed his legs and hugged his knees to his chest. "Another like me," he whispered. Suzy, Peg, and Patti came to mind.

"You are surprised?" Chiang stood and began gathering his things into his bag.

"Yes and no. I know of others, but someone attacking me? Why?"

"Come, let's walk." Chiang swung the bag over his shoulder and held out a hand, helping Jason to his feet. Side by side they moved down a path through the undergrowth.

"Jason, you are unique," Chiang said. "I am not talking about your abilities. I refer to the person you are at your core. With the limited control you have, you could have done great damage for personal gain. You didn't."

"Well, I don't want to get hurt or messed with, so why would I do that to anybody else?" He kept on eye on the path where flowing water had undermined part of it.

"My point exactly. You have your own lines drawn in the sand of your soul beyond which you will not go. Although you cannot describe it, I would call it a healthy desire to connect with people and do no harm." Chiang stopped abruptly and surveyed the surroundings. There was a noise, a small animal perhaps. "There could be people like you without this self-imposed limit."

Jason reached down and picked up a long stick about an inch thick, a walking stick. It felt good in his hand. He listened to Chiang as they headed for the small lake at the center of the sanctuary. The water's surface reflected the trees and sky. Across the lake, geese paddled among the water lilies. Others flew in and landed majestically in a whoosh of water and wings.

"So now what?" Jason swung his stick back and forth to part the thick carpet of ferns around the lake. He searched for a dry place on the water's edge where he could stand and watch the geese.

"To tell you the truth, I don't know. I have never known anyone like you." Chiang stood back, watching Jason. "I suggest you use your gifts very little. Keep doing the meditations. Stay out of people's minds except to defend yourself." He looked to the horizon and noted the dark clouds moving toward them. He added, "We should each return home." He turned, faced back up the path, and stopped. "But before we leave, tell me, do you know the man who has been following us today?"

"Yes." Jason smiled and wondered if Chiang had picked up on their tail. "He's my foster father. Not much of a father, though." Jason had sensed Frank's presence prior to the start of their meditation. "He is harmless, I think. Whatever Lydia, my foster mother wants, he does."

"They are trailing you because?"

"I'm not sure." Jason retreated from the lake's edge and stood next to Chiang. "You can bet it has something to do with money."

"So they will know about our meetings." Chiang looked concerned.

"I wouldn't worry too much about it. They will not want to upset me, since they think I will be good for business. We will see." They walked away from the lake. Close to their meditation spot, they parted company with a happy "See you tomorrow."

Jason wondered if he should erase Chiang from Frank's memory. He decided against it.

Chapter 12

/

"**N**o library card! What do you mean no library card?" Mary Tremont slapped the well-worn, ink-stained blotter on the counter. She looked stern with her strong chin, granny glasses, and short, silver hair. A sturdy woman, she was an imposing figure. "Has this child been made to live in the dark, under a rock?"

Books and magazines piled high like a great wall covered the long, mahogany counter. Louise Deloro joined Mary, and the two old women looked down over the published parapet to judge the capabilities of the boy brought to their attention.

"It is a long story, Mrs. Tremont," Miss Thompson said. "Jason is a mystery on many levels."

He blushed, unable to look any of the women in the eye. Earlier Miss Thompson had picked him up in front of his house. She wore a yellow, cotton skirt and peasant blouse, which he thought looked good on her. Her perfume reminded him of Mrs. Lim's backyard. Jason's words had failed him while they drove to the library. Miss Thompson did not give any indication that she saw her effect on him.

"What do you think, Lou? Can he handle it?" Mary Tremont pulled a piece of paper from a drawer below the counter and handed it to Miss Thompson. She gazed at the boy.

"Don't know, Mare." Louise considered the child skeptically, her arms folded. Smaller and thinner than Mary, Louise projected a quiet strength and confidence in her realm of books. She looked at Miss Thompson.

"What do you think? Is this subject"—she placed her hand on a thick textbook and nodded toward Jason—"something he can handle?"

"Of course, Mrs. Deloro." Miss Thompson smiled as she finished the paperwork for Jason's library card. "It would be best, of course, if a primer on basic biology might also be provided. He may need some basic definitions not provided in the text."

"I'm way ahead of you," Mary said. She tossed another smaller text on top. "Now, is there anything else we can do for you, young man?"

"Well ..."

"Come, come boy. Out with it." No one described Mary Tremont as a patient person. Get right to the point, or you were better off not bothering her. Louise smiled, benignly curious about the forthcoming request.

"I need something on World War II." Jason spoke fast. Before Mary could start interrogating him to narrow the scope of the search, he added, "Something on the B-17s or something like that."

Louise cupped her chin and looked around the room deep in thought. She came out from behind the counter and disappeared into the rows of tall shelves. Mary, her eyes closed, lightly touched the books stacked on either side of her. Suddenly she took off in the opposite direction. In minutes, they returned. Mary bowed slightly to Louise, intimating that she should go first. Lou nodded.

"This one just came to us. It is called *Night Fighters*. I have not read it. I will look to you for a review. Can you do that for me?" She handed Jason the book.

"Sure," he said, excited. He studied the cover of the book. It showed a Spitfire in a night sky with machine guns blazing.

"This book," Mary stated rather formally, "has been out for a while. Published in 1943 to be exact. It's about the twenty-five missions of the Memphis Belle."

Jason grasped the book. He stared at the sky-blue cover with the B-17 bomber flying, and smiled. Mary arched her eyebrow and then broke into a big grin. "My nephew flew in one of these. He thought this book was pretty fair, considering it came from the Air Corps." At last Jason would discover some things about his best friend's dad and not feel so stupid.

"Well, Miss Thompson," said Louise, "this young man will be busy for a long time, working through these." She pointed to the books cradled in Jason's arms. "So let's give him four weeks to get them back to us for renewal."

"Thank you, Mrs. Deloro," Miss Thompson said. "That is most kind."

"I think," said Mary, "that for the time being you may sign for his card. I trust that would not be too burdensome."

"No trouble at all." Miss Thompson handed back the completed page. Lou handed Jason a temporary library card.

"Come back in four weeks, young man, and we will renew your books for another four weeks." Mary and Louise, apparently satisfied that they brought another young soul into the light, started arguing about creating a unique designation for fictionalized history.

Outside on the sidewalk, Jason cradled his books, anxious to get to his room and start reading.

"I didn't know you were interested in war history." Miss Thompson fished in her purse for her car keys as they walked side by side.

"Russ's father was in the war. I didn't know anything about it. So ..." Jason watched, amused, as she argued with her orange purse.

"Did you know," she said as she extracted her keys, victorious in matching wits with the maze of her purse, "Mr. Downing is our resident history enthusiast. You might want to speak to him."

Jason frowned at the prospect of spending time with Mr. Downing. He remembered the testing earlier in the year and the grumpy old man's snide comments.

"Idiots," Jason had heard Mr. Downing whisper curtly. "We are teaching idiots these days. I could do this in second grade."

"I am sure, Mr. Downing, the children are not idiots," Miss Thompson had fired back forcefully.

"Well, it's all too easy these days. Too easy I tell you."

Jason had seen, in a brief flash, a child held over a desk and a yard stick coming down. The last thing he desired was to spend time with Downing.

"Yes, yes, he does take himself a bit too seriously," she said when she saw Jason's woeful look. "But he's a good guy when you get to know him. Besides, he could get you back on par on all the things you have missed or do not remember from social studies." They reached her car. She inserted the key in the door and then looked at Jason over the roof. "I bet he would even be able to help with some of the genetic material from a historical perspective. Will you give him a try?"

Jason melted under her sweet gaze. "Yeah, all right." He could not say no to her. "You gotta sorta set it up for me, okay?"

"Done!"

In the car, Jason gasped with the summer heat. Miss Thompson broke out her notebook. "Thursday evening looks good. I'll let you know." She started the car and let it idle.

Jason wondered how she set an appointment for Mr. Downing without checking with him and if his foster parents would give their consent.

"Mr. D and I have already spoken about you and … since I snatched you away from your house today"—she tossed her notebook into her bag—"Thursday evening will not be much of a problem."

Shocked, Jason just sat there nodding.

"What did you think of our library ladies? Quite a team, aren't they?"

"A little scary at first." Jason frowned.

Miss Thompson laughed. "Yes, they tend to have that effect at first, but they're really very sweet." She threw the car into gear and started to pull away from the curb. "They're sisters, you know, and run the library as volunteers. They keep up the stacks and add new books with money out of their own pockets. Fairly wealthy from what I can deduce." She reached into her bag, pulled out her sunglasses, and put them on. "Even the university professors go to them for support. They are the local information experts."

A cool breeze blew across the front seat. Jason inhaled Miss Thompson's scent. He couldn't describe how he felt at that moment, but he did not want it to end.

"Then," she continued, "if you ever get the chance to see them together, you will find out that Mrs. Tremont has feelings for Mr. Downing." Jason could not imagine such a thing. "It's quite touching in its way. Mr. D is oblivious, as most men are about such things. He'll get it eventually." She laughed. "Back to the house to read or out to lunch?" Miss Thompson took a right at the first corner and headed for the nearest diner, as if she could read his mind.

"Lunch!" Jason never turned down an offer of better food. The prospect of more time with Miss Thompson, of a full stomach, and of a good book to read later brought a satisfied grin to his face.

✼ ✼ ✼

Late Saturday night, Frank roused Jason from a deep sleep. Jason had spent the day moving furniture from the basement to the detached garage. Exhausted, he had skipped dinner and tried to do some reading in bed, but he'd fallen asleep on the genetics textbook.

"Come on, kid." Frank pulled him up from his bed. "It's showtime." The last page Jason had read stuck to his face. He still wore the clothes he'd worked in.

"Showtime?" Jason asked. He yawned and peeled away the page and then stretched his aching muscles. Bleary-eyed, he closed the book and got up. Frank pushed him toward the door. "What do you mean by showtime?"

"Never you mind," commanded Frank. "Just get downstairs. We have something for you to do. Someone to meet." In the hallway, Frank walked ahead and trotted down the stairs, two steps at a time. Jason heard his voice. "He's up and coming."

What now? He rubbed his eyes and stretched again at the top of the steps. Slowly he clumped down the stairs to the landing. Lydia and Frank stood by the front door. Lydia pulled back the shear curtains, looking through the etched-glass windows on either side. Jason sat on the lowest step and leaned against the wall, where he shut his eyes and drifted off.

"They're here." Lydia stood back from the door. "This should be interesting."

When Frank opened the door, Will Grossman entered.

"This kid's a big mess." Will looked at Lydia and then turned to Frank. "But I thought you couldn't handle any more with the Sutter kid in the house."

"The situation has changed." Lydia stood feet apart, hands on her hips. "Bring him in." Frank stood to the side, ready to jump, if needed. Will raised his hand and signaled. His assistant, who waited on the walkway, escorted a small boy up to the porch and through the door. Dressed in brown, corduroy pants with a bright-yellow T-shirt, the child looked harmless, and he showed no fear.

"This is Samuel Richardson. He's eight and has a little trouble controlling his temper." Will watched the boy cautiously. "Tossed out of four other foster homes in the last two years, he knows the routine. I'm gonna assume you read the bio I sent you. His last foster mother reported—"

Lydia held up her hand, palm out. Will stared at her, annoyed, but kept quiet. She leaned over close to Samuel and whispered in his ear. Then she pointed at Jason. "That's the kid that told the cops where to find your dad."

Sam's eyes shot toward the sleeping boy on the bottom step. Lydia stood upright and stepped aside. Like an arrow shot from a bow, the boy ran at Jason. Lydia put out her arm to stop Frank, Will, and his assistant from interfering.

"Wait," she said softly. "Just wait."

They watched as the boy landed punch after punch. Sam blocked their view of Jason, but they imagined he tried to defend himself from the onslaught. In moments, the fury of punches lessened as Sam's arms tired. Finally he stopped and turned away from his target. He sat next to Jason on the step, looking confused and weary. Jason remained against the wall asleep, untouched.

"What did I tell ya?" Lydia grinned, self-satisfied. "It's the boy, like I've been saying."

"Well, I'll be damned," said Frank, shocked that the toolshed kid looked like nothing happened.

Jason straightened up and got to his feet. He turned and headed up the stairs with his arm around Samuel's shoulder. At the top of the stairs, they disappeared down the hallway. The adults stood frozen below, waiting to see what would happen next.

Jason returned to the top of the stairs moments later and looked down at Lydia in disgust.

"Sam is in the room next to mine, asleep," he spoke aloud. *"If you ever use me like this again...!"* His words assaulted the minds of Lydia, Frank, and Will and brought them to their knees. They held their hands to their heads in a vain attempt to block the pain and ease the volume convulsing their brain. Will's assistant, whom Jason left untouched, stood mesmerized.

You got it?

Frank and Will nodded in quick agreement. Jason released them. They continued to shiver on the floor, tears on their cheeks. Eventually they managed to stand, shaken by the violence. Lydia, however, refused to surrender. Suddenly, in her thoughts she stood in a kitchen she knew all too well. Her father stood over her twelve-year-old self. "No," she whimpered but held herself together, refusing to give in to the terror.

You got it?

"Yes!" she cried. "Make it stop!" Lydia lay curled in a fetal position on the floor. Jason released her. Slow to get to her feet, she looked up at Jason and detested him. She refused to cry or show weakness. The others gawked at the boy who stood above them, awestruck by what had happened.

Jason eradicated the facts of that night from the four adults' minds, but he did not use the Etch-A-Sketch construct. Paper, pencil, and a large pink eraser sufficed. Working feverishly, the eraser undid the pencil description of Sam's arrival. Like a child just learning to write, anxious to fix his mistakes, Jason left behind a graphite haze on the page. He wrote over it, replacing the facts of the past ten minutes with another reality. Other refinements graced the modifications on Lydia's page.

No longer mindful of Jason's presence, Will and his assistant turned around and left the house, secure in the knowledge that the transfer of the child to the Dubois's care was routine. Frank and Lydia went and sat at the kitchen table. They calmly discussed the new boy, feeling good about how Jason had stepped in to help Sam adapt.

"There was something else? Wasn't there?" Lydia stared at Frank. "There was a plan, wasn't there?"

Jason came downstairs and eavesdropped in the hall outside the kitchen. "Just the usual," said Frank. "Get a difficult kid no one else wants and get all the money we can to take care of 'im." Frank shrugged. "No other plan you ever mentioned."

"The boy came downstairs," Lydia said, but then shook her head.

"He took Sam upstairs and that was that." Frank was beginning to worry about her. She had been obsessed with the toolshed kid lately.

"Yeah," Lydia said, giving up. "That's it. Just the usual set up."

Jason yawned, returned to his room, and collapsed on his bed—used up.

Chapter 13

᠁

The children returned from camp late Sunday afternoon, and Frank sat and listened at the kitchen table. Laughter, punctuated by sudden, hysterical, joyful screams tumbled from the toolshed. He checked his watch. Four o'clock. Dinner was next on his to-do list with the kids home. With an hour to waste, he relaxed. He thought, *Strange that I enjoy the sound of my children happy to be together.* The thought *my kids* caught him by surprise. He pushed the feelings away. It was always about the money.

Lunch, a quiet affair earlier that day, had found him sharing the table with the toolshed kid. The usual lunchtime fare was chicken noodle soup and peanut butter on toast, washed down with Kool-Aid.

"Excited about the kids coming home?" Frank held up a piece of toast. He studied it. "Happy to share some of the chores?" He took a bite.

"Yeah. Lookin' forward to catching up too." Jason spooned soup into his mouth, making sure none escaped.

"Hmm," Frank acknowledged. He took a drink. "How's Sam working out?"

"Upstairs asleep, right now." Jason did not look up as he broke off a piece of his toast.

"Yeah, the meds will do that." Frank stopped eating and considered Jason. "Lydia's out too. She said something about a headache and hit the sheets." A smile twitched across Jason's face. Frank missed it. "So it's just you and me for a while."

"I think," said Jason, raising his eyes to Frank's, "that I'll wait for the bus in front."

"Suit yourself." Frank felt oddly disappointed. A quiet moment ensued while he struggled with unfamiliar feelings. "You did a good job on the front rooms and basement. It made my life a little easier." His fingers lightly drummed the table.

"Thanks." Jason sat back.

"I guess your friend, Gus, Russ, whatever, will come over too?" The pace of the tapping increased.

"I hope so." Jason paused and looked at Frank. "Is that okay?"

"Yeah, sure. Just not for dinner, okay?" Frank sat forward and stopped tapping when he noticed the old habit had returned. He pulled his fingers into his palm.

"Yeah."

When they had finished lunch, and Frank said, "Just put the dishes in the sink. I'll rinse 'em."

"Thank you, Frank." Jason got up and put his dishes in the sink and then headed for the front porch.

Frank looked at his watch again. Five minutes passed. More laughter erupted from the shed, and then it got quiet in the backyard for a moment. Frank spoke Jason's name out loud. His fingers tapped the table again. Lydia had part of it right; there was something special about the boy.

He went to the sink and looked out the window. He could not remember a time when any physical ailment slowed Lydia, much less forced her to bed. Something had changed again. Try as he might, he could not figure out what might have happened to cause Lydia's headaches. Frank stacked the dishes in the dark-green strainer and glanced at the toolshed. Through the open door, he saw kids sitting around the workbench. A part of him yearned to join in the laughter.

✫   ✫   ✫

"Suzy kissed a boy!" Rachel screamed, throwing her arm around Suzy. "I thought he was pretty good lookin' too."

Suzy blushed. "It was just a cheek kiss." She, Rachel, and Jason sat on beat-up, wooden stools. Sam, who had awakened in the early afternoon, sat on the stoop and leaned against the door, still drowsy.

"You liked him." Rachel brushed Suzy's hair away from her face. "It was special. A good thing."

Jason watched the two of them, like sisters, the older encouraging the younger.

"So what about that Billy kid?" Suzy asked.

"Oh, pull-ease!" Rachel clapped her hands. "He was so full of himself." She moved closer to Suzy, and as if in confidence, she said, "I had my eye on Victor."

"The counselor in training?" Suzy covered her mouth with her hand, surprised.

"Yeah, but that Sylvia girl got there first." Rachel's eyes flashed in anger.

"Oh, I'm sorry." Suzy reached out and touched her hand.

"No big deal. Maybe I'll see him next summer." The talk stopped for a second, and then the girls turned to Jason.

"How was it here?" Rachel asked.

Before Jason could answer, Russ stuck his head in the door. "Hey, sports fans!"

Looking tan and healthy, Russ stepped over Sam, who was sitting on the threshold. "Who's the new addition?"

"This is Sam." Jason stood and walked over. "Sam, I want you to meet a good friend of mine. This is Russ."

"Hiya doin', man?" Russ stuck out his hand.

"Hey." Sam stood, shook it, and sat back down.

"A man of few words." Russ flashed one of his most winning smiles at Sam, which elicited no response. "Works for me." He shrugged and sat on one of the two remaining empty stools. "What'd I miss?" He looked around expectantly. When no one spoke, he shrugged again. "Okay. Where'd the stools come from?"

Jason returned to his seat. "I cleaned out the basement and found these. Thought they might be useful."

"Until our butts fall asleep." Russ shifted his weight on the decrepit stool.

Jason ignored Russ's comment and said, "Rachel had just asked what I was doing while you guys were away."

"Well, my time at camp was really somethin'," inserted Russ. He fidgeted.

"So tell us, Russ." Jason smiled, knowing he would not get a word in until Russ told his story.

In a blur of quick descriptions and personality profiles, Russ got them up to speed, ready for the finale. They were already laughing.

"Then, just to get back at those pain-in-the-butt counselors, we spiked their chocolate ice cream with Ex-Lax donated by Barton. The kid was a walking pharmacy with serious constipation issues."

Suzy started a giggling fit. Rachel caught it as Russ continued. "Well, all hell broke loose. Unfortunately all the toilet paper had mysteriously disappeared." Rachel laughed out loud, which started a chain reaction of laughter. As it faded, Russ added, "Did I tell ya that we nailed the outhouse doors shut." It was hard to breathe, laughing that hard.

"Anything else?" Jason asked. He wiped tears from his eyes.

"Nope. That about does it." Russ leaned back, satisfied with their reactions. "Your turn." He nodded to Jason.

"I met someone special," Jason began.

"A girl?" Suzy, Rachel, and Russ shouted together.

"No, no. He's a teacher over at the Penn State campus. He's Chinese." Jason leaned back with his arms crossed and described the time he spent with Chiang.

"Meditation, huh?" Russ asked, rolling his eyes.

"Ya know anything about it?" Jason was surprised that Russ knew the word.

"Nah, just what I remember from a book my mom was reading. Yogurt or somethin' like that." He shifted in his seat and tried to get comfortable.

"Yoga," Rachel said.

Russ ignored Rachel and asked, "So you just sit there for a long time and stuff?"

"Yeah … and stuff." Jason turned to the girls. "The thing is, I have no idea what happens when I'm doing it. I just kinda drop off."

Suzy frowned. "Can you just do it, or do you have to work into it?"

"I get into it almost at once."

"How do you keep your butt from goin' numb?" Russ asked. He stood up and pulled splinters from the back of his khaki shorts.

"What is it with you and butts?" Rachel looked exasperated.

"Well, maybe, if I could sit here in comfort." Russ slapped his shorts, knocking any potential wooden shards away. "Man, you ever hear of sandpaper?"

Suzy ignored Russ's complaints and said to Jason, "Show me. Maybe it's something we need to do too."

"Sure, but it'll be pretty boring to watch." Jason moved from his stool to the cot. He sat cross-legged and closed his eyes.

"He was wrong." Russ said as he stood and leaned against the bench. He refused to sit on the stools of torture. "This is not pretty boring. This is ugly boring."

"Shush," Suzy and Rachel said at the same time.

Minutes passed. A vague sense of well-being touched the children. Russ turned to see Sam's head lean back against the shed door with a muffled thud. A nap struck him as a good idea. He drifted and fell back on his stool, his head rested on his hand.

Suzy kept her eye on Jason, not knowing what to expect. She did not feel the same drowsiness the others felt. Something was coming, a storm of sorts, forewarned in the quiet, heavy air. She felt excited.

A spider dropped silently on its thin, silken tether to the cot. Suzy watched it intently. The creature crawled onto Jason's left leg. Eventually it disappeared under his knee.

"How?" Suzy choked when it reappeared on the right knee. She looked at Rachel asleep with her head supported on her hand. "Did you see?"

"See what?" Russ yawned.

"That spider on Jason's leg. It went under, not around."

"That's nuts. Couldn't have," Russ said.

Suzy rose from her perch, grabbed the end of the cot, and pulled. The cot moved. Jason did not.

"Holy …" Russ, shocked awake, went to the other side of the cot. With Suzy's help, they pulled it from beneath their meditating friend. For a moment, Jason floated in midair. He slowly settled closer to the floor. Rachel, roused by Suzy's and Russ's action, sat aghast.

"Well," said Russ, "that's the damnedest thing I've ever seen."

"What do you mean?" Rachel rose from her seat and stood by the sleeping Sam, ready to bolt. "What just happened?"

Russ and Suzy looked at each other and mouthed their "uh oh" in unison. They had forgotten Rachel knew nothing of Jason's abilities.

"Oh, this?" Russ improvised and pointed at Jason. "We've been working this trick for months, ya know. How do we make him seem to float?" He smiled, unconvincingly. "It's an illusion, a trick, and it looks like Jason nailed it."

"What? What are you saying?" Rachel said too loudly. She never took her eyes off Jason.

"It's a trick," Suzy repeated calmly. "Just a trick."

"Yeah? Good one." Rachel laughed nervously. "I think I'm going to go find something to eat."

"Good idea. Take our sleepy friend with you," he said as he pointed at Sam, "and bring back supplies."

"Yeah sure," Rachel said, desperate to get away. She roused Sam, who stood groggily. Rachel took him by his shoulders and pushed him toward the house.

Russ watched from the shed door as Rachel opened the back door and shoved Sam through. "That was close."

"I hate that I can't talk to Rachel about this stuff." Suzy looked sad.

"Well, maybe you can. Jason will have to be okay with telling her." Russ moved next to Jason. He leaned on his shoulder, tipped his friend slightly, and let go. Like a toy boat in a bathtub, Jason wobbled back and forth for a few moments. Russ laughed.

"I wonder if we should wake him up." Suzy sat on her stool.

"I wouldn't. He may be out for an hour. That's what he does with that Chiang guy." Russ thought for a second. "We could, ya know? Do something." Russ looked at Suzy and half smiled. The idea thrilled neither.

Suzy jumped off the stool and grabbed Jason by the shoulders. "Jason, time to come back." She shook him.

Jason's eyes fluttered open at the same time his body dropped a few inches to the floor.

Russ laughed. "This is just too much. So now we know what's saving your butt, man."

Not long after summer camp ended, Jason introduced his closest friends to Chiang.

"You have got to try this one. It's sooo good." Jason pointed at a white ball of what looked like raw dough. Russ and Suzy, skeptical of the unusual fare, sat around Mrs. Lim's table for lunch. A few days had passed since Jason had floated on the air while meditating in the shed.

Chiang picked up the identified dim sum with chopsticks and placed it on Russ's plate. "The adventurous palate is most often rewarded." Chiang smiled.

Russ lifted the delicacy and examined it. Resigned to his fate, he took a bite, his eyes closed. The sudden delight that registered on his face convinced Suzy to give one a try. After that, they devoured anything Mrs. Lim set in front of them. Jason, not very hungry, ate little but thoroughly enjoyed his friends' reactions.

Afterward on the back porch, Jason sat with Chiang while Mrs. Lim gave Suzy and Russ the grand tour of her garden.

"I like your friends," Chiang said. He smiled when he saw Suzy's face light up as she inhaled a small, white flower's fragrance. "The girl, Suzy?" He looked at Jason, who nodded. "She has something special about her."

"Even at my worst," Jason said, "I could be around her. She helped me a lot."

"Russell is a boy comfortable in his own skin. Unusual in one so young. He's genuinely a happy soul." As if on cue, Russ laughed out loud. Mrs. Lim clapped her hands and grinned at something Russ had said.

"Was he correct?" asked Chiang, referring to Russ's report on what had happened in the shed on Sunday. He focused on Jason, who thought for a moment before answering.

"I have no reason to doubt him." Jason watched Russ bend down to inhale something Mrs. Lim had cupped in her hands. "Besides, Suzy said the same thing." He turned back to Chiang.

"You had no idea you were not touching the ground?" Chiang sounded skeptical.

"None." Jason took a deep breath and let it go.

"Maybe it has something to do with focus." Chiang looked out at the garden. "Of course, how can we be sure? It is, however, something to try."

"Focus?" It was Jason's turn to be skeptical. "Is there something wrong with floating while one meditates?" Chiang laughed long and loud. Surprised by the outburst, Mrs. Lim, Suzy, and Russ stopped what they were doing and gazed at the two of them.

"Unusual? Yes." They sat quietly while the others resumed their garden tour. "What is your conscious destination?"

"I don't have one." Jason smiled. He watched Suzy clap and bounce on her toes in delight. "I just … drop off."

"It is time to choose a place for you to go." Chiang turned to him and patted his knee. "I have a few things for you to try."

Chapter 14

Suzy had begged Jason to talk to Rachel about joining them. She and Russ now waited for him on the back porch. Suzy paced, anxious to hear any news.

Jason found Rachel in the bedroom she shared with Suzy. Shoes flew through the air and thumped onto the closet floor. Music accompanied Rachel in her determined efforts to get things put away. "It's my party, and I'll cry if I want to …" Rachel sang along as she moved around the room.

"Rachel?" He knocked on the open door. "Can we talk?" A couple of wire hangers followed the trajectory of her footwear.

"Yeah, sure." She smiled but did not invite him in. Wearing jeans and an oversized, white, Penn State T-shirt, she piled clothes on her bed; they had previously lain strewn about the floor. Rachel tossed items from the bed into two open drawers of a tall, mahogany dresser.

"I wanted to say something about what happened on Sunday." Jason leaned against the door frame.

"Just a trick was all." She pushed and pounded the overflow of clothes into each drawer until they fit and then forced the drawers closed with a decisive thud. "Right?" She looked up.

"Well, no, not exactly." Jason waited. Rachel got down on her hands and knee and felt around under the bed. Her effort produced stray, unmatched, not-so-white socks. They piled up at the foot of the bed.

"Well, *what* exactly?" she asked and stood to face Jason with her hands on her hips.

He took a deep breath. "I can do things with my thoughts, or something like that." She stared at him. "I was floating in the toolshed on Sunday. Really."

Rachel looked at him as though he had just told her about the bodies of other children he'd murdered and buried beneath the shed.

"Suzy, Russ, and I formed kind of a club," Jason said. "Suzy really wants you to join us and see where all this floating, meditation stuff might go." He stared at her, waiting for a response. It did not come. "I mean, you saw what you saw. It was real. Now you know."

"I wish I didn't know," Rachel said. "I mean, I'd do anything for Suzy, and I kinda like you, Jason, but this is just …" A shudder went through her. She stopped. "I guess I'm not ready to go meditate or anything like that. I'm sorry I can't join you guys."

"So am I, Rachel. So am I." Jason watched as Rachel continued to straighten up her side of the room. The floating episode was forgotten. He returned to his waiting friends.

"Rachel no longer remembers what happened on Sunday," Jason told Russ and Suzy. "I'm sorry, Suzy. She just didn't want to deal with it. Maybe we can try to include her later. Maybe you can sort of bring up the subject slowly over the next few weeks. Give her a chance to get used to it." They stepped off the porch and headed for the shed.

"It would have been nice to have another girl to talk to," Suzy whispered. She walked with her shoulders slouched and her head down. The ensuing quiet cemented her isolation.

"Wait a minute," Russ said. He jumped ahead and turned around to face her. "I know how you feel." She stopped short. Jason hung back. He felt bad for Suzy; he was sure that Russ was not helping the situation. "I'm like you in reverse. I only have sisters who won't give me the time of day anymore."

"It's not the same." A storm rumbled in her voice. "You don't know what you're talking about. How could you know anything? You're just a dumb boy with a lot of friends."

"A lot of friends who don't know me at all! They don't know what I think is important." This vehement revelation surprised both Suzy and

Jason. "When it comes to things I really care about, there's been my dad or no one until Jason showed up. And even then, half of Jason's life is missing, and he can't relate." Russ turned to Jason. "No offense, man, but it's true."

Jason nodded, accepting the fact.

"I know that all-alone feeling all too well," Russ added.

Suzy looked at him differently. She calmed. "Okay, but you're still a boy and I'm a girl. There are things ... ya know? I can't just ..."

"What makes Rachel so special?" Russ asked kindly.

"I can't explain it." Suzy moved toward the shed. The boys fell into step on either side of her. "She knows. She understands, and she knows I understand too."

"Yeah." Russ sighed. The simple response contained a world of comprehension.

They entered the toolshed, silent with their own thoughts. Taking seats on the stools, they did not look at each other.

"Hey!" Russ yelled. "This seat is comfortable. What'd you do?"

"Old wrapping paper," Jason said, happy the silence was broken. "I found it in the basement, set it aside, and forgot about it until your butt complained so loudly."

Russ stood up and saw Santa Claus and Rudolf looking up at him from the thick, paper cushion. "Well, there ya go. Christmas all year. I like it." Suzy laughed. Jason smiled and appreciated Russ's genius for taking a difficult situation and nudging it into something else.

"I'm sorry for calling you dumb, before." Suzy did not look so upset. "I guess I just miss not having Rachel for everything that's going on."

"With sisters like mine, I've been called a lot worse." Russ raised his arm as if to give Suzy a hug but stopped, thinking better of it. "Wait a minute." Russ got a look on his face Jason knew all too well. "I got an idea."

☆   ☆   ☆

Later that night, Mrs. Lim walked into her living room to turn off the lights and shut the windows before retiring. Surprised, she found Chiang studying a composition notebook. She coughed softly into her hand to announce her presence. Chiang, who sat in a high-backed, comfortable chair, looked up and smiled.

"Professor, you will turn off the lights when you finish?"

"Certainly, my dear Mrs. Lim." He returned to his reading and added, "I will check the doors and windows also."

"Thank you, Professor." She turned to head upstairs. "You will find some hot water for tea on the stove, if you so desire."

"You are too kind, as always." Chiang turned a page.

She smiled and climbed the stairs.

Chiang fell into the story unfolding in the book. Jason had left the composition book behind to help his friend understand what had happened. He also meant it as a gesture of trust. The point was not overlooked by Chiang, who felt immensely flattered.

The handwriting at the start shocked him. The writing, in print style, reminded Chiang of a five- or six-year-old. Large, misshapen letters, little punctuation, and misspellings in the first ten pages slowly gave way to clear notes in small cursive. Jason's notes on his meditating brought a smile. Jason's flattery of his mentor, he passed over. It was the latter pages, however, over which he frowned and worried.

"They are setting me up for something, but what?" Chiang read. On the next page, with letters in tight, quick formation and the pen heavy on the page, the answer blasted forth. "They set me up to control another kid, and this will not happen again!"

Chiang read how Jason had dealt with Lydia and the other adults. Chiang imagined memories like wet clay melted, deformed, and reformed into what Jason needed them to be. Lydia had been left in a mental minefield while the others had escaped with new memories of that night Sam came to the Dubois house. Each misstep by this woman into the active pursuit of evil, as Jason described her actions, would bring on the detonation of a debilitating migraine. Chiang was disturbed that Jason's thinking had become so black and white concerning his foster mother. He needed to meet Lydia to make an accurate judgment of her. Whatever pain she might suffer as a result of Jason's actions could be considered self-inflicted, given the way the boy set things up. Or was it? Did she have a choice?

Chiang closed the notebook, holding the place with his thumb. He stared out through the living-room window. A streetlamp burned brightly, and shadows danced with the windblown branches. He sensed trouble coming but did not know what to do about it. What would he do if he had such power? Could he get Jason to control himself? Would power corrupt the boy as it had so many others down through history? It would be a long sleepless night.

He reopened the notebook and read the last entries. Chiang grinned and immediately felt better about what Jason might do. The water drop session, one of Chiang's greater focus experiments, had failed stupendously: Jason had tried very hard but hadn't managed a higher state with his eyes riveted to a droplet of water. He had given up when his legs fell asleep beneath him. Chiang wondered what his last entry might mean.

I don't know where I'm going and have no idea how to get there. Sorry, Chiang, your idea is a bust. Okay, Russ, now I see what you mean. I'll get some sandpaper.

Chapter 15

‎⚡

Suzy and Russ sat on the shed threshold, grumpy and bored. They watched Jason move back and forth across the yard, mowing the weeds. Russ picked up a small stone and tossed it in front of the lawnmower. The rumbling machine's vortex picked it up, and the blade batted the rock with a distinct ping across the yard toward the house. Jason stopped and glared at Russ, who studied the oak tree.

"Will you just stop?!" Jason hissed. The gasoline fumes made his head swim, and the mowing left him dirty and sweaty in the noontime heat. His T-shirt stuck to him front and back.

"You promised, man," Russ insisted. "I gotta go home soon."

Russ's great idea required Jason to create a special connection between Suzy and him. It was like a private phone number for direct calling. A little brain change was no big deal from Russ's point of view, if it helped. Jason disagreed but said he would think about it. He hadn't promised.

"I hav'ta get this done, okay?" Jason pushed the mower forward and ignored his annoying friends. In truth, he was trying to figure out a way not to do what Suzy and Russ had requested the day before.

Russ stood up and stretched and then slipped inside the shed. He pulled a book from the shelf underneath the tool bench. Jason told him that he sometimes used the shed to read, so he kept a stash there. Russ returned to his seat beside Suzy and waited. The book flew in an arc and landed in front of the lawnmower. Jason stopped abruptly and cut the engine. He took a deep breath, controlling his fury with Russ, or Suzy.

"Okay! Okay!" Jason gave up his attempt to dissuade them. "Both of you," he demanded, "into the shed. Sit on the cot and lean against the wall. Get comfortable."

Suzy and Russ scampered to the cot, excited; they would finally get what they wanted. Jason removed his T-shirt and used the driest spot he could find to wipe his forehead and hands. He put it back on, picked up the book Russ had thrown, and entered the shed.

"I'm not going to get a moment's peace until this is done. So …" Jason leaned against the bench and returned the book to its place. "Let's just do it." Russ and Suzy were all smiles and kept quiet.

"You will sleep for a while. When you wake up, I will have finished." Jason looked from one to the other as they nodded. "So close your eyes, abracadabra, hocus pocus, whatever." As he did with the bed-wetting boy, Jason nudged them into a sound sleep. Suzy did not put up any resistance; he'd feared she might.

With both friends sound asleep, Jason left the shed. The mower sprung to life, and he finished the backyard. With the mower parked next to the shed, Jason entered and stomped his feet. Suzy and Russ awoke.

"What time is it?" Russ asked. He yawned and stretched.

"Probably about one or one thirty." Jason got out of the way as Russ jumped to his feet.

"Oh jeez," he said, pushing his friend. "I'm late. I'll see ya tomorrow or something." Jason watched him run through the gate and pass out of his sight.

"How do you feel?" Jason crossed his arms and looked at Suzy. She took her time getting up.

"Will it work?" She slowly got to her feet.

"I really don't know, but time will tell."

"Thanks for doing this. I know you didn't want to." Suzy smiled at him and patted his shoulder. "Ewww, you're all wet." She wiped her fingers on her jeans.

"Hard work will do that." Jason smiled. He watched her cross the yard and disappear into the house. The books piled below the bench called to him. Of the ten in the shed there was only one he had not finished. He removed his soaked T-shirt and tossed it on the tool bench. With the paperback in hand, he plopped onto the cot. In seconds he was lost in the pages.

Chapter 16

⚡

The ping-pong paddle felt clumsy in his hand, but Jason readied himself. He and Mr. Downing were playing their third game in Mr. Downing's basement. Miss Thompson had finally managed to get the two of them together.

The first two matches had been shutouts. Jason never expected that a man of Mr. Downing's girth—his stomach prevented him from seeing his feet—could move so fast. Beethoven's Fifth Symphony blasted from a record player. Jason was determined to return this serve and not go scoreless a third time.

The ball came in low and fast. It swerved with the spin Mr. Downing put on it. Jason hit the white blur with counter spin and kept the ball in play as it cleared the net and bounced on the table at the center line. It returned, hitting hard but to the side of the table where Jason was not standing. He dove to save the point, missed, lost his balance, and continued into a shelf of paint cans. There was a crash, after which Jason returned to the field of play partially covered in white paint.

"My point, I believe, Mr. Sutter," Downing said, smiling calmly.

Jason wiped away paint about to drop from his eyebrow into his eye. He smiled and waved his paddle for the next serve.

"You know, Mr. Sutter, a great deal can be learned about a man in a one-on-one, competitive game such as this." Jason nodded. Downing served.

After ten games, with Jason sweaty, painted, and winless, Mr. Downing called a halt.

"I believe we have need of some lunch." Downing put away the paddles and ball. At the bottom of the stairs, he bowed and invited Jason with a flourish of his hand to precede him. "Let's see if we can't get some of that paint off you." He chuckled.

Thirty minutes later, smelling of turpentine and lava soap, Jason sat at the kitchen table. Mr. Downing searched the fridge and tossed cold cuts in brown paper wrapping on the table.

"There is some good rye bread in the bin behind you on the counter." He straightened up and placed two cans of Black Label beer on the table and a pitcher of iced tea. "The plates are in the shelf above the bread box." Jason faced the counter, found the rye bread, and gathered the plates. He placed them on the table and then sat. Mustard, mayo, pickles, and other condiments hit the table with knives and forks. A green glass filled with ice tea appeared before him, and a Black Label beer tab popped. "I think we're ready," Mr. Downing said.

Jason followed his example, piling the meat high on his rye bread and lathering it all with yellow mustard. After cutting the sandwich in half, he took a big bite. The explosion of flavor was wonderful. He chewed with his eyes closed. Mr. Downing smiled at Jason's apparent pleasure.

"I expected you two weeks ago, Mr. Sutter," Mr. Downing said. "It is the summer, after all, and you do not have all that much on your plate. Do you?" He drank his beer.

"Not at the moment, sir. The last weeks, however … things got messy, if you know what I mean."

"I am sure I have no idea." They ate in quiet for a while. Good food and company were enough. Mr. Downing finished his first beer with the last of his sandwich. He belched and said, "Rebecca tells me you are interested in biology and some World War II history."

"Rebecca, sir?" With his mouth full the name sounded more like, "R'boka."

"My godchild." Downing wiped an errant drip of mustard from his chin. "Miss Thompson to you."

"Oh, I didn't know, sir." Jason gulped tea from his green glass. Then he gathered his oversized sandwich and took another bite.

"Well, of course, you didn't know. Why would you? None of your business." Mr. Downing sat back in his chair, crushed his first beer can, and opened his second. "Now, what is it you want to know?"

Jason gulped his last mouthful, washed it down with the last of his iced tea, and reluctantly set the half-eaten sandwich aside. "I read a few books on fliers in World War II. Miss Thompson thought I might learn more about it from you."

"Why on earth would a boy your age pick up books on war?" He leaned forward, picked up the pitcher, and refilled Jason's glass.

"My friend's father flew B-17s in the war. I didn't know anything about it. I didn't want to sound like an idiot." Jason lifted his glass and drank.

"That would be Mr. Wyatt, I take it?" Downing tipped the can and swallowed.

"Yes, sir."

"Well, Mr. Sutter, I did not serve in the Air Corp during the war. Being older and college educated, I served on a variety of senior officers' staffs. I am most proud of my time serving with General Bradley." He coughed and cleared his throat. Then he stood and grabbed his shirt pockets and patted his pants. He went to the sink, where he found a pack of Lucky Strike cigarettes and matches on the window ledge. He sat, lit one, and took a deep pull. The smoke eased out in a long exhalation. "What did you think of those books?"

"They were exciting and everything, but ..." Jason shrugged. "Something was missing, but I can't say what."

"Reality, Mr. Sutter. Reality." Mr. Downing stared into space. "Do you think the books would sell if the truth were ever splattered on the page?" Jason could tell that Mr. Downing was lost in a painful memory. "What happens to friends on the receiving end of a bombing run during the London blitz is not something people want described in detail." Downing's eyes closed. His hands trembled slightly. "I usually do not talk about these things. You have turned me into something of an open book, Mr. Sutter." He finished off his beer and stood up to retrieve another from the fridge; his cigarette dangled from his lips. "I am sure Mr. Wyatt's experience was much the same as all of ours. There were long periods of hurry up and wait, short intense bursts of total horror, followed by a happiness to be alive one more day. The books tend to gloss over the horror part." He took a couple of deep breaths. "If you don't mind, let's change the subject."

"Of course, sir. I didn't mean to—"

"Think nothing of it, Mr. Sutter. I asked you, if you recall." With beer in hand, he moved around the table and put his cigarette out in the sink. "Disgusting habit really." He returned to his seat. "What else have you been looking into?" He popped the tab and a bit of foam shot out. He brought the can to his lips and drank the overflow.

"Well, I heard that there are these plants that grow in China but nowhere else. Now they are growing here, but no one knows exactly how they have managed it. So I have been reading about plants and stuff." Jason felt Mr. Downing's relief with the war left behind.

"Now, as it turns out, I know a few things about biology and plants. Did you know that animal cells tend to be oval in shape while some plant cells tend toward rectangles?" Jason shook his head. "Have you ever seen a living cell of any sort?"

"No sir."

"Well, that's your trouble, Mr. Sutter." Downing slapped the table and jumped up. "You need to see what you are reading about. And being a pack rat from way back, I happen to have a microscope for you to see exactly that." He waved at Jason to follow him back downstairs. "All the books and words on the page can never make up for firsthand experience, Mr. Sutter."

In minutes, Jason was staring through the eyepiece of an ancient brass microscope at a rectangular plant cell. Chloroplasts, little green ovals, circulated around the cell. The cell nucleus was clearly visible. He was mesmerized, and he increased the magnification while Mr. Downing spoke over his shoulder.

"You are looking at a very efficient solar-energy converter. Of course, a good many plants use photosynthesis."

Jason barely listened. For a time, he saw with his eyes, but as Mr. Downing continued to talk, he observed with something else. The nucleus became suddenly very clear and close. A ball of ribbon, like a hundred roller coasters twisting and turning in and around a hidden core, filled his view. Entranced, he let his inner sight take him where it would. He touched down lightly on one of the ribbons.

Mr. Downing stood by his side. He took the boy's silence and his sudden intake of breath as a sign that he might need help. "Well, my boy, why don't you let me have a look at what you have?" He laid his hand gently on his shoulder. His thumb made contact with the skin of Jason's neck. A connection opened between their minds, and for an instant, Mr. Downing rolled along behind Jason into an alien landscape. The contact lasted seconds but broke suddenly as Mr. Downing collapsed onto the floor unconscious. Unaware, Jason continued his travels through the looking glass.

✢   ✢   ✢

"Ah, good afternoon, Suzy," Chiang said when she opened the door to the Dubois house. "Is Mrs. Dubois available? I have something I would like to discuss with her and Mr. Dubois, if possible."

"Chiang?" Suzy did not disguise her surprise or her worry that he would come face to face with Lydia. "I … I'll see if either can come to the door."

"I am grateful." He bowed slightly and waited patiently. The wait was short.

"Yes? What do you want?" Lydia stood at the door.

Chiang stood silently for a moment before answering. "I am Professor Chin from the local campus. Your foster son, Jason, and I have been doing some meditating together. I thought I would introduce myself, since he and I spend time together." He held out his hand. "I am pleased to meet you, at last."

"Well …" Lydia stared at the proffered greeting and then looked up into his eyes. "He doesn't talk much about what he does when he's not around the house. Nice of you to come around—at last," she said sarcastically.

"I see." Chiang spoke calmly. He dropped his hand and then crossed both of them in front of him. "Do you have any objections to Jason spending time with me?"

The wheels in Lydia's head started turning but ground to a halt. The pain in the back of her neck shot up over the top of her head. She grimaced, and her whole body shuddered with the sudden jolt. With both hands pressed to her forehead she said, "No. You two can do what you like as long as no trouble comes of it."

"I can see you are in pain, Mrs. Dubois." Chiang was awed by the visible results of Jason's changes to her mind.

"It's nothing, just a minor headache. Is there anything else?" Lydia wanted to get away to a cool, dark place, take her medication, and lie down. She massaged her temples with both hands.

"I wanted to ask if you would allow the other children in the house to join me for a project sponsored by the town and the university. It is a little thing, but it would be fun for the children, I believe. A learning experience, at the least."

"Yeah, well, talk to my husband. He takes care of the things outside of the house." She turned and walked away. The door closed. Chiang waited a short time and then accepted the fact that Mr. Dubois was not likely to join him on the porch. He headed home.

The lack of common manners and civility surprised him. A few minutes in Lydia's presence unsettled him. A shower, a change of clothes, and time in the company of Mrs. Lim would be the cure.

Chapter 17

"**M**an! It's too weird." Russ sat across from Jason at a picnic table in the Wyatt backyard. Stacks of comic books lay all about the table surface. The covers flipped open in the breeze blowing across the yard. The afternoon summer heat tempered as clouds passed overhead in a bright, blue sky. The air smelled of newly mown grass with faint wafts of gasoline.

"What'd you mean?" Jason shrugged, proclaiming his innocence in the whole affair. He felt sorry for his friend's predicament. Music came from an open second-story window.

"These things girls do and … and what they think is so important. I mean …" He shook his head and then glanced up at the open window. "What did you do to me?"

"Exactly what you asked," Jason replied calmly, "if you recall." He reached out and scanned the stacked comics; his finger ticked off the titles. He sought Fantastic Four editions. Sue Storm sometimes gave him good ideas for understanding his gifts.

"Yeah, yeah, I know." Resigned to his fate, Russ looked over the stacks and moved a few Green Lantern comics from a Hulk pile to a stack with Superman and Batman. He whispered the lyrics of the song echoing from his older sister's room.

"I will follow him, no matter where he will …" He stopped abruptly and looked at Jason. "I was on your front porch with Suzy yesterday. We talked, talked, talked for an hour about stuff I can't even remember, but I enjoyed it. I mean …" Silence.

"Go on," Jason requested softly. He gave up on finding the comic he wanted and leaned on his elbows on the picnic table. He gave Russ his full attention.

"It's not natural. It's a disease, man! Now I'm listening to my sisters and having—conversations." He grabbed the hair on both sides of his head. "Now I got their music in my head."

"So? What's wrong with that?" Jason raised his eyebrows. He didn't move except to grin knowingly.

"Jason! Man! My older sisters?! A week ago they hated everything about me. Now they talk to me. My mom talks to me!" Russ crossed his arms on the table and laid down his head. "I'm into girly music, and my mom wants my opinion about what colors she should use in decorating the bathroom."

"But you like these ... talks and the music, right? You like your mom seeking you out." Jason smirked.

"Are you going to help or make it worse?" Russ glanced up and rested his chin on his crossed arms. He looked at his friend with a mixture of annoyance and pleading.

"Answer my question!" Jason insisted.

"Yeah, I like it." Russ hid his face again. Guilty as charged.

"Well, my friend, I have some good news and some bad news." Russ did not look up; his hand waved for Jason to continue.

"The good news is that I didn't do anything to you or Suzy. The bad news is that I didn't do anything."

"Huh?" Russ raised his head. A confused expression hung on his face.

"All you did was sleep. When you woke up, I told you that I worked it out. Remember?" Jason smiled.

"Yeah, I kinda remember." The details from the weeks before in the shed escaped him.

"I didn't do anything. You and Suzy worked it out yourselves, thinking I had opened some connection." Jason chuckled. "Solved it all by yourselves."

"You mean you never had us share thoughts or anything?" Russ sat up, not sure if he should be angry.

"I did nothing."

"Then ..."

"Face it, Russ, you have a way with people, both guys and girls. It's a gift."

"Ya mean I really like the girl stuff? I'm like ... a queer or something?" Russ practically squealed those last words. Desperate, he grabbed the edge of the table in an iron grip.

"Don't be totally lame!" Jason said, none too kindly. He leaned forward and pointed his finger in Russ's face. "You're not queer."

Neither knew exactly what that meant, but they'd gotten the impression it was something bad.

"It's how you are with people, all people," Jason said. "You like people. You want to know what they're about. You do it without thinking."

Russ relaxed a little and nodded. "Okay, okay, I think I get it." He took a deep breath. "I'm a people person, as my dad calls it." Jason nodded. "Whew, you had me scared there for a minute." He perked up and started to work the stacks again.

"It's the same for Suzy. The two of you found what you needed together."

"So I did it myself, believing it was you?" Russ stopped sorting the magazines and piled them up into two tall stacks.

"Yep." Jason grinned, happy Russ had caught on. His plan had worked.

"Does Suzy know?"

"I'm not sure. Maybe, but I'll tell her anyway."

Russ nodded.

"What are you gonna do with all these comics, anyway?" Jason asked. Some looked brand-new.

"My mom wants me to throw them out or put them somewhere out of the way." Russ put a hand on the stack and sighed. "Maybe I'll just chuck 'em."

"I thought you loved these. You couldn't wait for the continuing story."

"Not so much now." Russ smiled.

"How come?"

"Ha!" Russ stood, picked up one of the stacks, and turned toward the house. "How come, you ask? 'Cause …" He nodded at the second stack and asked, "Can you get those?" Jason got to his feet and hefted the second pile. "'Cause, I'm living in a comic book."

They carried the stacks to the side of the house near the back door. Together they stood around the gleaming aluminum garbage cans. Like bombs released through opened bomb-bay doors, they released their loads. The loud crash bounced off the walls.

"You're Superman as a kid trying things out. You're Spiderman learning how to use his spider power. Who needs comic books?" Russ replaced the can cover.

"I'm no superhero, Russ. I'm just me." Jason looked at his friend, who grinned at him like he knew something painfully obvious.

"That's the best part. We can be friends. Especially when things get tough, ya know? When you start saving the world and all." Russ took Jason by the shoulders and ushered him inside the house. "Let's find something to eat."

In the kitchen, Russ carried a large and colorful clown cookie jar to the kitchen table. He lifted the lid and pulled out two chocolate chip cookies. He passed one to Jason and asked, "How're Chiang's experiments coming?"

"Disasters. I can't even get into the meditation. I don't float." Jason took a bite of cookie. Russ put the clown back on the counter.

"Milk!" shouted Russ. "We need milk." In moments, two glasses of cold milk appeared. "Whoops, too much milk and not enough cookie." The clown gave up more cookies. "Ya know," mumbled Russ with crumbs lodged in the corner of his mouth, "you could be a superhero just waiting for the right things to happen. Ya know what I mean? An 'I got it' moment."

Chapter 18

"It wasn't your fault," Miss Thompson said. She sat with Jason at Mr. Downing's kitchen table. The family doctor was examining her godfather in the basement. Every time a noise came from below, Jason looked at the basement door. It *was* his fault.

Earlier, when he was at the microscope in another world, Jason hadn't registered the touch on his neck. Sometime later, his mind had tossed him out of his micro-state, as Rachel had thrown him out of her dream. The force pushed him and the stool on which he sat over backward. Mr. Downing's inert body cushioned his fall. After the shock, he found himself staring over Mr. Downing's chin into his nose. Clambering to his feet, Jason jumped back, barely able to breathe.

What happened? What'd I do? What should I do?

Jason stood over the unconscious man and struggled for direction. Mr. Downing's chest rose and fell, so he was still breathing.

How long will that last if I don't do something? Near tears, Jason turned away, trying to think clearly. He took two steps and then returned.

Finally he decided and raced upstairs to find nothing helpful in the kitchen. He rushed into the small room next to it. A desk dominated the space; it held a typewriter, a telephone, and some books. Frantic, he fanned through the books and found Mr. Downing's address book at the bottom of the stack next to the phone. Jason had never used a phone, but he quickly figured it out.

"Living under a rock," he whispered, frustrated. He found Rebecca's

129

number and dialed. She arrived like a shot and called Dr. Reynolds, their family doctor, who also showed up in short order.

Dr. Reynolds checked the patient's vital signs, as Mr. Downing lay on the basement floor. When the doctor said he was confident there was no imminent danger, they all struggled to move the unconscious Mr. Downing from the basement floor to an old couch on the other side of the room. Given his size, taking him to his bedroom upstairs was out of the question. Rebecca covered her godfather with the crocheted afghan that decorated the back of the couch.

"Should we call for an ambulance?" asked Rebecca.

"No." The doctor loosened his tie. "There's nothing to indicate he's in any immediate danger." The doctor rubbed the back of his neck. "This is strange. I gave him the once over at his yearly checkup only last week. I'll do a few more checks just to be sure." He shooed Jason and Rebecca out and suggested they wait upstairs.

Rebecca and Jason worried for twenty minutes in the kitchen.

"What on God's green earth do you think you are doing?" Downing's shout from below froze the two. "Reynolds, I'm fine. Let me up, and get out of here!" Rebecca and Jason dashed to the top of the staircase. Dr. Reynolds stomped up the wooden steps. He shook his head and stuffed his stethoscope into his black bag.

"There's nothing wrong with him that I can tell, Rebecca." He headed for the front door. Rebecca followed. "I have to get back to the hospital. I have several mothers-to-be going into labor any time now." He grabbed his coat, left lying over the back of chair by the front door. "What happened is anybody's guess. His vitals are fine."

"Thank you so much for coming. I was so afraid he'd had a heart attack."

"Heart attack?" Reynolds guffawed and stopped at the front door. "No family history. No indications. A neural upset of some kind more than likely, but as you can hear, it passed quickly. I wouldn't worry, Rebecca." He smiled and patted her shoulder. "He's stubborn but he takes care of himself. I must be off." She watched him drive off and then returned to the kitchen.

Shortly Mr. Downing appeared at the top of the basement stairs with his shirt unbuttoned, his hairy chest exposed. He glared at Jason and his goddaughter. "Well, what are you two looking at? I'm not at death's door."

He marched into the kitchen past the two of them and pulled a beer from the fridge. Popping the tab and taking a long drink, he looked at Rebecca and Jason over the rim. He gulped half the can, held the can out, and pointed with his index finger. "Rebecca, be a dear and run over to the drugstore. I need some aspirin. I have a terrible headache." He took another long swallow. "I'm gonna need some more beer too. You know where to get that."

"Sure. You'll be okay?" Rebecca watched him carefully, looking for any sign of distress.

"I am sure," he smiled and forced himself to relax. "Mr. Sutter here will take good care of me for the short time you are away."

"If you're sure." She picked up her bag.

"I'm sure." He took a seat at the table. Jason remained standing. Rebecca nodded to both of them and left.

Once her car pulled out of the driveway, Downing ordered Jason to sit. "You and I, Mr. Sutter, need to talk."

✳ ✳ ✳

The next day Russ stared at Jason, his mouth open, aghast. "So you're saying we can hitch a ride just by touching you and tour la-la land or wherever you go?" Russ sounded ready to give it a try. He, Suzy, and Jason sat around the toolshed bench.

Suzy sat between the two boys, and she had noted Jason's sour mood the moment they met. His description of what happened the day before at Mr. Downing's sent a chill down her back.

"Sure, Russ," said Jason, who hardly slept the night before. He worried about what had happened. Russ's attitude thoroughly annoyed him. "If you wanna wind up on the floor unconscious. And when you come to, go on and on about stuff you tried real hard to forget only to have it replayed over and over. Sound good?"

"Well, yeah." Russ gave him his *under a rock* look, reserved for his surprise at the simple things Jason did not know. "What do I have to hide, I'm only twelve. Okay, maybe the time when I was five and took my dad's staple gun and stapled the curtains to the wall or made a smiley face on the living room wall with a marker. C'mon!" Suzy smiled.

Jason waved him off in frustration. "What he told me was hard to hear. It was about the war. The one *your* dad won't tell *you* about."

"My dad," said Russ getting angry, "told me all about his time in the war."

"Oh yeah? Did he tell you about the blood of his good friend flowing between his fingers while he cried, helpless to save him?" Jason spread his arms with both hands so tightly clenched they looked like sledgehammers. "Did he tell you about the kid he helped uncover in the ruble of a bombed-out building, still alive, smiling, happy to be found, with his guts half out of his body?" He sat back, his hands tight on the edge of the tool bench. "Did he tell you about his nightmares about that boy—the smile that never left the child's face?"

"You're making that up." Russ fired back, visibly upset. "That never happened to my dad. He flew in a bomber."

"Yeah, Russ, maybe not. But something like that did happen to him, and that's what he doesn't talk about. Just like Mr. Downing didn't talk about it until yesterday. He also—"

"Well, I guess, that would explain why they call him old Down 'n Out at school," Russ said. "Too serious, no fun, if ya know what I mean."

"No, not really." Jason's anger broke out. "How can you be so ... so stupid about this?"

"Stupid?" Russ jumped to his feet, breathing hard, ready to fight.

"A moron!" yelled Jason, intending to hurt.

"Yeah?" Russ felt betrayed. He and Jason had never been angry with each other before. He struck back. "Well, you're the moron who didn't know how to use a telephone until yesterday."

"Stop it! Both of you!" Suzy yelled to lessen the damage from the evolving battle. "Jason, you're talking about Russ's dad. Of course, he doesn't like it. And you, Russ, you're making a joke about something that can't be made funny, no matter how hard you try. I think you're both stupid to go on like this."

Neither could find the middle ground to come back together. They stewed in silence even though they knew Suzy was right. Each was unwilling to admit that he might be wrong, and they waited for the other to make the first move.

So Suzy changed the subject. "Tell me, Jason, what happened when you saw the microscope thing?"

Bitter about Russ's reaction, Jason had to have the last word. "The war movies don't show you how bad it really was. Someday I hope your dad will talk about it."

Before Russ could fire back, Suzy interjected, "Jason, you never explained why Miss Thompson was there either."

"She's Mr. Downing's godchild," he said, looking at Suzy as if she had intruded into a private conversation. "She's the daughter of the friend he couldn't save." Jason glared at Russ.

"Oh my," Suzy said, sorry she'd asked.

"She was his friend's daughter, and Mr. Downing's been keeping an eye on her, helping her along, 'cause he promised."

"I ..." Russ swallowed his anger and was silent for a while. Then he said, "Wow. Talk about being a friend."

"Yeah, a real friend you can count on," Jason said, driving his point home. "Mr. Downing knows about me too. He figured it out 'cause of how things happened in his head when he touched me. I didn't feel right going in and redoing his memory. I didn't want to, and I don't mind him knowing."

"I guess he did open things up for you, right?"

Jason held the high ground and felt powerful, vindicated in his anger. He caught Suzy watching him and knew what she wanted him to do.

"I'm not sure yet." Jason started to let the anger go. He sat forward and crossed his arms on the table. "We'll have to see." He took a couple of deep breaths.

"Did you know," Suzy said quickly, "Chiang visited the house yesterday while you were with Mr. Downing?"

"No!" Jason sat back surprised. "What happened?"

"Yeah," said Russ, leaning forward.

"I didn't hear the conversation," said Suzy, " but I know Lydia headed up to her room like she does when she gets those headaches." She looked left and right at each boy.

"I have to go see Chiang tomorrow," Jason said, "and see what he thinks of my notebook. I bet he came here to check out Lydia and Frank. Now he knows, I hope."

"I'm sure he does," Suzy said. "Lydia's not as good at fake caring as she was before you showed up."

They sat in silence for a moment. Finally Jason said, "I like your dad, Russ. He did something way more scary flying in that B-17. That's probably why he doesn't talk about it much. It might help if he could. Maybe he's told your mom."

"Yeah, maybe," mumbled Russ. "I'll ask her."

A knock on the shed door brought them up short. Sam stood there. "Suzy and Jason," he said, "Frank wants you to come 'round the front of the house."

"What's up, Sam?" Suzy started to climb off the stool.

"Don' know. The guy who brought me here is with him. They're waiting in that guy's car." Sam turned around and headed off.

"I think I know what this is," Suzy said. She stepped out of the shed. "I did it last year."

"What?" Jason asked, following. Russ brought up the rear.

"We go to visit Frank's mother at the state hospital." She shivered. "That social worker turns it into a thing about how great Frank and Lydia are. How we're helping out the old folks."

"What's wrong with that?" asked Russ. "I visit my mom's father in the home now and then. It's kinda embarrassing but not bad. He just lies there and calls me Luke, for some reason."

"He has his own room, right?" asked Suzy.

"Yeah. So?"

"Words just don't go far enough." Suzy slowed and waited for Jason and Russ to come close. "The state hospital is not a nice place to live. The last time I went, I felt … trapped. The smells, the way some of them are tied to chairs. Old folks who can walk or shuffle start following you around, start touching you. It's ghoulish."

As they crossed into the front yard, they saw Frank, leaning on the open door of Will Grossman's Fairlane. He waved them over. As they neared the car, Jason saw Rachel in the backseat.

"Okay, kids, pile in. We are off to see my mom." Frank ducked his head and sat in the front passenger seat. He rolled down the window. "Sorry about this Ray."

"Russ, sir."

"Right, Russ. You'll see Jason and Suzy tomorrow." Russ nodded and waved to Jason. He turned away and headed home.

The backseat was barely big enough for three. With four it was shockingly intimate for near-teenagers. Sam and Suzy sat in the middle; they were the smallest. Suzy was next to Jason and Sam next to Rachel. The girls and Sam were dressed in shorts and T-shirts. Jason wore his usual jeans and T-shirt combination.

Jason crammed himself next to Suzy. His hand brushed her bare leg. They stared at each other, shocked, not knowing what would happen next, remembering what had happened last time someone touched Jason's bare skin.

"C'mon, guys," Frank said. "We gotta get goin'. Shut the door. It'll be a little cramped, but you'll survive. And when this is all over, we'll go for burgers on the way home." Oblivious to their gloom and discomfort, Frank faced front.

Jason pulled the door closed. Will threw the car in gear, and they drove away.

"Nothing happened," Suzy whispered, a little disappointed. "How come?"

"Don't know. I'm glad though." Jason felt a great sense of relief.

Chapter 19

"Okay, here's the deal." Frank turned around and faced the four disgruntled occupants in the backseat of Will Grossman's car. "Every six months or so, I go to the state home in Kearny to visit my mom. You guys come along to … to … to what, Will?"

"To be good little soldiers," said Will, who kept his eyes on the road. "You'll be helping out with the old folks while I take pictures of your worthy efforts."

"Pictures that get into paper." Frank smiled, satisfied that he had made his point. He faced forward again.

Will said, "It's good public relations and helps Frank and Lydia get the things you kids need."

Neither Will nor Frank heard the snorts nor saw the eye rolling in the backseat.

"Being used," Jason said just loud enough for Suzy to hear.

"Nothing new." Suzy concurred in a whisper.

"How long until we get there?" Sam asked.

"Thirty or forty minutes," Frank said.

The rest of the drive was quiet. When they passed through the gates, Jason discovered that the state hospital sat on a large campus with rolling fields of grass on all sides. It looked more like a warehouse. The building was huge, ten stories of beige brick and glass.

They all trooped from the parking lot into the main lobby, where they headed for the third floor, the geriatrics ward. When the elevator door opened, the strong odors of disinfectant plus human sweat and waste assaulted them. Jason didn't think he would ever get used to it. He covered his nose and mouth with his hand and managed to breathe and not gag.

Frank herded them to the nursing station just off the elevator. After a time, he found the aroma tolerable and dropped his hand.

"Frank Dubois to see Edna Richards." Frank watched the nurse check his name against her list.

"You'll want to tread lightly today. Edna's in a rare mood." The nurse checked her watch. "She's still in Room 316 down the hall and ..." She looked at Frank with a sympathetic expression. "Lunch just ended."

Frank thanked her. They moved down the empty corridor until a double door opened and a parade of wheelchairs poured into the hallway. The kids lined up against the wall to let the procession pass. Frank proceeded down the hall.

One elderly woman held to her chair by a sheet tied tight around her torso turned her head and caught Jason's eye. The skeletal, old woman raised her hand and pointed in his direction. No one paid attention to anything she did unless it resulted in a mess to be cleaned up. Jason felt sorry and repulsed by her emaciated face and pitiable condition. He looked away.

Behind the wheelchairs came the walkers. Few smiled or noticed the children, watching them pass. Will removed the lens cover on a 35 mm camera.

"Now, what I want you to do is mingle with the old folks," Will said. He looked down at the camera lens, adjusting the dials. He guessed at the settings to produce the best pictures. "If there are any drinks or snacks to give out, you walk around and give them out. Signal me so I can get a clear shot." He looked up. "And don't look so disgusted like you do right now. You're all gonna be this old someday. Smile a bit."

They all got in line behind the walkers and followed the shuffling train to the day room.

Jason and Sam stood just inside the entrance to the day room, not sure what they should do. Having done this before, Suzy and Rachel went to the small commissary, where they gathered up trays with cups of juice or stacks of chocolate chip cookies. Will gave a thumbs-up as the girls smiled for his camera and offered a drink or a bite to the elderly clients who barely noted their presence.

"Whada we do?" asked Sam.

"I dunno." Jason scanned the room. Some of the old people sat lined up in front of a television. Others sat around tables. A few looked like they might be playing a game of checkers, while others held cards. Jason saw the woman from the hallway off by herself by the windows. Her head lolled forward, like she might have fallen asleep. "I guess we just walk around and see if there is anything we can do for them. Maybe talk, ya know?"

"I'll just follow you, okay?"

"Sure, Sam." Jason walked over to the nearest table. Sam stayed close.

"Hi, I'm Jason and this is Sam. How are you all today?" None of the occupants registered their presence. A buzz and click made Jason and Sam look up; Will had snapped their picture.

He smiled and mouthed, "Good one."

With no response, Jason moved on.

"What's wrong with them, Jason?" asked Sam, trembling. "They're like ghosts."

"I guess it's because no one really cares." Jason headed off to another table where there was some activity. This time heads turned in their direction, but no one spoke a word. Jason leaned over the table at the game of checkers in progress.

"Who's ahead?" he asked, smiling. Will took another picture. When it became apparent that there would be no response again, Sam and Jason left. In this way they crossed the room and met up with Suzy and Rachel.

"Was it like this last year?" Jason asked. He took a cookie from Rachel's tray.

"Yeah, exactly like this to start." Rachel offered a cookie to Sam, who declined. "Don't make the mistake we made last time."

"What was that?" asked Sam.

"We tried to get some real conversation going. We even tried a little sing-along thing. That was Will's idea. That's when the shufflers started to come at us. It was gruesome." Rachel shuddered. "Will got the pictures he wanted. It looked like we were dancing with the geezers."

"Juice anyone?" Suzy joined them. Sam took a cup.

"Let's not do anything to get them excited." Rachel passed on to another table.

"Got that right." Suzy followed her.

Jason and Sam headed off in the other direction. They followed Rachel's advice. Jason moved to the far side of the room, where barred windows lined the wall. He leaned over the bookshelves that came up to the window sill. Trees moved in a breeze; white-coated men and women ate lunch in the sun.

Sam came up next to him and said, "It shouldn't be like this." Jason turned from the window. "They're so old, Jason."

"They're walking dead, Sam. It isn't right." Jason felt saddened by the life these people lived day in and day out.

"Who the hell asked you to?" screamed a wheelchair bound woman from the entrance to the day room. Jason watched Frank push her along. Her dirty, gray hair flew in all directions. She scowled and dismissed the gathering before her with a frustrated wave of her hand. Frank leaned in and spoke close to her ear. No one heard what he said. Her ancient face pulled back from his with a look that yelled, *Are you totally nuts?!* Thrusting her boney finger in Frank's face, she exploded. "I don't give a good goddamn about what anybody in this hellhole thinks! Why did you come here anyway! I didn't want you thirty-odd years ago! Why you comin' round now? What're you after?" Frank said something. "Just take me back to my room, doofus! Now!"

The nurses, aides, and kids watched, mesmerized by the little soap opera. Will knelt in front of the wheelchair and snapped away. Frank bent down close to his mother's face and smiled broadly for the camera.

"It's all about the money, isn't it you, little piece of sh—?" Her sentence went unfinished. Frank spun the chair around. The woman grasped the chair's arms for dear life. Frank whisked her into the hallway and out of sight.

In the quiet aftermath, Jason's world made a sudden shift.

Unnoticed, the woman secured to her wheelchair awoke and pulled herself along the line of books. She grasped a shelf and heaved with all her strength. As Frank spun his mother's wheelchair to escape, barely a yard away, she lurched forward and grabbed Jason's wrist.

The day room for Jason disappeared, replaced by an incredibly large, white-walled room with uncountable, parallel cables stretching across the ceiling. It was hard to make out details, since the lighting was poor. Fluorescent bulbs buzzed and flickered high above. Jason could not see the walls in the distance but figured they were as white as the one close by. The parallel rows of cables stretched on forever.

It was not, however, all that unfamiliar. Jason had slipped into or been hijacked into another's mind. This struck him as a better place to be than back in the day room, where he stood frozen against the bookcase. He explored the immediate area, secure in the belief he would figure out why he was there.

The nearest cable a yard above his head came to an end and meshed with another cable, moving on through the wall behind him into another room. Where the two came together looked like the roots of two trees connected through a blob of tar. Unafraid, Jason reached up and touched it. It was a sticky, gray substance. It reminded him of chewing gum.

"Interesting," he murmured. Then he walked along the length of the cable to the next junction of roots. It was a long walk. Jason spied more globs of the tarry substance, enveloping the middle of the cables. He did not think this was correct. At the next juncture, he found no sticky stuff between the roots.

Just behind the roots, on one side of the juncture, a large bulge stuck out. It contained what looked like a cell nucleus similar to the one he'd seen in the microscope in Mr. Downing's basement. The cable extended from the cell nucleus to the next junction far in the distance. This struck Jason as the way it should be. The tar did not belong. It messed up the roots. Probably made a person unable to do much but sit. Jason felt sure he knew the owner of the mind he shared. He waited beneath the cables for help. He needed more information. The scene changed to an earlier time at the Dubois house.

"Oh, just sit still and stop crying. The hair will grow back. This is the only way to get the gum out." Lydia yanked the hair, annoyed with the child's reaction. Holding it out, she snipped the tress.

"Could try ice," Frank suggested, a little too late.

"Doesn't work with hair, and why don't you just shut up." Lydia brushed the hair back into place. "Can't hardly see it." The scene faded as the girl got up from the chair to look in the mirror in the bathroom. When she saw her reflection, she gasped. Everything blurred and changed again.

In a school hallway, Russ leaned over to whisper in Jason's ear. "Don't you wish you could try this out to see what might happen?" Russ pointed at the fire extinguisher behind the glass door, with its garish warning label about subfreezing temperatures upon release of the gas. Russ's smile and the hallway became fuzzy and melted away. Help had arrived.

Back beneath the cables, Jason returned to his starting point and found a red, glass cabinet door behind which the fire extinguisher waited. Over the top of the door was a fireman's axe. Jason opened the emergency door and hauled out the canister. He pulled the axe from the wall.

He aimed the nozzle at the nearest tar blob and blasted it. Aside from changing color, a whitish opaque rather than a dull gray, it looked unaffected. Jason set aside the extinguisher, took up the axe in a two-fisted grasp, and swung at a point where he would hit no roots. Upon impact, the tar blob shattered like glass into a thousand crystal shards. He covered his head as the shrapnel fell all about him. When all was done, he looked up and found the roots exposed and the tar mostly gone.

Jason looked down the line of cables and realized there was no way for him to fix every connection. He needed more help.

Jason stood in the bathroom off the Dubois kitchen, where he looked at himself in the mirror. He recalled the infinite number of his reflections in the mirror on the door behind him. Mirror within a mirror presented the solution. Without his willing it, the act of knowing the answer to the problem created the resources.

Two mirrors, like the one hanging from the door in the Dubois bathroom, faced each other just behind Jason. He laughed. This was too easy.

He stepped between the mirrors and saw his reflections stretch on to infinity.

"Okay, boys. We got a job to do." He stepped out from between the mirrors, and his reflections followed him into the room. The red emergency cabinets and axes duplicated themselves for each reflection, now real in this mind.

"You know what to do." All of the Jasons threw him a salute and grabbed the tools they needed to remove the tar blobs. In moments the sound of shattering glass enveloped the room.

"Hey, Chief!" Jason looked around for the source of the call. He discovered a radio microphone attached to his belt. He pulled the gray, oblong box out of its holster and held down the side button.

"Yeah. What's up?" He released the button. The speaker squawked and scratched; then a voice came through.

"We got those tar balls coming down on us from above. Thought you oughta know and go up a floor. See if you can do anything." For an instant Jason faltered when he heard himself on the radio. It was weird. He let it go and got back work.

"Okay. I'm on it."

"Roger that, boss. We got you covered down here."

A door appeared next to the emergency cabinet behind Jason. He holstered his radio, banged the door open, and walked into a stairwell. Up the steps, he discovered another large space but better lit. The space, crammed full of brass pipes of varying sizes, looked like a boiler room with little space to move in any direction. Climbing over, under, and around the plumbing, Jason discovered row after row of large piping. Piles of tar overflowed the sides of metal tubes that looked like bathtubs designed to gather and carry the material away. Something had failed to perform its normal function.

Jason, though a statue in the hospital's day room, was working feverishly to unclog the brain's plumbing. A control panel was needed—something he had always found when invading other's minds. He sat among the large tubes and controlled his breathing. A blueprint flashed in his awareness. What he sought lay beyond a wall of smaller pipes.

They pushed up through the floor hidden behind a barrier of pipes. They looked like the switches used to move trains from one track to another, with a gear at the bottom that meshed with others to move the track. Three stood in the forward position and leaned away from him while one was back toward him.

This was not the time to worry about what might happen. Jason grabbed the down switch and pushed it forward like the others.

Immediately liquid flowed through the pipes. The tar blobs stacked up in the bathtub pipes started to collapse, as if the bottom had melted and collapsed. In moments, the tarry substance in the pipe dissolved and disappeared, but the flow stopped. Jason turned around and found the switch set to "off." He grabbed the handle and pushed forward again. This time he jammed the ax, still in his hand, into the gear to keep it from moving.

The fluid ran again in the pipes; clanks and clangs came from all directions. Jason looked left and right, and like the room downstairs, it stretched on forever with more switches to throw and more tar to be dissolved.

"Now what am I s'posed to do?" Jason felt exhausted. He collapsed against a pipe and sank to the floor.

"Not your problem anymore, young man." Shocked, Jason looked up.

"Sally Tilghman." She held out her hand.

Jason took her hand, and she pulled him to his feet. She wore an orange hardhat and looked at him with a huge grin. "Can't thank you enough," she said. "But I'll take it from here, okay?"

Jason no longer leaned against a pipe with machinery clanging, but found himself braced against the bookshelf. It was quiet. He looked down and stared into Sally Tilghman's eyes. Once dead to the world, she smiled up at him with tears flowing down her cheeks. She let go of his arm and pointed a finger at him. "I will remember you, young man." Her rough voice was barely audible. "Yes, Jason Sutter, I will remember you." She sat back in her wheelchair. Before Jason could answer, an aide whisked her away.

Sam looked concerned. "Jason? What happened? You were like ... gone for a while."

"Don't worry, Sam. I was just shocked by being grabbed." Jason watched Sally wheeled out and wondered how his actions would come back to haunt him. Her smile would stay with him the rest of his life.

Chapter 20

Kyle Downing knocked on the white door. Mrs. Lim opened it the length of the chain latch.

"Mrs. Lim, I believe." He cleared his throat and watched her study him carefully. "I was hoping I might speak to Professor Chin? This is where he lives?"

Mrs. Lim closed the door. Downing heard her footsteps move away and return. The chain scraped in its slide. She opened the door slowly and pointed the way. Downing found the man he had felt compelled to meet, sipping tea in Mrs. Lim's kitchen. His Asian features had flashed into his conscious mind for days after his encounter with Jason at the microscope.

"It is not hard guess." Chiang smiled. He invited Downing to take a seat. "You're here about Mr. Sutter, I presume."

Downing nodded. He thanked Mrs. Lim for the steaming cup poured and placed before him. She quietly exited the room.

After a sip of tea, Mr. Downing said, "Well, what are we to do with our Mr. Sutter?" He cradled the warm cup and thought carefully. "He needs guidance and direction. If left to his own devices, he—"

"Might do much more harm than good." Chiang finished the thought. They sipped their tea in unison, each with his thoughts about the potential harm.

"I do not believe," Downing said, "that either of us knows his full capabilities, but I've got a good feel for what he can do." He set down

145

his cup and described everything he recalled from the episode in his basement.

Chiang sat rapt as he listened to Downing's journey down the rabbit hole. The wonderland landscape amazed him.

"I don't have Jason's permission, but I don't think he will object, given what has happened between you. Read Jason's journal." Chiang placed it before Downing. He looked up at Chiang, opened the book, and read.

"My God!" he declared after studying the pages. "What has happened to this child?" He closed the journal and pushed it away. "Used by his foster parents, a target for armed criminals, apparently his family is in some sort of trouble, which he escaped. It's a miracle he survived at all."

"It is a miracle," agreed Chiang. "One of many. We are fortunate that he has not struck out at the injustice of all that has happened to him."

Downing looked pale. "Would you know, my friend, if Mrs. Lim might have something stronger than tea? I feel the need of it." The shock from Jason's touch remained, and the stress induced from what he read in the journal unsettled him. His hands trembled.

"Yes, of course." Chiang rose and returned with two small glasses and a bottle of Jack Daniels. Expecting a foreign concoction, Downing questioned him with a look.

"It is something I have sampled while in your country and found I like." He placed the glasses on the table and filled each to the brim. "Like you, however, I am torn about what to do." They both polished off the bourbon in one shot. Chiang filled the glasses again. "There is no reason Jason has to be the only one."

Mr. Downing finished the second drink. Chiang refilled the glass. "How would we know?" He pointed to the journal. "Our memories are easily modified."

"Jason has reacted only in defense. I have no worries about him using his abilities just because he can." Chiang slowly turned his shot glass; he lifted it and sipped. "I wonder if there is any way we can know if we have been visited by others like him."

"If I were to start somewhere …" Downing rubbed his chin, his mind working like a well-oiled machine. "Look for the miracles, the unexplained. We should check in with the sisters Grimm."

"Who?" Chiang asked.

"The library sisters." Downing sat back and sipped the bourbon. "I've known them for years. They have a knack, like magic, for pulling in irrelevant references that often lead to an answer to the question at hand."

"Yes, yes. I've found them to be quite useful, as well as, entertaining." Chiang smiled with the memory of working with Louise and Mary.

"So we are agreed. We look for miracles." Downing raised his glass. "Maybe we can find an answer to our Mr. Sutter."

Chiang raised his glass in response. "To miracles and those who can work them."

"You know why you are here?" asked Rodney Davenport. "Here" was the Tarrytown Community House. Large and hunting-lodge elegant, it provided distance from the loud, hyperactive City.

Rodney sat back with his elbows, resting on the arms of his executive desk chair. His fingers were steepled, partially hiding his face. Samantha stood behind him and to his right.

"Yes," said Riley, a blond young man eager to please. His black T-shirt hugged his muscular body.

Constance—petite and pixie pretty—sat next to Riley and nodded. Quiet and reserved, she lived to serve the Community.

Rodney smiled. Of the two, Constance radiated greater strength. Riley would be her backup.

"We have confirmed the report from Central." Rodney raised a hand and signaled Samantha to come forward. "Fill them in."

"It's a child ... a gifted child."

Rodney watched their reactions.

Riley sat back and shrugged. "Let's do it."

Constance gave no indication that she might have concerns killing a child.

"Good," Rodney said. "Logistics."

"Saturday," Samantha said. "Here." She stepped back.

"I expect this to be a quick action but energy intensive. Do what you have to do to prepare." Rodney waved them away.

Constance, Riley, and Samantha exited the office, closing the sliding doors as they left.

Rodney spun his chair to face the picture window. The evening sky darkened. It had been a long time since he last eliminated any of his kind.

"What must be done will be done." He leaned forward and pulled a ledger from the shelf beneath the window. The accounts required his constant attention.

Chapter 21

⚡

The library doors opened, and Chiang and Mr. Downing entered. A young girl clutched a book to her chest and scurried out. They held the doors for her. It was near closing time, a week after they shared a drink at Mrs. Lim's house. Down the hall from the front door they saw Mary Tremont and Louise Deloro bent over a book. As they neared the mahogany counter, the two ladies debated energetically.

"I'm saying that he's got some talent that's very special. Look at the books he goes through." Louise leaned on her elbows and looked up at her sister.

"I don't know, Lou. Look at the source. Not the most prestigious publication." Mary leaned over to get a better look at the document. "It's not a very good photo either." She shook her head. "Indeed, he's a reading dynamo."

"My good ladies, how good it is to see you again." Mr. Downing paused. They looked up in unison. Louise smiled. Mary's smile warmed the room. Downing cleared his throat, uncomfortable beneath Mary's gaze. Chiang hung back.

"Well, if it isn't Kyle Downing after all this time," Mary said. She frowned and folded her arms. "As usual you have come when there is little time left." She sounded genuinely disappointed. "We are about to lock up."

Mr. Downing coughed, embarrassed. "As it turns out, Mrs. Tremont, we have come at the best possible time to seek you and your sister's help to solve a mystery."

"A mystery?" Louise glanced up at him and then looked over Mr. Downing's shoulder. "Good afternoon, Professor Chin. As always, it is a pleasure." Chiang bowed slightly at the waist in acknowledgement.

"A mystery, you say?" Mary found her smile again. "As it turns out, we are working on one of our own."

"Well." Downing gave his most gracious but mischievous grin. "Perhaps we can help each other."

"Perhaps," Louise said. "Please tell us more." Mary stood there dreamily. Louise nudged her sister with her hip to get her to focus.

"Professor Chin and I are in need of help to list any miracle cures in Pennsylvania in the last few decades. Medical miracles reported by the press or some other publication."

Mary and Louise looked at each other. Louise raised an eyebrow. Mary nodded, accepting their silent agreement.

"Does this have anything to do with our young Mr. Sutter?" Mary asked.

Both men froze, surprised.

Mary chuckled, amused by their reactions. "Well, Kyle Downing, it would seem we are all well met."

"What do you mean?" Chiang asked.

"Since Kyle's goddaughter, Miss Thompson, introduced us to Mr. Sutter, he has been ..." she thought for a moment to capture the right words, "devouring books as fast as we hand them over."

"Can you be more specific?" Mr. Downing laid his hands on the counter. He looked from one sister to the other. Mary's hand covered his. With the other she pointed down to the end of the counter.

"Each one of those carts holds about sixty or so books, depending on the size of the volumes." Downing and Chin followed her gesture to the carts and nodded their understanding. "Those four carts"—Mary pointed—"are the books Jason took out and retuned in a four-week period."

Chiang asked, "You are telling us that this boy read over two hundred books in four weeks?" They nodded. "Are you sure he actually read those books."

"By all means at our disposal," Louise said. "We shared tea and cookies in the back and discussed the books in some detail." She leaned forward and looked from Downing to Chiang. "I assure you, he read them."

"Of course, we think he may have read a good many books already in the Dubois house before he ever came through our doors." Mary came around the mahogany counter. She looked the two men over. "So we are working on the same mystery?"

"Yes," Downing said, still shocked by the amount Jason had absorbed.

"Are we to work together then?" asked Professor Chin. They looked at each other and exchanged nods. "If so," he continued, "please call me Chiang. What has Jason been reading?"

"Let's see," mused Louise, her hand on her chin. "He started with biology and genetics, and some books on World War II. Then he started asking for more books on biology. Lately he has shown interest in plant and brain anatomy. He still has those texts. The fiction and history books he takes out one day and returns the next."

"Don't forget the chemistry text. He still has that one too," chimed in Mary.

"My God." Downing shook his head in disbelief.

"He started with genetics based on something I told him," Chiang stated. "In short, I had some plants that changed mysteriously in his presence. It looks like he wants to know how."

They stood there in silence and contemplated the enormity of Jason's abilities. Mary pulled them back from their own thoughts. "What is your part in the Sutter story?"

"We believe," Chiang said, "that Mr. Sutter is special." He paused. "Very special and requires equally, special guidance." Louise held up her hand for him to stop. She came from behind the counter with a heavy set of bright, brass keys.

"Let's go into the staff lounge to discuss this further," Mary suggested in a hushed voice, like there might be prying eyes watching and unwanted ears listening to them. She turned away and passed through the door behind the counter on the left. "Lou will shut the place down so we are not interrupted." She indicated that they should follow.

"Some tea, gentlemen?" A porcelain tea service graced the table around which they sat. The cookie tin was opened, and a plate layered with chocolate chip and oatmeal cookies appeared. Louise stepped into the room.

"So, Kyle," Mary said sweetly, "Earl Grey I believe is your preference from your years in England?" She loaded a shiny tea ball with loose leaves. "You know, I still have a rain check from our missed date. I save it in my desk at home." She poured and handed the cup to Downing.

"Well ..." He coughed. "That was 1943, Mary. You were married by the time I got back from the war, and I ... umm thought it best not to complicate things."

"Jasmine for you, Chiang?" She worked on the next cup. "My Harry has been dead for the last five years, Kyle," she said matter-of-factly. "I expected you to claim your check, but you have not yet." She handed the simmering cup to Chiang but held Downing's eyes.

"Thank you, Mrs. Tremont." Chiang smiled.

"Call me Mary, please." She smiled, turning to him.

"Cookie, either of you?" asked Louise, rescuing Downing from any further embarrassment. After each took one or two from the plate, she poured her own a cup. "I think, Mary, we should allow you and Kyle to work this out at another time." She sat back and stirred her tea. "Kyle, for pity's sake, call. Neither of us will have any peace until you do."

Downing nodded reluctantly and grumbled something under his breath. Mary looked delighted.

"We need to come clean, so to speak," Louise continued, "on what we know or think we know. It will be more helpful to our investigation, don't you think?" She looked around the table.

"Given what you have already observed," Chiang said, "I agree you need our part if you are to be most helpful." Downing nodded.

Chiang paused, considering where to start. "Our Mr. Sutter is, as far as we can tell, a gifted telepath. We know, for example ..." Chiang provided the details found in Jason's journal, after which a long silence ensued as the women absorbed the enormity of Mr. Sutter's condition.

Mary leaned forward and put her cup on the table. She rose and left the room and then returned with a newspaper opened to the middle pages. She folded it closed and held it up to display the headline. It was a tabloid found in grocery stores across the country. The headline read, "Miracle at Kearny." The picture of Jason Sutter with his wrist held by a frail, elderly woman covered most of the front page.

"We were discussing this when you walked in." Both men leaned forward.

"What does the article say?" Downing asked.

Chapter 22

T he Dubois foster children watched from the living-room windows. Strangers crowded the front of the house like supplicants at a holy shrine. Some knelt on the sidewalk, hands clung tightly in prayer. Others stood with placards held high, crying out for help in bold, bright colors, "Save my Henry" or "You are a gift from God! Help us!"

Frank and Lydia watched from Lydia's bedroom window.

"I'll kill that fool Will Grossman." Lydia seethed. "Everything we've built here will be blown away with all this attention."

"Can't blame them," Frank said, nodding at the people below. "They're probably desperate."

Lydia stared at him, furious with his stupidity.

"Shut up. You're as pitiful as Will. I don't give a damn about those fools out there. I'm talking about losing everything and going to jail." She could not believe how difficult Frank had become in the last few months.

Three weeks had passed since the trip to the State Hospital at Kearny. Will had followed through as always. The pictures featured on the front page of the *Franklin Chase Messenger*, a weekly publication. The words "Deprived and damaged kids give back to the community" accompanied the pictures. The article wound up in Will's offering to his bosses at the Department of Social Services, along with an assortment of his pictures. When the unexplained, miraculous cure came to the attention of the tabloids a week later, and their reporters discovered that someone had taken pictures, Will was contacted. He offered up the snapshots willingly; he would not leave five thousand dollars lying on the table. Frank and Lydia got two thousand.

"Can't blame Will." Frank ignored Lydia's venom. "I wouldn't have turned down that kind of money either. We got our cut." With no response from Lydia, he continued. "This will work itself out like those other times. Besides, who takes those papers seriously."

"Apparently they do, you jackass." She pointed to the crowd. "Please, God," she continued as she rubbed her forehead, "don't let them sing again." As if on cue, "Amazing Grace" filled the air. "Oh damn."

When the first pilgrims found the house, Lydia's first impulse was to drag Jason downstairs to lay his hands on the people at one hundred dollars each. When the headache hit her like a sledgehammer and forced her to bed, she changed her approach.

"Where's the boy?"

"Jason? He's in his room, so far as I know." Frank listened to the hymn as the crowd began the second verse. He was moved by the feeling in the voices.

"He's got something to do with this," Lydia said.

Frank had heard that before. "Give it a rest, will you? This is all a tabloid-created craze."

Frank gave vent to his annoyance. "This is coincidence and nothing more. People will interpret the picture as they need to. These people need a savior. They believe they have found one. I just wish there was some way to let them down easy."

"Screw 'em. I tell you, this boy has something to do with it." Lydia moved away from the window and sought a calm, quiet place to stop the budding pain. Frank wondered if the miracle at the hospital might have touched his mother.

☆ ☆ ☆

Jason sat at his small desk, surrounded by his latest round of books, and stared at two newspapers. One was the afternoon paper. The other showed a photo of Jason firmly grasped by Sally Tilghman, their eyes closed—Sally, the desperate child gone wrong, pleading for forgiveness and healing from Jason, the benevolent father. He studied the photo to learn more about what happens when he is off on one of his mind trips. The photograph showed Sally clearly, but he looked fuzzy, like he was vibrating faster than the film's ability to capture his image. He heard the singing.

"Damn. I can't heal everybody," Jason said to himself and set aside the paper. "I just got lucky with Sally." This whole thing gave him a headache. He rubbed his eyes and sat back. His hand rested on a paperback book of historical fiction about a boy, alone, growing up at the turn of the century in rural Canada. He thumbed through the pages, having just finished the story. Jason loved it and felt cheated when the final page arrived in under an hour. The boy's life was one he would have cherished, if given the choice.

He felt trapped by the people on the curb in front of the house, but there was nothing he could do. Down deep, however, he wanted to run out and promise to heal everyone at the hospital. He fought this impulse; it felt like a dangerous thing to do.

A chemistry textbook stood at an angle against the wall, opened. The section described covalent bonding between atoms. Jason ran his finger over the words for the umpteenth time. He failed to capture the meaning and its relationship to what he had read in the genetics text. What was the connection to the wad of ribbon he observed through Mr. Downing's microscope? Something escaped his ability to comprehend. He could not grasp how the molecules held together.

Pounding footsteps on the stairs interrupted his focus. He turned to face his door. As it got louder, he braced himself for the inevitable knock. He would not go down and face those people.

"Jason!" Suzy called. She banged on the door frantically. "Come quick, it's Russ. Something's wrong with his sister Patti!"

He bounded to the door and threw it open.

"He's in the shed out back, waiting." Suzy ran after him. He shot down the hall, took the steps two at a time, and rushed through the kitchen. Before the screen door slammed, he was across the yard.

In the shed, Russ paced. When Jason got there, the tear tracks were still fresh on Russ's face. He grabbed Jason's arm and started dragging him out. "Something's wrong with Patti. The doctor can't get there till later today. You gotta come and help. This has to do with what you do. Come on."

"Wait." Jason and pulled back. "I can't go out there. I'll be mobbed. Tell me what's goin' on while I think of what to do." Russ started to argue but instead collapsed onto one of the stools, obviously exhausted.

"Last night, really late, she started crying out in pain. I mean screaming." Russ rubbed the tears off his face. "She stops for a while; then it all starts up again. It's awful. It's killing my parents 'cause they can't help." He straightened up, feeling better that he would soon bring help.

"Okay. Suzy, how do I get away from here?" Jason asked.

Suzy stopped worrying about Russ and thought. She smiled. "I've got just the thing."

Fifteen minutes later, Russ and two girls from the house walked down the side of the house from the backyard and talked loudly about going to the candy store near the A&P grocery. The people chanting on the street continued while some watched them carefully. They recognized the boy who had raced into the backyard earlier. They didn't recognize either girl, not the one wearing jeans with the pigtails or the other one in the long, blue gingham dress with the rosy cheeks under a wide-brim summer hat. They wanted "the boy," so they lost interest in the kids walking down the street.

"We'll shoot back around to your house, Russ, in a few blocks," Jason whispered. He glanced back. No one watched. "You better let me have my clothes to change before we get to your house."

"Yeah, good idea." Russ wore two pairs of jeans and two shirts for the getaway.

Jason nearly tripped a few times on the dress's hem. Fortunately his worn-out sneakers did not show. "Suzy, can you get this makeup off me?" She nodded.

Behind a line of bushes a few blocks over, Russ stripped off his top set of clothes.

"Are your older sisters home too?" Jason asked. He stepped into his jeans and then pulled the dress over his head.

"No. They're spending the night at their friends' houses. It's just my mom and dad, me, and Patti." Russ handed him the shirt. Jason balled up the dress and handed it to Suzy for their return journey. He put on his shirt and then sat on the curb. Suzy joined him. She licked a cotton handkerchief and wiped the rouge off his cheeks and eyeliner from around his eyes.

"Okay," she said, looking at her handiwork. "You're done, as best as can be expected." The three children dashed the remaining distance to Russ's house. They heard the screaming from the Wyatts's front door.

"Russ," said Mr. Wyatt, who opened the door, "there's nothing Jason can do here." He looked worn out, with dark circles under his eyes. "This is an adult situation that—"

Jason took control of Mr. Wyatt, and he led the children upstairs.

"Work your magic, man," Russ said. "Work your magic."

Chapter 23

Jason sat cross-legged, meditating. Patti's screaming stopped moments after he started.

When Jason first entered the room, Mr. and Mrs. Wyatt, who had remained steadfast by their suffering daughter since the early morning hours, relinquished her with a sudden, desperate need to sleep. Jason had injected that insatiable need. Fear for their daughter generated countless questions, which slowed Jason's rescue. He needed them out of the way, and they went hand in hand to their room.

After they left, Russ and Suzy sat on the bed with Patti, who was wrapped in her white summer blanket. She slept, her arms clinging to a large, floppy-eared, stuffed dog. Her features, earlier distorted by pain, were now relaxed. She breathed softly in a deep, forgetful sleep.

As he focused on Patti, neither of Jason's friends saw the blood trickle from his nose. Only when he settled on the floor and fell back against the wall with a thud did they notice anything wrong with him.

"Jason!" Suzy screamed, running to him. She knelt and wiped the blood from his upper lip and then patted his cheek. "Jason, say something." He did not respond.

"Oh jeez," Russ said, as he knelt at his side. "There's blood coming out of his ear too." He gently pulled Jason's head to the side so Suzy could see his other ear.

"Yeah, it's there too." She started to cry. "What should we do? We can't just leave him like this."

"Let's stretch him out of the floor and raise his legs. He may be in shock or something." Russ put his arm behind Jason's shoulders and leaned him forward enough to turn him so he could lie flat on the floor. Suzy grabbed a couple of pillows and put them under his feet.

"Now we gotta wait," Russ insisted. "There's nothing more to do. At least I can't think of anything." He sat on the floor at Jason's head and leaned back against the wall so he could keep an eye on his sister too. Suzy took up a post between Jason and the bed, resting her arm on the mattress. They waited in silence.

An hour passed before Jason showed signs of coming around. Suzy and Russ drifted deep into their worry and fear, waiting for something to happen. Jason's cough brought them to full alert. He opened his eyes and took a deep, desperate breath, as though drowning in a raging sea. Eyes wide in terror, he looked at Russ and Suzy. His mouth moved, but no words came. His eyes rolled back, and he fell unconscious again.

Suzy controlled her fear and stated calmly, "He's healing himself."

Russ nodded. "Yeah, he's on automatic like those other times."

Suzy felt less confident than she sounded. She and Russ returned to their vigil.

Scared for Jason and Patti, Suzy focused on Jason. "Whatever it was, he's fighting back." Unable to sit still any longer, she got up and paced. She wanted to say something or wanted Russ to utter the right words to make their waiting feel like the right thing to do. Jason had never showed such vulnerability before.

Thirty minutes later, he moaned and rolled onto his side, facing the bed. His eyes opened. "I can't see."

"Oh, Jason," Suzy cried. She went to her knees next to him and put her hand on his shoulder. "We thought you might be really hurt."

"Glad to hear anything from ya, man." Russ stood up and walked around to kneel next to Suzy and check on his sister. Patti slept undisturbed. "Gave us a scare," he said, looking down on his friend.

Another few minutes passed until Jason raised himself on his elbow. He sat up and waved his hand before his eyes. He slowly got to his feet. He was unsteady, so Suzy supported him with her hand on his arm.

"My vision is back, but pretty blurry," he said. "My legs feel weak. I'm gonna need some help getting around. How's Patti?" He stooped like an old man and struggled to get his legs in motion and face the bed.

"She's okay," Russ said. "You saved her."

"Good." Jason nodded. "I have done all I can. Help me get downstairs. We need to talk." He stopped, stretched, and rubbed the back of his neck. His muscles complained, as if he had hauled heavy cases of ammunition to the front lines while dodging enemy fire every step of the way. "She needs to sleep now." Jason turned toward the door and hobbled out into the hallway with Suzy's support.

"So what happened?" asked Russ, following behind.

"I thought I was getting a headache with all those people in front of the house begging for help. I was wrong about that." Jason's feet dragged on the rug. He stumbled, and Russ caught him around the waist. With effort he righted himself and started down the hall again.

"I'm thirsty."

"Let's get you downstairs to the kitchen," Russ said. With Suzy on one side and Russ on the other, they navigated the stairs and made it to the kitchen without Jason collapsing.

"I can see things better now." Jason dropped into the nearest chair at the kitchen table. His legs were beginning to regain their strength.

"You want me to wipe the blood off you?" Suzy took a dish towel and soaked one end in water and then rubbed soap on it. She stepped closer.

"Blood?" he asked. "What blood?"

"Take a look." Russ handed him a small mirror he'd taken from a utility drawer next to the fridge. He turned back, pulled a glass from a cabinet, and filled it from the tap while Jason examined his face. Russ's hand shook when he set the drink in front of him.

Jason took the towel from Suzy and ran the soapy end over his face and ears. Then he used the dry end to clear away the soap. He set the towel down in front of him.

"It was an attack." Jason picked up the glass. "Patti was under attack." He gulped the whole glass, then got to his feet, grabbed the towel, and shuffled to the counter, where he set both down. He arched his back. His bones cracked.

Through the window, the Wyatt backyard looked the same, with its trees, garden, and picnic table. How could that be? Nothing would ever be as it was. Weariness took hold of him. He closed his eyes and dropped his head.

"Oh jeez," Russ said with his hands flat on the table. He leaned forward. "Attack from what, from who?"

"Well," Jason said after a moment, "it looks like I am not the only one who can do what I do." Jason raised his head and stared out the window. A summer breeze gently swayed the trees. He reached over the sink, unlatched the window, and raised it. The clean, warm air brushed by his face. It felt good. He breathed deeply. "I guess some of those people are not very good."

"You mean dangerous," Suzy said, scared.

"Yeah, very dangerous and very strong." Jason ran his hand through his hair and wondered what he should do. He turned around and leaned back against the counter.

"When I entered her mind, it was like hammers pounding. The force and pain were more than a child could survive. I threw up a shield construct." He grinned for a second; he remembered Russ's Fantastic Four comic. "That's when she stopped screaming." He closed his eyes, shuddered, and remembered the pain.

"Then the force of the attack doubled. The only way to save Patti was to throw myself in the way." He shook his head and remained silent. Suzy and Russ watched him intently and waited. The room tensed.

After a time he continued. "I could do nothing. I had to take it, blow after blow. It was like … like getting in the way of an oncoming car to protect a little kid who stepped into the street. The driver kept backing up and trying again. It was attempted murder. I'm lucky I made it through." He came back to the table and sat down.

"For now, it's all fixed … but at a price." Jason shook his head slowly. He felt horrible. It was the only thing he could think to do. "She had to look dead to her attacker."

"What?" Russ's lower jaw dropped as his hands curled into fists.

"I had to wipe part of her memory, Russ. I had to take away that part of her that does the mind stuff." He paused to collect his thoughts.

"If I stayed in her mind, she was safe. But ... I couldn't do that forever." Jason looked at Russ for understanding. Russ did not register that he got it. "Her talents, like mine, made this attack hurt her. Regular people don't feel anything. People like me with these abilities only get a headache because we protect ourselves. Patti's too young and couldn't do that."

"I don't know what you mean. Why her? They musta known it was just a kid, right?" Russ watched Jason carefully.

"I don't know, Russ." Jason looked away, afraid of the implications in his friend's question.

"Then," continued Russ, "how come they came here?"

"I believe it had something to do with what I did to help that old lady. 'Course, I'm not sure." Jason folded his arms. "I picked up a few hints."

"Like what? What has happened to my sister! Did you help her or not!" Russ's anger, born of fear, rushed out. He could not comprehend what Jason said. "Tell me what happened!"

"Let's all calm down," Suzy said. She laid her hand on Russ's arm and looked at Jason. "Jason came to help."

"Yeah? And you did what, exactly?" Russ eyed his friend suspiciously.

"I protected her by hiding her abilities from her own mind. I put them away so any future attacks will not affect her." Jason looked at Russ. "You will have to help her through this."

"Like how? I can't do what you do?" Russ felt shocked and dismayed that his powerful friend could not just wave his hand and clear up the mess.

"You don't need to have my abilities." Jason got up and refilled the glass. He took a long drink. He stared through the opened window at a beautiful summer afternoon. It calmed him.

"Teach Patti to meditate for a start," Jason began, holding the glass. "That will help her. Eventually her talents will leak out from the hiding place. She will pick up people's thoughts again. It may scare her, and if she tells your parents, it may frighten your mom and dad into sending her to a hospital or something. You must be there to tell her it is okay and she's not nuts. Tell her what she is. Keep your parents from overreacting or knowing at all, if possible." Jason paused for a moment to let this sink in. "Then come and get me."

Russ accepted that he had a job to do. In a way he felt better; he had a part to play in helping his family. "How long?"

"Maybe a year, maybe two. I'm not sure."

"But she's safe now, right?" Suzy asked.

"Yeah, she's safe. She's dead to my kind." Jason glanced back over his shoulder at Russ. "Your parents will awaken later today but will remember nothing that happened. Neither will Patti. It will be just another day. You will be the only one in your family who knows."

Russ nodded.

"Jason," Suzy asked, "what else happened inside Patti's mind? You said there were hints?"

"Once the attack ended, I followed the trail of energy that generated the hammering and traced it to the owner fairly easily. I don't think he—it was a guy—expected to find someone like me. He didn't even know I was there." Jason looked from Suzy to Russ. "I sensed he was older, maybe your dad's age, Russ. I kept getting images of a large, gray building with these pillars lining the walls on the outside. The shield I put up blocked the blows, and I guess with me in the way, he no longer sensed Patti's mind's abilities. He stopped. Probably thought she was dead or something."

Jason shuddered. The man had enjoyed the destruction. "I could have attacked him. He let his guard down. But there was something … something that held me back."

"What? Why not give him what he deserved?" Russ wanted payback for his sister's suffering.

"I didn't want to reveal myself. He could've been too powerful for me." Jason paused. "With the blood comin' out of me"—he looked at the stained towel on the table—"it was the right thing to do." Jason returned to the table and picked up the mirror again to make sure the bleeding had stopped. "I bet he is not the only one out there, and he must be powerful to reach so far."

"How far do you think?" Suzy asked. She scanned Jason for any blood marks elsewhere. She found none.

"Maybe Philadelphia. Maybe somewhere else. I don't know." Jason sat and let his thoughts drift. His whole body shivered.

"Jason?" Suzy caught the sudden frightened look on his face. "What?"

"This guy had the same feel as Lydia. You know what I'm talkin' about." He looked at Suzy, who nodded. "He would've tried to kill me too, if he knew I was there." Jason felt very unsure about what he should do next. "I think I got lucky." Something gnawed at him at the edge of comprehension.

"I guess," Russ said, less upset. He understood and had a plan. "My job is to make sure Patti doesn't turn out like you."

"What?" Suzy and Jason asked at the same time.

"Ya know, like Jason." Russ thought he'd said something wrong. He looked from one to the other. "No memory. Not knowing what he could do. Nutsy. That sort a stuff."

Comprehension like a strong tide rose in Jason. He stood, every muscle stiff, and glared at his friend. "That's it!"

"All right, I'm sorry, man." Russ raised his hands as if he might have to ward off an attack. "Don't get all messed up about it. I didn't mean anything bad."

"Bad? It was the worst possible thing!" Jason tossed the small mirror on the table and then leaned forward and stared intently at his friend.

"I don't think it was all that bad," Russ said. "It was the way you were, man."

"It wasn't what you said. It was what someone did to me." He paused aghast at what must have happened so many years ago. "Maybe she did it to protect me 'cause she wouldn't be there."

"She who, Jason?" Russ asked.

"I know." Suzy reached across the table and put her hand over Jason's.

"My mom, Russ. My mom did this to me, so they couldn't find me. She did what I did to Patti. She … hid me." Jason stood straight and paced about the kitchen.

"What d' ya mean?" Russ asked.

"The shrink I saw for a while, Dr. Lipton, sent a letter saying he had found her in a psych hospital in New York somewhere. She's been hurt bad, probably because she took the time to hide me first." Jason let the feelings sweep over him. "I've got to find her and help bring her back."

"How will you do that, Jason?" Suzy asked.

"I don't know. I think I need to talk to Chiang or Downing about it." Jason nodded; he felt better; he had adults to advise him. "They may be able to help me."

"Maybe we better get back," Suzy said. "We never told anyone where we were going."

"Let's skip the dress and makeup this time." Jason stood. "And I don't want to go back to the house just now." He could not face the chanters or his bleak life in the Dubois house. He needed somewhere open and welcoming. "Let's go to the library. I want to talk to the ladies there."

"Okay," Suzy said.

"Russ, you wanna come along?" Jason saw that his friend was torn. If he could have split himself into two people, he would have done so.

"I'll stay," Russ finally said. "One of these guys might wake up and will need to be told everything is fine."

"I think you should try to sleep some yourself, if you can," Jason said.

Jason and Suzy headed for the front door. They stopped on the threshold and looked back. "You gonna be okay?"

"Yeah, don't worry 'bout me. I'll see ya tomorrow." Russ watched them head down the walkway and then out of sight around the corner.

"Thanks, Superman," he whispered.

Chapter 24

⚡

The walk to the library was a solemn affair; both Suzy and Jason were quiet with their thoughts. With little street traffic, the air smelled clean. It was quiet, with only the occasional whoosh of a car passing. The sun stood high overhead. No cloud marred the blue plane of the sky. Jason guessed it was near three o'clock.

"You feeling all right?" Suzy asked. The library was a few blocks away.

Jason stared at the sidewalk. "Yeah, I'm much better." He looked up. A determination crept over his features; he understood at last and accepted his fate. He might not be able to solve these problems; he might not survive. Something, he felt to his core, had to be done.

"What are you thinking?" Suzy asked.

"I hate not knowing." Jason's frustration came out as anger. He slowed and looked at her. "Why am I the way I am? Why would someone like me try to kill a kid? How many are there? Are they all dangerous?" He shook his head, frustrated and afraid of what almost happened to Patti. "I gotta find out some of this stuff. Guessing may get me killed next time." Jason stuck his hands in his pockets and walked faster.

"Okay, but remember." Suzy fell behind a step. "You're just a kid like me and Russ. You need help." She sped up and fell into step next to Jason.

"There's only one problem with that: I'm not just a kid. Not just a normal kid anyway." Jason stopped abruptly. Suzy passed and then turned to face him.

"You know what this is like?" Jason asked. Suzy shook her head. "You remember the goons that came to the house?" This time she nodded. "What did the dogs or cats roaming the neighborhood care about that little episode?" Jason pulled his hands out of his pockets. He ran one hand through his hair to rustle a resistant thought free. "We could be killed, but they wouldn't care or even register that there might be a problem."

"You think people, normal people, are like animals?" Suzy stared at him like he was talking crazy.

"In a way." Jason became calm "When your memory can be wiped and changed to be anything we want, anything I want, normal people are defenseless like those animals are defenseless against human plans to get rid of them. They have no defense against normal folks' tools and no thinking ability that would allow them to see it coming."

"Where do Chiang and Mr. Downing fit into this?" Suzy turned away and started walking slowly. Jason followed.

"That's the hard part. They are among the cats and dogs. I hate that, but they can be manipulated as easily as anyone else. Unless—"

Jason caught up with Suzy, who finished his thought. "You are there to defend them." She suddenly felt the enormity of the power at Jason's disposal and the weight of his responsibility.

He nodded and said, "There's Patti, Patti's mom, that guy who tried to kill Patti, and you."

"Ha! Not me, Jason." Suzy was happy he included her. She wanted to belong but feared the notion that she might not be entirely human.

Jason grabbed her arm. They stopped, face to face. "I can't read you. That's important. I don't know why, but I am sure it is." He looked deeply into her eyes. "You are one of us."

"I don't wanna be one of anything but just people … good people." Suzy did not smile this time; she felt even more frightened.

"Yeah, I know." Jason shrugged and nodded. "You get used to it." He took her hand and pulled her along up the steps of the library. "Let's just try to find out a few things first, okay?"

"Okay," she choked out.

As they entered the library, Mary was manning the front counter. Jason saw Louise walk off somewhere.

"Well, well, Jason Sutter. Back again so soon?" Mrs. Tremont smiled. "Surprisingly, I may actually have something new for you." Jason dropped Suzy's hand, embarrassed.

"That … that would be great, Mrs. Tremont, but I need something else. Something you and Mrs. Deloro may be able to provide." Jason glanced around the area, trying to remember where he had seen what he needed. Mrs. Tremont waited patiently. Jason snapped his fingers and headed into one of the reading rooms off the lobby.

"Well, my dear, you are Suzy, if I am not mistaken?" Mary Tremont asked.

"Yes, ma'am." Suzy looked surprised.

"Your name came up a few times in our discussions with young Mr. Sutter." She leaned over the counter and raised her hand to her mouth as if she did not want to be overheard. "You gave our Jason a good head start with your teaching. I think you could be an excellent teacher, if you want to be." Suzy blushed and grinned ear to ear. No adult had ever told her she was good at anything.

"Thank you." She looked down at the floor, not knowing what to say.

"Here." Jason had returned. He laid a number of comic books on the counter.

"Hmm, interesting. And you want me to do what with these?" Mary asked.

"Let's say one of these guys"—Jason pointed to the Green Lantern— "wanted to find others like him. Where would he start to look?" Louise came from the back room and joined the discussion.

"What do you think, Lou?" Mary faced her sister and raised an eyebrow. "Should we?"

"Yes, I believe we need to." Louise turned from her sister to Jason. "I believe, young man, the question is more, 'How do you find people like yourself?'"

Jason and Suzy stood before the counter, stunned.

"Don't be so surprised," Mary said. "We puzzled together some of your abilities, and Mr. Downing and Professor Chin confirmed them. Your reading prowess alone signaled you were different."

"And they are on their way here now to join us." Louise gathered up the comic books and set them aside. "Let's get comfortable in the staff room. We all need to talk, don't you think?"

Jason did not think much at that very moment. He and Suzy followed the ladies into the back and sat, waiting for Mr. Downing and Professor Chin.

"I should call Frank," Jason said, "and let him know that Suzy and I are here." He was itching to get moving and figure things out.

"I took care of that," Louise said. "Frank knows you are here." She and Mary pushed two more chairs into the circle around the table. "We guessed the crowd at your house had you fenced in. I knew you'd sneak out."

"Is it so—" Jason feared many people might have figured him out.

"Obvious?" Mary finished his question. "No, we have inside information, so to speak. We observed you closely, Mr. Sutter. Only the four of us know."

It did not take long before Mr. Downing and Professor Chin joined them. With the front door locked and tea and cookies spread out on the table, all focus turned to Jason. He described everything he could remember about the attack on Patti.

He strove to recall every detail. "I got the impression that the old guy knew exactly what to do. He had done this before. But he didn't know about me."

"So how many of you are there?" Mr. Downing asked. He sat on the edge of his seat. "So far as you can tell."

"Well, there's me, Patti, Patti's and Russ's mom to some degree. Then this other guy." Jason paused and looked at Suzy. She nodded. "And Suzy. I can't read her without her allowing it. That means something, but we don't know what."

"And this other guy is associated with a building with columns?" Chiang asked. "Perhaps it is a museum or a library."

"No, my friend, I think not." Mr. Downing sat back, crossed his legs, and brought the tips of his fingers together. "We must think in terms of power. A court or financial institution of some sort makes more sense. It would be easy money for someone with Jason's abilities."

"Yes, Jason's abilities." Chiang leaned forward. He considered his words carefully. "I think we need to be honest with you, Jason. We are concerned with those abilities. You have done some good, much good in fact, but—"

"There is an old saying," Louise interjected. "Absolute power corrupts absolutely."

All eyes focused on Jason.

"You think I might …" Jason could not finish his thought. The shock overwhelmed him. Betrayed by the people he trusted, by the people he needed. He could not speak; he could not breathe. It was like losing another family. They did not know him at all.

"No!" Chiang shouted. He got up, knelt in front of Jason, and looked him in the eye. "No! We know your caliber. But even the most saintly of those among us, in an effort to do great good, often go astray, thinking an end justifies the means. And Jason," Chiang said and took a deep breath, "you have great power at your disposal. There are very few who could stand against you."

"How could I …" Jason said, swallowing his urge to cry. His eyes searched the faces of each adult. He made a decision. In the blink of an eye, he read the details of every mind in the room except Suzy's. A great sigh flowed from him, and he relaxed, pleasantly surprised. *They care about me.* Only Suzy could tell what Jason had done.

"We apologize, Jason," Mr. Downing said. "Our fear got the better of us." He rose and went over to give Jason a firm grip on this shoulder. "We adults, in haste to control our fear, sometimes overreact. We forgot that you have been through a great deal of unpleasantness. You deserve better from us. I apologize."

"I want you with me, not against me," Jason said. These were no dumb animals but normal people, powerful in their own right. He would gladly sacrifice himself to defend these good people.

Mary and Louise looked at him sympathetically, their eyes welled with tears.

"Don't worry," he choked out. "I'm gonna be okay now." He could not find the words to tell them what their thoughts, their feelings meant to him. He cleared his throat and changed the subject. "Mrs. Deloro, you said something about finding others like me?"

"Well," she said, "let's start by using first names. Call me Louise."

"Mary," followed her sister.

"Kyle," said Mr. Downing as he returned to his chair.

"Call me what you have always called me." Chiang smiled.

"You said that the attack was an attempt to kill," said Downing. "Tell us more about your sense of it."

Jason sat forward, his body still sore. "The blows I absorbed were definitely meant to kill, but I don't know why."

"Kyle and I have been discussing your situation," Chiang said. "Based on your writings and, now, this very selective targeting of a child, it sounds like a brutal, crush-all-threats attack." Chiang chose his next words based experience. "There may have been a war or an uprising of some sort with a clear winner." He sighed. "This aligns with what you wrote about your mother. Imprisoned, maybe?"

"So it would be like …" Jason paused as he thought for a second. "The Nazi regime in Germany winning World War II. Look at what they did in occupied countries." *What are these people doing to my mother?* He felt scared and helpless.

"Exactly," Downing said.

"So they are killing the …" Jason looked to the Downing and Chiang to finish his question.

"The resistance," Chiang said. "At such times the losing side runs to safety or hides in plain sight. The men and women on the losing side survive but live in fear of betrayal."

"You have experienced this?" Jason looked from one to the other of the men.

"The French resistance during the war," said Downing.

"I have friends who did not make the crossing to Formosa when our battle with Mao Tse Tung was lost." Chiang rested his head back in the chair. He stared at the ceiling, seeing the faces of long lost friends. "They still live in hiding."

"So you are saying—" Jason began.

"What we are saying, young man," interjected Downing, "is that there is a culture, maybe a whole other civilization, living under our noses. They had a war or revolution or something. Who the hell knows?" He threw up his hands. "It left the wrong people in power. These people will kill children to maintain their order."

"And we poor mortals," Louise said. "Never know about any of it except through odd happenings reported in stories hidden in the back pages of newspapers."

"Do you know, Mr. Sutter?" Mary asked in a forceful voice. All eyes turned to her. "There are twenty-two stories so far this year of unexplained miracles at a variety of medical institutions around the state." She paused. "There are seventy or so stories about mysterious murders and unexplainable mayhem in the same period."

"I didn't know," Jason whispered.

"So we have to assume that the enemy believes the Patti girl is dead and they have reported it." Downing assessed the situation as a military strategist. "There is a higher authority somewhere, a command center. This local guy checked in with his boss. We will have time to decide what to do."

"Wait a minute. You can't go anywhere with this." Jason looked each person in the room in the eye. "You can't do anything." Jason shook his head, his fingers tightened on the arms of his chair. "You cannot win. Hiding is the only way to go. Hiding me will be the best possible thing to do."

"Spell it out for them," Suzy said, thinking of cats and dogs. "Fighting back would be useless."

"She is right, Kyle," Jason insisted. "I can arrange for you and Chiang plus these helpful ladies to leave this building with nothing more than a sudden interest in the last works of Shakespeare. It would be easy."

"It probably has already happened," said Downing. "How would we know?"

"Exactly," Jason said. He stood, frustrated. "You are not in jeopardy. You can be manipulated easily. It's me and Patti and Suzy who are at risk.

If we are killed, what would you know about it if the killers are like me?" Jason challenged them with his question.

"Not a thing," Chiang said, unafraid faced Jason. "You and your kind are too powerful. We would know nothing. What do dogs or cats know of their owners' problems?"

The conversation died with these words. Jason stared at Chiang, shocked to hear his words echoed back to him. Chiang sipped his tea, apparently lost in thought, while Downing considered his shoes. Mary and Louise studied everyone in the room, especially Jason.

"What am I to do?" Jason shut his eyes, weary with the obvious. It would be his task to confront this evil. He suddenly wanted his mom to point him in the right direction.

"You, my friend," Chiang said, "must do nothing. You must not be found. You are hiding in plain sight. You must not be betrayed. It is you who will have to fight the good fight," Chiang said as he looked over at Downing, "while we will know nothing of your battles."

"We will help as we can," Downing rushed to add. "In the end, of course, it will be your war, my boy."

"Surely not a war, Kyle," Mary pleaded.

"Our memories, the details of our lives, which include Mr. Sutter as we know him, are in his young hands." He looked at Mary, suddenly aware that he had wasted a good deal of time not calling her.

Louise said, "I believe we have nothing to fear. Our memories are faulty enough even without manipulation. It is Jason who is most at risk." She looked around the circle of adults. "I pledge myself to do whatever he needs to support the good he does." The other adults nodded solemnly.

"Until you tell us differently, Jason," Chiang said, "we are on a war footing. We do not, cannot understand the violence you have endured, but we are at your command."

"Th-thank you," was all Jason could get out. He was touched by their unconditional support for what he might need or have to do. Silence filled the room.

"Uh, can Suzy and me get a lift home?" Jason smiled, embarrassed. *So much for being so powerful*, he thought.

Laughter erupted in the room. Mr. Downing stood, pulled his car keys from his pocket, and ruffled Jason's hair.

"Of course, son. It's the least I can do."

Chapter 25

R odney stared at the blinking light on his office phone. The fifth button across the bottom flashed, demanding action. He hated it when she called.

At his desk in his office on the sixty-sixth floor of the Empire State Building, he finished the balancing of the accounts for the Communities around the United States. It was a simple task to provide the funds; all would live well. There were not that many.

The phone demanded attention again.

He snatched up the receiver. "Yeah?" He glanced out of his window, seeking any distraction.

"Rodney, dear, don't be petulant," a female voice said. He envisioned his spit sliding down her smiling face.

She waited patiently for Rodney's hello.

She sighed heavily, giving up on civility. "Is it done?"

"Yes." He would never confront her directly, of course; she was stronger and very dangerous. Rodney discounted anything weaker and feared greater strength. He followed the rule of keeping enemies closer than friends, except in this case.

"Completely?" Her pleasant, mellifluous voice belied a cobra-swift strike capability. Rodney had disappointed her before and paid a price. He could reach across hundreds of miles if he knew what he sought. She was global in her capabilities. "Who was it?"

"A preschool child." *Volunteer nothing,* he thought, *give only the basics.*

"Certainly, this has happened before." She spoke from experience and more to herself. "A child might put out that level of energy. Our children are so ... uncontrolled." There was an extended pause. "Nothing else?"

"No." He controlled his loathing. "No psychic signature remained. It is a total blackout in Pennsylvania. It is over." He held the receiver away from his ear and, in pantomime fury, screamed obscenities.

"Anything suggesting a rogue family of our kind?" All resistance to Community rule was to be squashed. Rogue families would never again rise to challenge the good of the Community.

Rodney stopped his quiet tirade. "Nothing," he said ready to slam the phone down. "It ... is ... over." *Let it be,* he thought.

"Okay, Rodney dear. It's over." A perfunctory click broke the link.

Rodney knew she would not leave well enough alone. She would send someone to check his facts. He stared at the black receiver still in his hand. *Let her do what she wanted,* he thought. He slammed down the receiver. "Go to hell!"

☆ ☆ ☆

Two days had passed since Jason helped Patti and shared his story at the library with the only adults he trusted. At home, in the toolshed, Jason got together with Suzy and Russ to figure out what to do next.

"It has become clearer to me what must be done." Jason considered his next words carefully. He looked one to the other. "It has all become too big for me to control. Mr. Downing, Chiang, and the library ladies have a clear picture of me in their minds. Too clear."

"Yeah? What does that mean?" Russ's world encompassed Franklin Chase, his family, and friends. The outside world did not register yet. He sat on his hands, pushed up, and supported his weight as he adjusted to a more comfortable position on the stool.

"If I was looking for someone like me," began Jason, remembering what he saw in the minds of those who cared so much for him, "I would find out pretty quick by scanning ordinary people's minds." Jason rested his hands on the benchtop, finding the hard, rough surface an anchor. His current world, unglued from anything normal, was battered and filled with enemies. "My face will jump out real clear. It is no longer safe for me here. Too many know."

"You're leaving?" Suzy whined, reaching out to grab his hand. The thought of his not living in the Dubois house crushed her. Her eyes filled.

"Yes and no." Jason grinned at the perplexed expressions on their faces.

Russ smiled. "You can come live with me if ya need another place."

"It is not the house I intend to leave. I plan on leaving people's minds." Jason leaned back on the stool. "I need both of you to help me. I intend to set off a memory bomb that reaches all the way to Kearny."

"Wow," Russ said, clearly attracted to the idea of setting off an explosive of any sort. He stared blankly as the cogs in his mind sped up. A mischievous smile curled his lips. He envisioned the flame as it slowly touched the fuse on a cherry bomb the size of a house.

"Do you know how to do it, Jason?" Suzy asked, looking askance at Russ while he envisioned a long line of detonations.

"I know how to modify a small group of people's minds but not a whole town." Jason pictured the outcome he wanted, and he suddenly felt old and worn too thin. He looked up abruptly and focused. This was not the time to give in to weakness. "I will have to practice and work out the details. One big detail is determining if I have the strength to do this thing."

"Practice?" Russ asked, ready for action. "On who?" The devilish smile never left his face.

"On you, on the chanters out front, on as many as possible," Jason said. "Start small with little stuff at first." He smiled and looked directly at Russ. "I need your ideas." He wanted all of his brilliant, zany ideas.

"How soon do you want to set off the bomb?" Suzy asked. Her gaze switched from one boy to the other, as though she sat at a tennis match and followed the ball across the court.

"Before school starts," Jason said, rubbing his chin.

"Ya got two weeks." Russ's legs started to twitch.

"Yeah, that's not very long." Suzy looked to Jason.

"Ya want to try something now?" Russ asked.

Jason could tell he had something bubbling in his mind.

Russ vibrated with his idea, already laughing. "Like, on the people out front?" he said. "There must be about twenty still out there. Maybe you could get them to go away."

"Good idea, Russ," Jason said cautiously as he leaned forward. "But something small just to see if it works."

"Well …" Russ's eyes sparkled. He laughed and then took on a serious demeanor. "You could give all of them the notion that they need to go pee … really bad."

"Russ!" Suzy screamed, unable to hide her smile. "That's so gross."

"Yeah, but it won't really hurt anyone, and we'll know real quick if Jason can do what he needs to do."

Jason laughed. "Why not?"

✯   ✯   ✯

Fifteen minutes later, Frank came out of the second-floor bathroom, still reading an article on the economy in the local paper, when a body rushed past him. The door slammed shut. He looked up and wondered what happened; he saw kids lined up. Each child did a dance in place to make it easier to control his or her bladder.

"Why not use …" Frank began.

"The line's longer downstairs," said Rachel, who stood with her legs crossed and bounced against the wall.

"Oh." Not wanting to go any further into the issue, he folded the paper and marched downstairs. When he reached the bottom step, he saw Suzy and Russ. They were peeking out of the living-room windows. Frank pulled aside the sheer curtain at the side of the front door and looked out.

"Well, well," he said, delighted, "our crusaders seem to have given up." The kids at the living-room window erupted into a fit of giggles. As he turned toward the kitchen, he wondered why Jason was not with his friends.

✫   ✫   ✫

Russ and Suzy returned to the shed and sat at the tool bench. They looked down on an inert Jason, unconscious on the cot.

"How long do you think he'll sleep?" Russ asked.

"Hard to say." Suzy looked concerned.

Jason had performed the experiment from the shed. He had finished floating, stood up, and stretched— and then crumpled to the floor. Together Russ and Suzy had lifted him onto the cot. They remained with him for a while until Russ suggested they go check on the people who crowded the front of the house. The experiment had worked. That's when they took up their stations in the shed and stood guard until Jason came around.

Russ turned to Suzy. "So I guess he bit off more than he could chew. This is good. Now he knows his limit on this one."

"Yeah, I kinda got a feeling he was getting weak." Suzy drummed her fingers on the benchtop.

Russ grinned, about to make a moronic comment on Suzy's relationship with Jason, but thought better of it. Instead he said, "We haven't had a good talk for a while. It looks like we might have some time on our hands. What do you think?"

"That's an idea." She stood up. "There's an old deck of cards in the kitchen. We can play Gin or Crazy Eights or something and … talk."

"Good. I'll sit tight and keep an eye on our man here."

Suzy left and then returned minutes later with cards, a pitcher of Kool-Aid, and glasses.

"What will it be?" Russ asked.

"Crazy Eights." Suzy handed him the cards, and he started shuffling them. As Suzy filled the glasses, Russ dealt.

"So," he said, "you'll be going into Mrs. Needham's when school starts."

"What's she like?" Suzy laid a queen of hearts on the two of hearts face up on the bench.

"We were pretty hard on her. Called her Needles. But she really wasn't so bad." Russ changed the suit with a queen of spades. "She really likes kids who read and try hard. And she likes girls better than boys, but that's not unusual."

A single loud snore erupted from Jason. Both kids turned their heads and smiled when they realized it was nothing.

"Clearing the boogers," Russ said. "Nothing to worry about."

"Yeah." Suzy concentrated on her cards. "I like to read. So I guess maybe Mrs. Needham will like me."

"Are you kiddin'? She'll *love* you."

Russ and Suzy talked continuously as they finished several games of Crazy Eights and Gin, not caring who won.

Jason finally woke up. Still woozy, he sat on the edge of the cot. "What'd I miss?" He looked from Russ to Suzy.

"A whole lot of flushing, my man." Russ was happy to see his friend recovered. "A whole lot of flushing."

The next afternoon Frank sat at the kitchen table. He read the paper and enjoyed a fresh cup of coffee. It was not long before Lydia found him. "See this?" she said acidly.

"Yes, what of it?" Frank had finally begun to tire of Lydia's constant negativity.

"It's the boy." She snatched the paper from him and showed him the front page. The headline read, "Water Pressure Plunges." According to the article, the water pressure for the whole of Franklin Chase dropped dangerously low for about twenty minutes when the whole town flushed their toilets at roughly the same time. "He had something to do with this. First, those people out there." The petitioners for Jason's intersession had returned. "Now this. Why are you so blind to what is going on around here?" Lydia rolled the page tight, slapped the top of the kitchen table with it, and threw it down in disgust. "What's with you?"

With great care, Frank picked up the paper, opened it to where he had been reading, and looked directly into her eyes. "I see a great many coincidences that may mean nothing, or they may point to the boy being a miracle worker. His name, by the way, is Jason." Frank took a sip of his coffee. "If Jason is a living, breathing saint able to do these things you say he is doing, then we better take damn good care of him so we can enjoy some of his blessings."

"What ..." Lydia gaped at him. For the first time, Frank had stood up to her.

Frank held his cup in his right hand and slowly swirled the coffee. "Let me tell you what I see, especially since you have been incapacitated by your headaches. I figure since about March, the kids in this house have been doing better. That was about the same time the lock came off the toolshed. I haven't had to restrain any of them. That's a good thi—"

Lydia interrupted. "It's also cost us—"

"All of them are working together to help each other. I've been able to work more overtime. In fact, we have made money and increased our savings." He set down his cup. "The load on me for laundry, meals—all that stuff—is much less. The kids are helping out." He stood up and said forcefully, "And I am damned glad we are well out of the drug business. It was more trouble than it was worth and downright dangerous."

A silence grew in the room—the calm before a storm.

"It's better in this house," Frank continued. "I will not mess that up. So get over it. Whether Jason had anything to do with all this is not important." He paused. "I don't believe for a second he did. He's just a kid. The fact is, things are just better."

"Now you listen to me, you twit." Lydia shook as rage flowed through her body, reverberating with no outlet. She aimed her index finger at Frank.

"Stop!" he shouted before she attacked. "That's enough!" Frank let his words echo in the room. "If you no longer want to be here, then I will split what we have with you, and you can go your own way. I am sure you don't want the children. You've made that clear over the years."

"You want me to go," Lydia choked out. The radiating headache made it hard to think.

"It suddenly occurred to me," Frank said, sitting back down, "that spending time in your company was not all that different from spending time with my mother. Now, why would I want to endure such abuse?" He leaned back in the chair and glared at her.

Lydia said nothing. She turned, stumbled on her first step but regained her balance, and left the room. Moving swiftly to her bedroom, she popped open a pill bottle taken from one of the children. She poured a number of the sedative pills into her shaking hands and swallowed. She did not feel the tears as they ran down her cheeks.

Frank watched her go and then returned to his article and coffee. Something had changed, and maybe it *was* Jason, but he didn't care. He liked what he had found in himself. Lydia would have to get with the program or go.

It made him sad to think that she would probably go. They had pulled through some tough times together over the years, but things were different now.

"Money's not everything, damn it," he said to no one in particular.

Chapter 26

T he metal plate cover shot across the hall in an upward trajectory like a flying saucer escaping Earth's gravity. It crashed into the wall and clanged its way to a landing on the tiled hallway floor. Seconds before launch, the nurse's aide flew out of the patient's room, running for her life.

"Well," said the charge nurse behind the chest-high floor desk. She set aside the chart where she had updated the day's dispensed medications and looked over the tops of her reading glasses. "I guess Edna did not like her lunch again."

"No, she didn't." The young aide had her hand on her chest and was taking a few deep breaths to calm her racing heart.

The two looked up when the white ceramic plate followed the cover, hitting the wall food-side first. It stuck a moment and then slid down the wall. A trail of red sauce mixed with lines of broken pasta like bleeding white worms followed the plate to the floor.

Wednesday was pasta day at the hospital. A whiff of cheap tomato sauce, not unlike tomato soup, wafted down the hall.

"Just a bad Edna day." The nurse picked up another chart as she thought, *I wouldn't eat that stuff either*. She looked at the stressed young woman and said, "Take a break, honey. Let her calm down. You know the drill."

The aide nodded and left the floor, using the stairs to go to the cafeteria. When she was gone, the charge nurse let her glasses dangle from the chain around her neck, left the nurse's station, and steeled herself. She found Edna in her wheelchair, sipping a cup of orange juice.

"Edna, what are we going to do with you? You've got to stop throwing stuff at our aides." The nurse sat on the edge of the chair next to the elderly woman.

The three other beds in the room lay empty. Their occupants were kept busy in the day room. The staff worked hard to get Edna's roommates up and out early. After the cantankerous, old woman fell asleep, her roommates went to bed. It was easier that way. A battle avoided made for a better day.

Edna looked her over and said, "Give me some decent food, and I won't have to chuck it." She hated the white uniform, the white stockings, and the dinky white hat they all wore. Edna drank more juice.

The nurse realized her most difficult charge was every bit as angry and put out as she was when her son visited. If anything, his visits did more to unsettle her than make things better. She made a mental note to discuss this with Mr. Dubois. Maybe he should not visit as often.

"Well, let's not forget what Dr. Watts said about getting too excited and your blood pressure. It's high enough to cause trouble. You need to calm down." Edna waved her off. The charge nurse stared at the wrinkled woman in the wheelchair and shook her head frustrated. She used to think no patient was a lost cause, but this one had proved her wrong. She stood and left the room.

Twenty minutes later, the aide returned. She checked in with the nurse at the front desk.

"Quiet as a mouse," the charge nurse said. "Not a word or projectile since you left. She probably fell asleep." She smiled and nodded in the direction of Edna's room. "Go check."

When the aide entered the room, she stopped short. Edna lay on the floor surrounded by scattered photographs, pulled out of a bottom dresser drawer. She shook with sobs. Tears poured down, dripping onto the floor.

"Edna?" the shocked aide asked, almost in a whisper.

"What have I done?" the old woman moaned. "None of them have come to visit." She picked up some pictures and held them out to the aide, who made no move toward the stricken woman, and then tossed them away. She pointed to others, an array of photos with her and children smiling. "They don't come. They don't care. I shoulda done better. I shoulda been better."

Her chest heaved. "Get my Franky!" She started to crawl to the aide, frozen at the door. "Did ya hear me! Get my Franky now! He's the only one who cares." She cried and whined like a four-year-old. "Get me my Franky!"

Wednesday afternoon, the day that spaghetti slithered down the walls at the state hospital, Frank took off like a rocket for Kearny. Jason watched from the side of the house as Frank dashed across the front yard. The car burned rubber as it pulled away from the curb; it shot down the street.

Jason returned to the shed, satisfied. He was ready. With borrowed mental energy from Suzy and Russ, who felt fatigued afterward, Jason had opened one targeted mind fifty miles away with pinpoint accuracy. Doors long closed in Frank's mother's mind had swung wide, and like junk in an overfull closet, the wreckage of the past had tumbled into her frontal lobes. Awareness had overwhelmed her denial of long-imprisoned truths.

A short time after he made the changes, Jason sat in the toolshed with his friends and waited. Just after Edna had struggled from her wheelchair onto the floor, squirmed across the floor to the dresser, and scattered the pictures from the bottom drawer, Jason had heard the phone ring in the house. The nurse told Frank that his mother had demanded, cried, and shouted that her son must come to her. Frank had revved up the Valiant and sped down the highway, pushing the speed limit. He was headed toward a dream come true.

"I guess this is it." Jason looked at Russ and Suzy as he entered the shed after Frank took off for the hospital. "We need to pull everyone together and do this thing."

"Jason, what exactly are you going to do?" Suzy asked. She sat at the bench, her head resting on her outstretched arm.

"Yeah, I was kinda wondering myself." Russ sat on the stool next to her. He rubbed his eyes and yawned.

"I want to try to be a normal kid for a while." Jason plopped onto his usual stool, mildly amused by their lethargy. "So I need folks to know me as just a regular kid. Some will know a bit more, like Chang and Mr. Downing. Only you two will know everything about what has happened."

"Yeah?" Russ said. "The only problem with that is you're not a normal kid."

"I will stop using my abilities, Russ, and be normal." Jason stared out of the shed door. He longed to fit in and be safe. Small birds—wrens, he thought—congregated around the garbage cans at the side of the house. They chirped loudly and flapped their wings. They fought over half-eaten pieces of bread lying on the ground. "Besides I need to hide out from the bad guys. Ya know?" *Fight to survive,* he thought. He watched the crusts get pounded apart and the crumbs devoured by the stronger birds.

"Oh, right." Russ yawned again. "I forgot. You're in hiding." He waved his arm to signal that nothing more need be said. "Got it."

"What about Frank and Lydia?" Suzy closed her eyes, unable to fight the desire to drift off to sleep.

"Yes, there are a few people who will need custom work, special treatment. If I do things right, I'll be a dumb, likeable kid just like Russ." Jason smiled.

Russ sat up straight. "Hey! Wait a minute!" Suzy raised her head, eyes wide, startled awake by Russ's loud complaint.

"Just kidding, man." Jason winked at Suzy, who looked at Russ fondly. "You're one of a kind."

"When and where?" Suzy asked. Her head floated back down onto her arm. She smiled dreamily.

"I need to get those who know the most gathered at the sanctuary by the big oak tree where Chiang and I meditate. I will set it up." Jason ran down the list of names silently; he used his fingers to keep tally. "With you and Russ, that makes six in all. I will plant the suggestions for everyone to come together on Saturday afternoon at three o'clock."

"Zero hour," said Russ, who abandoned his stool, unable to resist the siren call of the old cot. He climbed onto the mattress and was snoring softly a few moments later.

"How are you holding up?" Jason asked Suzy as he gazed down on his sleeping friend.

"Tired some but keeping up." Suzy felt physically weak from Jason's use but mentally energized in his presence. "I will take a nap later."

"So now we come down to it." Jason felt ready and excited to leave his current life as far behind as possible.

On Sunday morning, Frank stood on the front porch and leaned on the railing. His mother had died quietly in her sleep late Saturday night. After hearing the news, he had hung up the phone and stumbled out the front door. The walls had closed in on him; he couldn't breathe inside the house. He paced the front yard, threw his arms to the sky, and prayed. He kept moving and muttering to himself. He screamed at the injustice of it all until he calmed. He wound up on the porch confused, not knowing what he should do or feel.

The last four days with his mother had been a marvel. She begged his forgiveness. They talked for hours about what had happened and why it happened. Everything he believed he would have to claw out of her, she gave willingly. What he needed in order to get on with things in his life, she provided without cost. If the nurses had not insisted that he leave, he would have stayed all night every night to be with her. Frank needed time to work things out in his head for both of them. Fate decided four days was enough.

Frank stared out over the street. He did not react when he heard the front door creak on its hinges.

"So the old hag is dead?" Lydia, in her usual stance—hands on hips— looked at Frank. He turned slowly to face her.

"Yes, Edna is dead." Frank waited for the venom to pour out of her mouth.

"She never cared very much for me—or you either, for that matter. Why all the fuss?" Her mouth twitched. She sensed his vulnerability. A laugh would have escaped, but for her self-control. Pleasure in others' pain wrapped around her psyche like a welcoming embrace.

"Yes," Frank said. "She detested both of us for a long time. But—"

"Damn right she did. That old …" Lydia stopped. Something was not right. "What's goin' on?" she said slowly.

"She changed." Frank straightened up and faced her. "She begged me to forgive her for being such an uncaring—"

"Bit—?"

"Shut up, Lydia!" Frank fumed at her. He would not back down. "*Mother*, I was going to say."

This was different. Lydia had seen it coming, but she refused to believe that Frank would ever find the backbone. He did, and now he refused to bow to her demands. She tried another tack—to break him.

"I'm starting to feel like my old self." She sought Frank's weaknesses. "My headaches are going away it seems."

"Good." Frank did not like seeing her in pain, but he liked being in charge when she retreated to her bed. "You can help out more."

"I was thinking more along the lines of getting back to the money." She studied him carefully.

"The money," he scoffed and shook his head. Frank recognized her pose, like a statue; she had not moved an inch since she started her rant. This was so familiar. "The money is fine. The principal grows. It's the kids that need some help."

"The kids?" she snorted derisively. "Since when—"

"Since now! Haven't we had this conversation before?" Frank sensed a repeating pattern that he could not quite recall. There was something, but his memory failed him. Her discounting the children was not right. Doing right struck him as important.

"You're nuts," Lydia fired off. "The kids have always been a means to an end. What are you … getting all high and mighty?" Her voice rose an octave. "Remember who got us this far."

"Yeah, I know how we got here." Frank returned his attention to the street. A car drove by slowly. *Probably heading to church*, he thought. "Stay or go. Things have to change around here." He stood his ground, though his legs felt weak. His body sagged an inch as his knees bent. Frank suddenly realized how bone weary the last few days had left him.

"Wait a minute!" Lydia sensed his unfamiliar assurance; he had failed to fall into line behind whatever she wanted. *What has been going on?* she asked herself. "You've changed." She wanted to tear him down, watch him wilt before her. "So all of this happened, you, your mother … what? All of a sudden, out of nowhere?"

Frank stopped ignoring her and faced her. He wanted to smack the smug look off her face.

"Ya know what I think?" Lydia asked.

"No, what do you think?" Frank asked sarcastically.

"The boy had something to do with this." She felt absolutely sure.

"Jason, you mean." Frank glared at her intently. "Just give it up. If it's anything, it's coincidence."

"You are such a—"

"Yeah, I am, and you're stuck with me unless you have plans to take off?" Frank turned away from her. "You ready to make a decision—right here, right now?"

Instead of going for the jugular, Lydia left the porch silently without a word. The desire to hurt and control had triggered a massive headache. She slunk away to find darkness and quiet.

Frank remained on the porch, out of the suffocating house. Something had changed, something he could not comprehend. His thoughts returned to his mother, and the tears started flowing down his cheeks. This surprised him. This time he did not stifle them. He wept for the joy of the last four days and the sorrow. There would be no more.

Chapter 27

⚡

At three sharp on the day Frank's mother passed, Jason surveyed the people who genuinely cared about him. They sat in a circle beneath the old oak tree in the sanctuary. He could not have wished for a more beautiful day or a better cadre of friends. Suzy and Russ sat next to him to his right and left respectively. Mr. Downing took a position next to Suzy. Jason smiled as his older friend found it difficult to get into a comfortable sitting position on the ground.

"You have to give us old folks a minute." Mr. Downing chuckled and finally managed after much grunting to get his legs crossed in front of him. Next to Mr. Downing sat Mary Deloro, perched on the bright-blue blanket she'd brought with her. Louise sat on a green blanket next to Mary. Like her sister, she wore beige cotton pants, a white blouse, and a big, floppy hat.

"Speak for yourself," responded Louise, who easily found the correct meditation position, legs crossed, back straight. The circle finished with Chiang in his usual black attire, ready to begin.

"I cannot tell you how much it means to me that you agreed to allow me to use you as I will," Jason began. They nodded and smiled at him. "You will not feel much of anything." *You will, however, hear me as you are now.* His last words registered in their minds.

"Oh my," both ladies said with a sudden intake of breath.

"I'll be damned," came from Mr. Downing.

Chiang and Suzy showed no reaction.

"Cool." Russ said.

Please close your eyes, relax, and try to clear your minds. It will be quiet for a time.

Jason watched as they tried to calm themselves without much success, except for Suzy and Chiang. The forest around whispered the comings and goings of life. The birds called among the trees. Chipmunks dashed from cover to cover amid the ferns. The wind gently jostled the leaves overhead. A limb creaked.

Jason helped where needed to push his circle into a meditative state. Once done, he did not wait; he took over his friends' minds. They would remember nothing of his activities inside their heads.

The first stage was the easiest. Like sending out the urge to use the bathroom, Jason constructed the memory modifications. He extracted the energy from the circle of minds. The power increased exponentially. Like the metal casing around a bomb is unable to hold the blast once triggered, Jason reached his limit to hold it back and let it go. The force of it affected every human being for miles around.

Jason relaxed. He took a moment to recoup. The weariness came on him suddenly. He opened his eyes, stood up, took a step, and stumbled. Throwing out his left arm, he steadied himself against the tree's trunk.

"Stupid." Passing out was not something he could afford. "I should have prepared for this," he whispered. He walked around the great oak and stretched, fighting the mind-numbing fatigue. At least his cohorts sat oblivious to what had happened. He yawned and returned to his position in the circle. Stage two began.

Jason jumped from one mind to the next, starting with Mr. Downing. Certain memories evaporated. In each case, he found himself in a large room full of filing cabinets. He wore a white coat and carried a clipboard.

"Ah, yes." Jason scanned his list. He placed a check in the small box beside every needed change. As the pencil flicked in the box, the change took place. Jason also pulled files from several cabinets identified ahead of time when he placed the suggestion to meet at the bird sanctuary.

The library ladies, Mr. Downing, and Chiang no longer knew of his abilities. From now on they would recognize him as a bright young man with a good mind for learning. Jason also tagged one sheet with a special instruction and placed it into Mr. Downing's file. His work within his immediate circle was complete.

Jason felt sad that he would no longer be able to confide in these good people. At some point, however, he would restore them if he survived. He placed them all into a deep sleep, except for Suzy and Russ, who were needed for his final effort.

Jason's radar thoughts reached out and found Lydia Dubois's mind easily. She hid her head under a pillow, blocking all light in a desperate search for relief from her migraine. She slipped into a deep sleep at Jason's insistence. He worked her files and added a few new suggestions. He jumped out of her filing area when done, into a bleak landscape where Lydia willfully sought others' destruction for her gain or pleasure.

There the vestiges of the force fields and triggers he put in place glowed. Jason had stopped her worst behavior, but it was evident that she fought her way into these tracts anyway. The explosive aftermath, huge holes in the landscape, lay all about. *No wonder she spent so much time in bed, debilitated by the headaches,* he thought. Jason removed the force fields over most of the area, but not all. She would be her old self, almost. Finished with Lydia, Jason sped off to settle things with Frank.

Frank was not close. Jason stretched his abilities more than ever before. He took more energy from Suzy and Russ. He discovered Frank by his mother's bed in Kearny, watching over her as she slept.

The work on Frank turned out to be the most difficult. On his own, he had managed to change some of his own files regarding Lydia and his mother. Jason needed some of those pages restored for things to get back to normal in the Dubois house.

"No, you can't." Jason heard Suzy's voice. "Let it play out, Jason. You can make changes later if you need to."

Shocked, Jason turned and saw Suzy's face. It floated as if on television. She looked down on him. "How are you doing this?" he asked.

"I … I don't know. I just suddenly woke up and knew what you were going to do, and I had to stop you." Her image frowned down.

"Why?" Jason felt his security threatened. Leaving Frank's emotional improvements in place was a risk.

"Do no harm, Jason." Suzy's face faded; her words echoed to silence. Jason was free to choose. He scanned his clipboard. One item remained unchecked; the power was his. The risk that he might be found through Frank scared him. What happened to Russ's little sister would not happen to him. One check and Jason would be safe. Frank would be back in his hell hole with Edna and Lydia lording over him, and Jason would breathe easier.

He tapped his pencil against the clipboard. He rocked back and forth on his heels, unsure which path to take. Finally he touched pencil to paper. *I'm gonna regret this no end*. With a quick stroke, Jason crossed out the issue. It faded from the list like disappearing ink as it dries.

He knew Suzy had it right: the high road no matter what. *Besides, I am not like Lydia*. Jason pulled back to the confines of his own mind, satisfied that his actions had worked as intended. He disconnected from Suzy and Russ and managed to open his eyes a moment. He saw his circle of friends asleep. Satisfied they were safe, he fell back, unconscious.

Chapter 28

"I may have killed her," moaned Jason on Sunday morning. The rumor of Frank's mother's death spread quickly through the house. He fretted in the kitchen with Suzy as Frank braved Lydia's onslaught.

"No, you didn't," Suzy insisted. "You would have seen it. You would have fixed it if you saw it coming. It wasn't there. How could you know?" She touched Jason's shoulder as he sat at the table.

"How can I know? How ... how can you be so sure?" Jason stuttered. He felt guilty and fearful beyond anything he had known. His actions might have killed someone. His stomach churned. He felt like he might throw up.

"Look at me," Suzy said. Jason bounced his forehead on the tabletop. "Look at me!" she yelled. Slowly he raised his head and turned to look at her. "When have you ever done anything to hurt anyone? When you had Lydia completely in your control, did you hurt her?" Suzy waited a heartbeat. "No, you didn't. You did something to help all of us."

Jason stared at her; he could not comprehend what she said. He felt responsible. He was the superhero. *Superheroes don't kill people.* Frank's mother was dead.

"She was old! She died, but you had nothing to do with her death. If anything you made things better as you always have when you do what you do. Do I need to remind you?" Suzy fumed, frustrated with Jason's stubbornness.

"I need to talk to Frank." Jason jumped to his feet and started for the porch.

As if on cue, the front door opened and closed. They heard Lydia's footsteps on the stairs to the second floor. Jason headed outside and found Frank crying. His foster father straightened up and glared at Jason as he walked out onto the porch. Jason stopped, ready to back off and leave him alone.

Frank smiled and waved him over when he saw who it was. He wiped his eyes. "Sorry, I thought you were Lydia coming back for round two." The two just stared at each other for a moment, neither sure what to say.

"I am so sorry about your mom, Frank," Jason finally said. "I mean, that's the last thing I wanted to see happen." He fidgeted under Frank's intense gaze.

"Thanks. I had hoped to hear something like that from … someone else." He nodded toward the house. Then he let it go, knowing that blood never comes from a stone. After a pause he said, "I knew it was coming. Her dying, I mean."

He thought for a second and realized that he really liked this kid. He looked at Jason for a moment and thought that if he had a son, he would want him to be like the toolshed kid. He smiled and remembered what he and Lydia used to think of him.

"I thought," Frank continued, "she would pass on and leave nothing settled—settled for me, that is." He took a deep breath. "She gave me a gift, then died before I could say thanks." He choked on his last words. Jason said nothing; he waited. "It was a CVA, 'cause of her high blood pressure. A cerebral vascular accident, the doctors called it. They were surprised she lasted as long as she did." Frank stared off into the distance and whispered, "Four days is better than nothing."

"I'm still sorry, Frank. You shoulda had more time." Frank just nodded, his tears flowing again. Jason left him alone.

A few hours later, Jason met Russ and Suzy in the shed. "Looks like, I probably didn't kill her," Jason said as he entered.

"So what happened with your foster dad's mom?" Russ asked from his usual spot at the tool bench.

"She was sick. I didn't look for it." Jason sighed and took a seat. "I might have saved her, but I just didn't take the time to look."

"You're being too hard on yourself." Suzy would not allow him to take responsibility for any part of this death. "You had no reason to look for anything. As a matter of fact, you simply tested your abilities and did Frank a big favor. So ..."

"Okay, Suzy," Jason said harshly. Then he said more softly, "Okay." Jason never wanted to feel this way again. He would never be less than thorough in the future.

Fortunately Russ decided it was time for a change of subject. "I have no idea what happened by the oak tree." He scratched his nose with his fingers and looked at Jason. "I kinda recall carrying you somewhere."

Russ and Jason turned to Suzy. "Fill us in," Jason said. "What happened? I have no memory of it either."

"Well, I woke up first," Suzy said. Her annoyance with Jason slipped away. "Russ was half awake. You," she said as she pointed at Jason, "were lying across the roots of the tree, out like a light. The adults were asleep too." She took a deep breath. "I pushed and tugged on Russ to help me half drag and half carry you beyond the hedge where the broken fountain is. Then I waited. Russ fell asleep again on your shoulder. It was kinda cute, you two leaning together."

"Oh God," moaned Russ. "Don't you ever repeat this outside of our little group."

Jason just chuckled.

Suzy continued. "The adults woke up before Jason came around. They acted confused at first; then they got up and walked away as if on a mission."

"When did I come around?" Jason asked.

"Not long after the adults left." Suzy smiled at Jason. It made him uncomfortable. She knew something he didn't.

"Yeah, yeah, yeah," Russ said. "So what happened with the bomb? Did it all work?" Russ squirmed in place, ready to jump out of his skin in anticipation.

"Yes, Russ," Jason said, turning to his energetic friend. "It worked. I'm just a kid to everyone. A very smart kid to a few." He returned his gaze to Suzy.

"And, and …?" Russ wanted details.

"Well, I did a few special things for you." Jason nodded to Russ. "The girls are going to love you, my friend. You're going to start wearing dresses and growing your hair long and …"

"Sonuvabitch." Russ believed every word Jason spoke.

Suzy laughed out loud. Jason's serious demeanor gave way to laughter too. Russ was just too good a target.

"Just a regular kid, Russ. Nothing more than that." Jason slapped his back and laughed at his reaction.

"Hey, man, don't do that." Russ ran his fingers through his hair. "Like, I take you very seriously. The girls like me well enough, ya know?" He calmed and sat quietly for a moment. "So what did you tell the adults in our circle to do?"

"Basically I set things up so they would return to a familiar site, like their homes or the library. Once there, they'd do a few little familiar things. About then their memories of me would change." Jason smiled sadly.

"What more did you do?" Suzy asked, suspicious.

"Let's just say that Mr. Downing will be visiting the library a lot more."

"Mary?" Suzy asked.

"Of course."

"You set up ol' Downer and Mrs. Tremont?" Russ laughed.

"Do you think that was wise?" Suzy sounded worried; she ignored Russ's amusement.

"It will be the greatest thing he will never thank me for." Jason felt good about his little action on Mary's behalf.

"Hey," Russ yelled, "I may want to never thank you sometime too. I'll let you know for what."

"So," Suzy said, "that explains it."

"Explains what?" Jason asked.

"Why Mr. Downing and Mrs. Tremont left the park arm in arm. It was dear." Suzy dropped all her opposition and acknowledged Jason's action on Mary's behalf as a good thing. "It was probably long overdue."

"Thanks," Jason said, smiling broadly. He could not read Suzy's mind, but he imagined what she described nevertheless.

They spent the rest of the day enjoying each other's company. They joined Rachel and the other Dubois house inmates for lunch. Later even Frank joined and insisted that Russ stay for dinner. The plans for his mother's funeral could be set aside for a time. He taught them how to play poker.

First he broke out a new deck of cards and strands of uncooked spaghetti. He snapped the pasta in half and laid the pieces in the middle of the table. "Why don't you guys divvy those up," he said, as he headed to the basement. "I need something from downstairs." He returned after a few minutes with a bread-basket-sized off-white box. "Too quiet, don't you think? We need some music." He placed the old radio on the counter next to the sink, plugged it into the socket under the cabinet, and fiddled with the dials. A song blasted out. "I left my heart in San Francisco ..."

"Aw, that Tony Bennett can sing a good tune." He turned down the volume and returned to his seat. "Are we set?"

"All set," many voices said simultaneously.

"Whoever wins the most eats the best tonight, my friends." Frank laughed as the kids around the kitchen table giggled. He hadn't felt this good in a long time. He could not remember when he last laughed spontaneously. "Five-card draw is the name of the game. Everyone ante up. One piece will do."

Spaghetti strands rolled to the middle of the table. The cards slid across the tabletop. Jason saw no ghosts haunting the occupants at the table. He heard only what was said aloud. This was the best time he could ever recall. Easily bluffed, he turned out to be a lousy poker player. But the big winners, Suzy and Sam, shared their winnings. Everyone ate well and everyone laughed.

Chapter 29

On a rainy Saturday afternoon late in September in a suburb of Bismarck, North Dakota, children concentrated on their tasks so they could meet the deadline. Reena Sorenson supervised her crew of eight- and nine-year-olds, gathered in groups of four around her enormous kitchen table. The kids, boys and girls, laughed and giggled. They squished cookie dough through their fingers, certain to mix all the ingredients well.

A boy leaned closer to his partner, a girl wearing a pink dress under a white apron, and said, "Like sticking your hands down a clogged drain full a fish guts?"

"Ewww, gross!" cried the girls around the table. They laughed. Quickly the game became who could find the most disgusting description of what they pressed between their fingers. Worms and three-day-old mashed potatoes with gravy had given way to fresh, warm cow pies when Mrs. Sorenson stepped in.

"Enough, my dears; we have a schedule to keep." She tapped the kitchen counter near the sink with her large wooden spoon.

"Oh jeez, Mrs. S, we were just 'bout to get to the good ones," whined a brown-haired boy at the end of the table.

"Don't be petulant, my dear Edward." She frowned at the eight-year-old.

"Yes ma'am. Sorry ma'am," the boy said quickly.

Reena went from bowl to bowl and checked the consistency and readiness of the cookie dough. The neighborhood kids loved her. Mrs. S's kitchen could be fun, and you might learn a thing or two. Having fun, of course, trumped learning. Some of the parents of these children had made cookies in Reena's kitchen when they were eight or nine.

"Cookie sheets, everyone. Start shaping the balls. You are all doing very well. There will be cookies going home today." She smiled as the children cheered. A mountain of chocolate chip or oatmeal cookies poured out of her oven for the end of the summer festival.

Reena, an attractive woman with black hair falling just below her ear—a practical cut, she called it—showed streaks of gray. She had been around for a long time, but her face did not betray her age. The gray she added with hair dye, a sensible thing to do in her opinion. She stood five feet six inches and could be described as sturdy in her build but not overweight. A whirlwind of activity, Reena stood as the standard by which other women were measured. To be told you had pulled off a Mrs. S. was the highest of compliments in her neighborhood.

Every head turned when someone knocked at the kitchen door. Mr. Bill Sorenson stepped into the warm room full of magnificent odors. He clapped his hands in appreciation.

"Are we going to make it this year?" He glanced at the children in mock skepticism of their ability to deliver to Reena's exacting specifications. Like his wife, his full head of brown hair possessed the marks of aging at his temples, but his face told another tale. No shadows of wrinkles or laugh lines touched his pleasant face. At six feet tall, he emanated health as he stood in the kitchen entry in his green T-shirt dotted with wood splinters. When not working for their Community, Bill spent his days shaping wood into beautiful and useful pieces of furniture. He often disappeared into his workshop behind their house for days. Bill returned to the house only when a piece was finished, the first layer of stain drying.

A quiet man, he and Reena suited each other well.

She leaned over and kissed Bill on the cheek. "We're already ahead of schedule." They stood and watched the kids for a moment. Then Reena whispered to Bill, "I need to talk to you." He nodded. They stepped back into the hallway.

"I spoke to Rodney," she said softly. She let out a long, disappointed breath.

"He messed up again?" Bill frowned. He brushed the wood debris from his shirt.

"Maybe." She shrugged. "Maybe not. You know how he is." She shook her head, disappointed. "I would have left it alone except I picked up a whisper of another event. By the time I was able to focus my full attention, it was gone." She shook her head, crossed her arms, and sighed. "Either I mistook some background noise as something significant, or there is a new power with which we must reckon."

Bill nodded. "What do you need done?"

"It's not what I need," she said, suddenly cross. "It's what the Community needs." Reena defined all her special actions as "good of the Community."

"Of course," he said. He sensed her concern and her need to rationalize her actions.

She looked into his pleasant face and calmed. Bill had that effect on her. She said, "I want you to take the next month or two and scout in Philadelphia and the area south of the city for any signs of our special abilities."

"I may not be the best choice for this task." Bill leaned back against the wall, clearly a bit shocked by the request. Reena showed no concern. "You know I can't read thoughts to discern what has happened. You may want a more talented scout."

"You can't be read, is more to the point." She placed her hand gently on his chest. "If Rodney got it wrong, there may be a very powerful person living there. We need to know—and you, my dear, are perfect for the task."

"I understand. Makes sense." His hand covered hers affectionately.

"I would expect you to be back by Thanksgiving." She pulled her hand out from under his and put her arms on his shoulders. She pulled him into an embrace. "Just take your time and settle this for me, okay?"

"Okay, hon. I'll take care of everything. I always do." Bill leaned down and kissed her lips, hugging her tight.

"Mrs. S?" asked a shy voice from the kitchen entrance.

"What now, Edward?" She let go, stepped back from her husband, and turned to the child.

"We think we're ready for the next batch to go into the oven." The boy's face showed clear signs of having sampled the raw cookie mix. Chocolate started from the corner of his mouth and gave him a brown, painted smile. Reena chuckled.

"Then by all means we need to get this train rolling down those tracks. Into the oven they go." She shooed him back into the kitchen. She turned and smiled at Bill, who returned her affection with a grin of his own. He headed upstairs to start packing. When Reena asked, everyone—especially Bill—jumped. Tomorrow he would be in Philadelphia.

As Bill collected his things and packed his bags, Jason shared the backseat of the blue Valiant with Suzy and Rachel. Jim, the eldest of the foster children, sat in the front with Frank. The mood was somber; the kids wore their best, which meant the cleanest jeans, shirts, and socks available to them. Frank wore a navy jacket over a white shirt and tie. He drove fast toward Kearny. It was the last time.

When Frank pulled up in front of Heaven's Angels funeral home, he killed the engine and took a deep breath. He turned to the kids. "Thanks for coming along. I hope you know ... well ... you didn't have to. I appreciate it."

"It's okay, Frank," Rachel said.

Jim nodded. "Yeah, we all agreed."

As Frank opened his door, they all climbed out. They stood under the awning and waited for him to lead the way.

"Mr. Dubois, at last," said a smiling, heavy-set man in a dark, gray three-piece suit. It made his pale complexion look even more ghoulish. His dark hair receded. His meaty jowls suggested he missed few meals. "Your dear deceased mother lies in our Assumption Room. The wake will last until six p.m. We would greatly appreciate you staying until then." Frank nodded. "Excellent. Please follow me."

The fat man, who ignored the children, had the good sense to say nothing more. He led Frank to Edna. The thought of staying for three hours did not appeal to the kids, but they had accepted Frank's invitation and would not complain.

Edna lay in an open bronze casket. There were flowers on either side. A podium stood off to the right as they walked past four rows of metal, folding chairs on either side of the aisle.

Frank stepped up to the casket. He looked at his mother.

"Mr. Rupert," Frank said. "You did a good job."

"Thank you, Mr. Dubois," the man said from the rear of the room.

"Where is the music, Mr. Rupert? I believe I asked for some Benny Goodman or Cole Porter for my mom." Frank turned slowly to confront him.

"Oh my, you are correct, Mr. Dubois. Allow me but a moment to correct the situation." Mr. Rupert shuffled off to fix the oversight.

"Please, kids, sit," Frank said when they were alone. In short order, the speakers in the corners of the ceiling came to life with a lively, if low volume, rendition of "Take the 'A' Train." "She really liked this kind of music." Frank sat down next to them.

"Do you expect anyone else to come, Frank?" Jason asked.

"No. I sent word to as many names and addresses she had in her dresser. I called the phone numbers she had too. None of these people seemed the slightest bit upset. None will be showing up."

They all sat in line in the front row. The kids looked at Frank, who stared at the casket. No one spoke. They stared at their shoes or studied the room. They did not know what to say.

A middle-aged man in a black suit came into the room and walked up to Frank. "Excuse me, Mr. Dubois?" He offered his hand in greeting. He wore his silver hair short. His laughing, green eyes missed nothing and hinted at mischief. "I am so sorry about your mother." Frank nodded, not comprehending who this man might be. "I am Reverend Timothy Smithford from Trinity Methodist Church. I work with the elderly at the state hospital. Your mother and I had an … interesting acquaintance."

"Oh yes," Frank said with a nod, "we spoke on the phone. Thank you for coming. How well did you know her?" Frank turned his attention back to his mother's face.

"Hmmm," said the reverend. "I would have to say, as well as anyone at the hospital."

Frank nodded. He gazed at the coffin, lost in the world of might-have-beens. The reverend was forgotten.

"I would like to start in a few minutes," the reverend said. "I will say a few words, then let you talk about Edna—unless you think anyone else will be coming?" Frank nodded, barely registering the question. "Okay, then, I will be back shortly and we can begin." Reverend Tim patted Frank on the shoulder as he left. He smiled and nodded at the kids on his way out of the room.

Jason looked back over his shoulder and watched the reverend leave. He had no memory of a death in his family. Scared and not sure of the right things to do, he stood and approached the casket. The kids watched him, curious.

Jason wanted to see the face of the woman he had not saved. He desperately wanted to know that things had turned out for the best. The dead, however, do not give up their secrets, and Jason was not ready to seek answers in what, if anything, was left of her mind. He just stared at the woman's face.

The song "What'll I Do?" started. Jason remembered the first time he saw her across the room, ranting at Frank from her wheelchair. The lines of her face were in a permanent frown. The hint of a smile now on her relaxed features gave him hope. Maybe she died happy.

"Jason," Suzy said, tugging on his shirt, "the reverend wants to start." Jason and Suzy found their seats. Reverend Smithford stepped behind the podium and looked over at Edna. He took a deep breath.

"Every morning," began Reverend Tim, his hands on either side of the podium, "I would say 'Good morning.' Edna answered in the same special way every time: 'Get the hell out of here and leave me alone.'" That got everyone's attention. There would be no sugar coating from this man. "She could turn a sunny day to gloom and doom at the drop of hat."

The kids looked at Frank and wondered how he might react to what had been said. He rubbed his forehead with his thumb and forefinger like he had a bad headache. The strong beat of many drums banging out a Big Band era rhythm echoed off the walls. Frank's shoulders started to shake. When he laughed out loud, the kids were shocked.

"Amen to that, Reverend." Frank clapped his hands.

"Well then, Frank, it is time for you to say a few words. You knew her better than anyone." Reverend Smithford stepped down and sat with the children.

"What can I say?" Frank started. He leaned on the podium. "This woman, my mother, wasn't any better and probably worse than any of yours." He pointed at his foster kids. "We have that in common." He stopped and looked over at his mother. "But sometimes … every once in a while, miracles happen. The last few days of her life …"

Four weeks after Frank's mother's wake, Jason sat on the threshold of the toolshed, writing in his old composition notebook. The new school year was underway. The weather remained warm. A thunderstorm had passed through late the night before. The air was clear and refreshed.

No one disturbed him while he scratched his notes on the pages. Water dripped over the tops of the blocked rain gutters and played a tattoo on the metal cellar storm door. At first, annoyed, Jason ignored the drumming.

He wrote,

1. My new teacher, Mrs. Hatcher, does not like me very well. I'll bring her around.
2. Frank was right. Fast, quick, and good hands make a good receiver in football. I think I have convinced Coach Gunther. Running every day has made me faster. Frank, knowing so much about the game, has been a big help too.
3. Being just another dumb kid is not so bad—yet. Russ certainly gets a kick out of my playing things down.

4. Lydia has been Lydia. Frank seems to have her under control for the moment. Suzy was right about Frank. Do no harm.
5. Mr. Downing has moved with us to the middle school. Nice surprise. Still trying to understand what I saw in his microscope. The textbooks I read ...

Jason continued writing, going over the things that had rumbled around in his head over the last few weeks. Finally the constant clatter on the metal door started to grate like fingernails on a blackboard.

"Oh, just stop it, will ya!" He went on writing. When the silence replaced the wet slaps against metal, he noticed, stopped, and looked up. "Well, I'll be damned."

Two puddles of water had accumulated not on the ground but three feet above the storm doors. Jason set aside his notebook. This was something new. *Russ and Suzy should be here to see this,* he thought. He dared not move. The puddles might crash to the ground.

Excited, Jason released the abilities he kept hidden and concentrated. He pictured the drops following each other to form two Ferris wheels of racing water. The two rings immediately took shape. He played with them, reshaping the water wheels into links like a chain. He laughed and turned the chain into a water locomotive with water-vapor smoke. It poured out of its stack. The locomotive pulled four cars on a water track. It all exploded upward and then splashed to the ground. Jason collapsed back against the door frame, exhausted.

"Cool."